THE SECRET SURROGATE

STEPHANIE MITCHELL

I0694254

Published by Alter Ego Publishing, Inc.

ISBN-13 (Paperback): 979-8-9851307-0-6

Cover design by Cormar Covers

HER SURROGATE HAS VANISHED, ALONG WITH HER UNBORN BABY

As a generous and respected philanthropist, Brooklyn Taylor is well aware that image is everything. Married, successful and living a life she created from scratch, Brooklyn only needs one thing to feel complete- a baby. Unable to have one, she hires a surrogate in secret. And then she gets a positive pregnancy test of her own. But, just weeks before their due dates, Brooklyn's surrogate vanishes and her perfectly crafted life begins to crumble.

Desperate and running out of time, she does everything she can to find her missing baby before it is too late. But as she also tries to keep the disappearance, and her connection to the surrogate, under wraps, the media pounces on the story.

Almost immediately the headlines turn against her in a flurry of secrets and lies. Her life, her business, and her family are all under attack. Why was the owner of an exclusive adoption center keeping a surrogate a secret? What happened to the heavily pregnant surrogate and Brooklyn's unborn child? Does her agency have anything to do with it?

Does her husband?

Does *she?*

Prologue

The letter opener descended toward her in what seemed like slow motion. Everything slowed down, even the sound of her own blood throbbing in her ears in rage seemed to slow. An eternity passed between every heartbeat, and yet she had no time to get away. Her hands and arms were being held behind her still, so she couldn't fend off the attack or protect herself. She was totally exposed. Vulnerable.

Her round, hugely swollen belly was all that stood between them. It almost seemed to be reaching out toward the pointed blade that was headed straight for it. She was past-due. Over her due-date now by almost a week. She couldn't help but think that if she wasn't, if everything had gone on as scheduled, if everything had *gone according to plan,* she wouldn't be here at all.

But nothing had gone like it was supposed to. Not even from the very beginning. And so here she was, watching it all come to an end as time slowed down and then stopped. At least for her.

She didn't even feel it. She saw it though. She couldn't help but see it as time seemed to stop for her completely.

The tip of the letter opener first touched the fabric of the maternity dress she was wearing, indenting it, pushing against the tautness for one helpless split-second before sliding deep. Up to the hilt.

Seeing it like that was surreal. The beautifully entwined filigree of its handle just sticking out so obscenely finally broke her trance.

She screamed.

Part One

Chapter One

Brooklyn rubbed the palm of one hand mindlessly over the large, swollen protrusion that was her belly, drawing comfort from the knowledge that she really was this close to getting everything she'd ever wanted.

She'd already created a successful, multimillion dollar company from scratch with nothing but blood, sweat and tears and along the way gotten the handsome, charismatic husband, too. All that had been missing from her life-long goal of attaining the holy trifecta of career, husband and baby was the baby, and it was almost here.

She couldn't believe she was finally this close. After so many years of helping other couples become a family, she was finally going to have a baby of her own to love. She was almost breathless with excitement. Although some nights, like this one, she wasn't sure if it was the excitement of everything that was to come that made her breathless or if it was the weight she was carrying in the form of the huge beach ball bump she was smuggling under her formal, flowing tent of a dress.

As happy as she was mentally, physically she felt like an irritated elephant. She waddled her way around the ballroom, socializing and making nice with all the donors who seemed to think that copping a feel of her swollen stomach should come with the price of admission. She had many avoidance maneuvers in her bag of tricks, and over the evening she had to use almost all of them to keep from being touched.

She kept a smile firmly in place as she deftly avoided each and every hand that reached out toward her, even as she wished she could stab some of the pushier donors with her cocktail fork. Putting on a good face came with the territory though. She'd have never gotten where she was without cultivating the art of not letting her true thoughts or emotions show. It was a skill she learned early and learned well. Plus, it just wasn't a polite way to utilize the cocktail fork.

She caught a glimpse of her husband Peter

through the well-dressed crowd. He stood head and shoulders above most of them, so spotting him was rather easy to do.

His eyes met hers every now and then, smiling at her over everyone's heads as they each worked the crowd, stopping at each small grouping of people to say a few words and shake a few hands.

Peter was a big reason these things always raised so much money. Getting people to part with very large sums of cash was what he excelled at. She always thought he could go into politics if he ever tired of being an attorney. The consummate host, he could charm the pants off of anyone he set his sights on.

She smiled back at him when she'd catch sight of him through the crowd, watching with envy as he wrapped everyone in attendance around his little finger. Between his skill and her belly, she was quite sure that this year's fundraiser would top the charts on donations for the center.

When their paths eventually crossed again he stopped beside her. He put a hand on her lower back and leaned in to whisper in her ear, "Everyone keeps telling me how radiant you look. And they're right. I know it's cliché, but you are glowing."

"I'm pretty sure it's the sweat. Is it hot in here to

you?" She asked, turning her whole body slowly, like an ocean barge, to face him.

He laughed at her under his breath. "Well, there is a whole lot of hot air in this room tonight, to be sure, but thankfully they've all brought their equally bloated wallets."

She laughed as his eyes left hers to focus on something behind her.

She turned to follow his gaze and saw Carole, one of her employees who'd been with her since almost the very beginning, take the stage.

"What's going on?" she asked Peter quietly. "What is she doing?"

"You'll see."

"I'll see? You know I don't like surprises. Peter, what did you do?"

"Hardly anything at all," he responded as Carole pulled the microphone attached to the podium down some and prepared to speak. "I just kept the secret."

"What secret?"

His only response was to again place his hand on the small of her back.

"May I have your attention, please," Carole began. "I know that most of you believe that you're here for The Brooklyn Taylor Center's annual fundraising dinner, and you are, so don't tuck those checkbooks away where they'd just burn a hole in your pockets just yet."

Brooklyn's eyes darted around the room as the sound of gentrified laughter enveloped her. She shot a glance back at her husband before turning her attention to Carole once again, as she resumed speaking.

"First, a huge thank you to all of you for being here to help support this great cause. Your donations allow our birth mothers, usually homeless women or teenaged girls who've been turned out from their homes and have nowhere else to go, to be able to give birth in a kind, understanding, home setting where they receive not only the monetary and medical support to have their children, but emotional support as well. Most of them also receive additional legal support in doing the amazingly unselfish work of making other families complete through the act of adoption. But tonight you all get to be a part of even more than that. As if that wasn't enough, right?

"But, tonight there is more. Tonight we are also here to celebrate something that has been so hard for me, for all us, to keep a secret," Carole said, taking a moment to single out other employees of the Center, as well as Brooklyn's husband, as Brooklyn looked on in confusion.

"Tonight we get to honor our very own Brooklyn Taylor with a lifetime achievement award from the state. Brooklyn, could you and Peter please come up here? I want to continue to embarrass you face to face."

More laughter rolled across the room, changing over to applause as Peter took her hand in his and led her through the crowd, up the few stairs and onto the stage. Carole said a few more words that largely escaped Brooklyn in her surprise and nervousness at suddenly becoming the center of attention.

Old instincts were kicking in and it was everything Brooklyn could do to fight them.

Calm down. Deep breaths. Smile. Being the center of attention, all eyes on you, is not dangerous in this situation. It's ok. You're ok. Breathe.

She grew more and more aware of the room again as her tunnel vision relaxed. As the sound of her blood pounding in her ears started to fade she was able to pay more attention to the kind words Peter was now saying, after Carole had turned the mic over to him.

He'd handed her a heavy clear glass award in a wooden base at some point. She was grateful she hadn't dropped it. Instead, she was holding onto it like it was a lifeline, her knuckles white as she finally got her heartrate slowed and her breathing calmed enough to give a thank you speech to the expectant crowd.

"Wow, I am shocked. I had no idea. Thank you. Ummm, I don't know what to say."

"That's a first," Peter said, leaning into the mic to tease her, causing more laughter to ring out.

"Very funny," she said, narrowing her eyes at him, warming up somewhat to the crowd. "Yes, I know I can ramble on when in private, or when talking to prospective adoptive parents as they look to begin their journey, but this is different. When I'm speaking like that, it's not about me. It's easier when it's about a cause I very much believe in.

"I don't know how many of you all know my story, but I, too, was put up for adoption. I won't get into all the details, as I'm sure the announcement that dinner is served should be coming any second now and I, more than anyone, know better than to get between hungry people and food."

Her statement brought out more laughter so she added, "And I certainly know better than to get between donors and food when that food is costing them a thousand dollars a plate."

She smiled at the crowd as the next wave of laughter died down, though she couldn't help but wonder if she was pulling herself together that well, or if everyone was just being polite. She decided to wrap it up quickly, either way. She wanted to end on a high note and put herself out of this misery of public speaking, allowing them to turn their attentions to the food, or really anything else but her.

"Seriously though, I'm so very grateful to all of you. None of our work could've happened without your donations, and as you all well know, tonight's food is only the tiniest bit of what your money goes toward.

"The girls who come to us are often in desperate situations. As Carole already mentioned, your donations allow us to help them physically, medically and emotionally and they also help to match their beautiful babies up with loving, adoptive families, allowing their desperate situations to become selfless acts that benefit both our amazing birth mothers and the families that welcome those beautiful babies into their lives with open arms.

"And that has most certainly felt like a lifetime achievement to be very proud of. But this award should have all of your names on it, too. Although in that case we'd need a much larger award, to be sure."

At that final bit of laughter she thanked them again and released everyone to eat and drink their fill, glad to finally get off the stage. She looked toward Peter, seeking reassurance that she'd done well, but she didn't see it.

The look on his face was troubled, but his attention wasn't on her. He was looking off to the side, to the base of the stairs they'd climbed.

She turned her head and locked eyes with one of their private security team members, and he looked anything but happy.

Chapter Two

"The intruder alarm went off," Charles told Peter. His eyes swung to Brooklyn to include her as well before going back to Peter's.

"At the house or the center?" Peter asked.

"The house. We've already checked it out, no one got inside, but there was a brick thrown through a window."

"A brick? When?" Brooklyn asked, baffled. "Why would someone break a window but not go inside?"

"About ten minutes ago is all I know, ma'am."

"Did the cameras catch who did it? A license plate? Anything?" Peter asked.

"Nothing identifying. There was no car seen on camera, whoever did it came on foot. We're still reviewing the footage, but I wanted to let you know immediately. But there's something else..."

"How did they get past the gate?" Peter asked, interrupting him.

"We don't know yet; they're pulling that footage as well. Although it's definitely easier to get around a gate on foot than with a car. But there's..."

"What do you mean you don't know? What do you know? What are we paying you for if someone can get past all of your security to get close enough to throw a brick through our window..."

Peter's voice was low but his obvious agitation was catching the attention of nearby donors so Brooklyn interrupted him.

"Peter, calm down. People are looking. And maybe if you'd let him finish a sentence we'd know more."

"Don't tell me to calm down, and who cares if someone is watching? If we've got a security issue I've every right to be upset..."

Brooklyn ignored him and addressed Charles. "You said a couple times now that there's something else. What else is there?"

"There was a note attached to the brick."

The couple stared at him but nothing else was added until Peter erupted.

"Well? Are you going to make us guess what it said?"

"No, sir. Sorry, it said *You can't get away with this. I'm going to tell.*"

"Well, what does that mean? Tell what? Get away with what?"

"I don't know, sir."

"Maybe we should go home and deal with this, Peter. See the videos and the note ourselves."

"We shouldn't have to. Our security team gets paid well enough that they should've prevented this from happening to begin with and at the very least they should already have someone identified. Or better yet, detained. We shouldn't have to go and do their jobs for them. This is a big night..."

"Be that as it may, it did happen and it needs to be dealt with."

"Fine. I'll go, but you should stay here. It's your night, they'll want to see your face around for a while after that award. Make my excuses and smooth things over so everything looks good. You're good at that."

He must've caught her look because he backpedaled. "I just meant that one of us should stay here. That's all. Don't make it a thing. I'll send the car right back for you so it'll be here whenever you're done, ok?"

"Fine."

Once he'd left she did as she'd been told. She mingled, accepted congratulations, smiled and put everyone at ease. When anyone asked about Peter's sudden absence, or mentioned they'd seen him getting a little upset, she made sure to stick as close to the truth as possible. Everyone knew it was easier to keep one's story straight that way.

She told them that they'd had a glitch in their home security alarm, most likely a false alarm, and as upset as he was at having to leave her on this special night he felt it was his duty to make sure their home was safe.

She rubbed her swollen belly as she spoke, ensuring that everyone's responses were positive praises about what a great guy he was, making sure his soon-to-be growing family was safe, as she smiled and nodded right along with them. But underneath every conversation she found herself thinking about the note that had been attached to the brick. *You can't get away with this. I'm going to tell.*

She had as many questions about the situation as Peter did, she just kept her questions to herself instead of getting all obviously upset and angry, as he had.

Who had done it and why? How had they gotten past the security gate and avoided all the cameras? Had they actually avoided the cameras, or had the cameras just not gotten good, clear footage?

At her earliest opportunity she excused herself to the restroom. She spent a few minutes running cold water over her wrists, checking her hair and adjusting her makeup. She patted a bit more powder over the small scar that followed the curve of her cheekbone, just under her eye. It was a thin, barely there reminder of a long ago car accident, but it always seemed to stand out more when she was stressed, because it didn't flush with color when the rest of her face did.

That tended to, she pulled out her cell phone. She quickly located a hidden app and waited for the tracker to load. When she didn't see what she expected to see she began to get nervous.

I knew it. I never should've relaxed, I let my guard down. Things were going too well for too long, of course they'd fall apart now.

Once she was finally on her way home it took everything she had in her not to redirect her driver to where she really wanted to go. Needed to go. She needed to see things for herself, but that would have to wait until she could take the car and go alone.

The house was quiet when she got there. The window had already been replaced and all remnants of anything uncivilized happening had been swept up and disposed of, one of both the perks and the responsibilities of their station. God forbid one of the neighbors saw.

She found Peter in his study. He slid something across his desk toward her without saying a word. She crossed the room and picked it up.

It was the note, opened and flattened out of its creases from where it had been folded and rubber banded around a brick. It was enclosed in a large plastic bag. She assumed that was to protect any fingerprint evidence possibly on it.

She started to open the bag and he exclaimed, "Don't open it! It's bagged for a reason."

"I know that. I don't intent to touch it," she said, raising the opening to her nose and inhaling. To her surprise it held no scent.

"What are you doing?" he asked as she resealed the bag and looked it over before handing it back to him.

"Nothing."

He continued to look at her as she stood before him, thinking.

"Do you think it has anything to do with... her?" she asked him.

"Her who? You mean Kristine?"

"Shhh, don't say her name."

"There are no cameras or recording devices in here, Brooklyn. And I still don't understand why we can't discuss her in the privacy of our own home."

"Because our home isn't private. You know that. We have on-site security, I know Charles is still here; Jeff just brought me home, he could knock on your door. So could the cook or the housekeeper."

"Most of them have already gone home and I'm sure the rest of them will be gone shortly, as well. You're just being paranoid."

"It's gotten us this far, hasn't it? We're too close, Peter. I don't want anyone to know."

"Fine, whatever," he said, appeasing her. "But to answer your question, no. I don't think it has anything to do with *her*. How could it? *You can't get away with this? I'm going to tell?* Why would she tell? We're paying her a lot of money for her silence, Brook."

"Well, what else could it be?"

She had other suspicions but didn't want to be the one to raise them. Not this time.

He just raised his eyebrows at her as he continued to watch her. She started to pace around the room.

"Would you relax?" He finally said. "It could be any number of things."

"But this is our *home*," she said, with a sigh that could've been anything from exasperation to exhaustion. "We're supposed to be safe here."

"Maybe it was thrown at the wrong house," he said, trying to reassure her. "We both know that there've been a lot of bodies buried in this neighborhood. We live two doors down from a husband and wife pair of horny senators and across from a reality TV slash YouTube star. It's entirely possible that one of their fans isn't intelligent enough to read an address correctly."

She didn't push the issue as she didn't know if she could even trust herself or her constantly swinging emotions right now. There was too much going on.

"Was there anything helpful on the video cameras? Can I see the footage?"

"Of course you can, but there isn't anything worth seeing," he said. He grabbed a glass she hadn't noticed from the corner of his desk and leaned back in his chair. He took a drink, watching her over the rim and making no moves to show her anything.

Amber-colored liquid swirled gently as he lowered the crystal high-ball glass from his lips until it was cradled in both hands, held against his stomach. He noticed her staring at it so he offered her a drink.

"Very funny."

"What? You look like you could use one."

She didn't push to see the security footage. She preferred to look it over later, alone. When she could take her time with it, without him watching over her shoulder or breathing down her neck.

"Will they be able to get any prints off the note, do you think?"

"It's a fifty-fifty shot," he told her.

She raised her eyebrows in question, like she didn't know what was coming next.

He raised the glass to his lips again and drained it. He placed it back on the desktop, opened the large drawer near his right leg and pulled a bottle out. He refilled his glass about three-quarters full and sipped on it again before answering himself with one of his favorite annoying sayings, "They either will or they won't."

It's going to be one of those nights, is it? She thought, watching the light from his desk lamp glint off the facets in the crystal between his fingers. *Good. How about you pour yourself another after that one? I've got information of my own I need to gather tonight, and you passed out drunk in here for a few hours will only make it easier.*

"Ok," she said, after a few moments of silence. "As fun as this has been, I'm going to turn in. Are you coming up?"

"In a bit. I've got some work to do that I didn't get finished before the fundraiser and I don't want to have it hanging over my head tomorrow. Tomorrow is supposed to be beautiful and I plan on spending it outside, on the golf course."

"Ok, well, don't stay up too late. It's been a long enough day already."

She let herself out without another word, closing the door behind her. Once she reached their bedroom, on the opposite side of the house and upstairs from his study, she closed the door and pulled her cell phone out. She sat on the bed as she waited for the hidden app to load itself again. And again she was disappointed.

Where it normally showed a blinking dot on a

map, pinpointing the location of her biggest secret, it now showed nothing at all for the second time today.

Tracker offline, it said instead. *Please check your connection and try again.*

She planned to do better than that. She didn't fully trust technology, she only trusted her own eyes, so she made plans to go see for herself as soon as she was sure that Peter wouldn't hear her leave and she could get away unnoticed. The way he'd been drinking she was certain it wouldn't take long.

Chapter Three

*L*ess than an hour later Brooklyn was well on her way. None of their staff lived-in, and she'd waited until they'd all gone home for the night, so no one saw her leave. As she grabbed the keys from the hook by the door to the garage she paused, briefly entertaining the idea of turning off the cameras to keep it that way, but she knew that would be harder to explain than just saying she'd needed to run an errand if anyone ever noticed her leaving on the video.

As she drove she let her mind wander back to her conversation with Peter. She didn't give his possible explanation much thought, the odds of someone throwing a brick through the wrong window seemed pretty slim. She figured that anyone going through that kind of trouble, taking that kind of risk, would at least make sure they had the right house.

So, assuming they hit the house they'd intended to hit, was it meant for her husband or for herself? Could it be tied to the business?

The Brooklyn Taylor Center was a joint venture maternity home, midwife hospital and adoption center that she'd personally built from the ground up. She'd come from less than nothing and risen to the very pinnacle of a hugely profitable enterprise. That kind of success could easily have made them a target. She was proud of what she'd built, but she knew from personal experience that not everyone believed in her cause the way she did. Some people had very strong opinions when it came to babies and adoption and were not shy about making those opinions known.

But, if it was tied to their business, wouldn't they have attacked it instead of their home? Granted, there were a lot more people always around at the center. It would've been much harder to get away unnoticed if an upset father had aimed the brick at a window where his current or ex-girlfriend was staying while she quietly had their baby away from prying family eyes.

No, she thought. *'You can't get away with this. I'm going to tell'* sounded personal.

So, back to the original question. Was it meant for her or her husband?

Is he cheating on me?

The note hadn't scented of perfume or lotion, and she had no other reason to think he was currently cheating on her. But, who knew what men got up to when their wives weren't looking? Although he could say the same thing about her, just as many wives cheated as husbands. But throwing an *I'm going to tell* note through a window sounded more like a feminine thing to do. That seemed more woman scorned than wounded male pride.

Not that she was seeing anyone, anyway. When would she have the time? Plus, one would think the huge pregnant belly she was sporting would be a deterrent. Or not, she guessed, allowing her thoughts to veer off track while she drove. Maybe some people were attracted to big, pregnant bellies. Who was she to judge? Plus, there was the added bonus attractant that they'd obviously assume she wouldn't be able to get *more* pregnant, she thought with a laugh.

She shook her head to try to bring her thoughts back to their current reality. She wasn't seeing anyone, and he was questionable, but there were other things, more important things, that she'd prefer didn't get out.

Like Kristine.

Peter didn't know she tracked Kristine with her phone. He'd have likely said it was a violation of her privacy, and maybe it was, but she didn't care. She was too invested in this going well to care about a little thing like privacy. This was too important not to keep track of and try to control. If this didn't go as planned...

No, she couldn't even bear to think about that. Everything depended on this being ok. She knew she wouldn't be able to relax until she saw for herself that the woman who carried her unborn child was safe.

She rested one hand on her stomach as she drove with the other, thinking how crazy this whole situation would look to an outsider. What a mess, right? Who hires a secret surrogate while pregnant, and then puts a tracker on her to keep up with her every move? And why would she venture out alone in the middle of the night to check on the baby Kristine carried instead of protecting her own by staying safe and sound, at home in her bed, until she inevitably got the news that the one Kristine carried was perfectly fine?

It's a good thing there are no outsiders asking questions then, isn't it?

Peter was right about one thing; she was probably just being paranoid. The tracker going offline at the same time they'd had a brick thrown through the window was most likely just an odd coincidence. It had to be. It made no sense that they were connected.

But still.

She loved the baby in Kristine's belly just as much as her own. Which made perfect sense, since it *was* her own. It was her and Peter's DNA that Kristine carried, of course she'd love it. And of course she'd come to care for Kristine, as well. That was only natural.

Just because her and Kristine's relationship started out as a business transaction that she'd wanted to keep secret, *still* wanted to keep secret, didn't mean she didn't care about the woman. One couldn't go through something like this with another and not come to care.

For some reason a line from a movie she hadn't seen in years came to her. It was an old movie her mother had loved, back before. Back before the accident. Back before her mother had died and she'd been put up for adoption.

"And you say I used you, but what about you using me? Everybody uses everybody, don't they?"

Wow, she hadn't thought about her mother in years. Too painful. Apparently even now it wasn't actually a thought of her mother that bubbled up, but a line from a movie she'd adored. Brooklyn could hear it playing on repeat in her head, accent and all.

"Everybody uses everybody, don't they?"

Where had that memory come from? And why now?

Yes, she was using Kristine, but Kristine was using her, too. She was being paid well for her services, even more so for keeping who was paying her quiet. They *were* using each other, but that didn't mean she didn't care for Kristine. Of course she did.

She was practically family.

Kind of, anyway. And she definitely carried their family inside her. Her and Peter's family. Their future. Or part of it. Just because that particular part of them was in Kristine's belly instead of her own didn't mean her baby was any less loved, or shouldn't be checked on just because it was late at night. Family was everything, after all.

Wasn't it?

It must be. It had to be. Otherwise what was it all for?

She'd learned over the years that money wasn't everything. Money was a lot of things, yes. And it was far better to have it than not, but it wasn't everything. Love wasn't either. No matter what songs and movies led you to believe, love *isn't* all there is. No more than money is.

No, family was what was most important. It had to be.

She was almost there.

Her mind kept trying to tell her that all was well. What could be wrong at this late stage? They'd already done all the hard stuff, after all. She was too near the finish line for things to go wrong now.

But her gut was saying something else entirely. Her gut was saying she should've known better than to even try. Who was she to think she could get away with such a thing?

She was glad to see Kristine's apartment complex finally come into view, a reprieve from her unproductive thoughts and memories. It almost looked more like a jail complex than an apartment complex. Usually gated communities gave off a feeling of being exclusive and expensive, but this one wasn't in the best neighborhood. No, with this one Brooklyn could never decide if they were trying to protect the residents by keeping the world out, or if they were trying to keep the often rather interesting residents in. Being so near the university campus it really could've gone either way.

Once there, she pulled into the driveway and took a left when the driveway T'd in front of the apartment office. She had no remote issued, since she wasn't a resident, so she rolled her window down at the drive-up gate. She entered the code she knew by heart into the keypad on the dented, leaning and paint-peeled pole. She rolled her window back up as she looked around, cautious but impatient as the arm blocking her way slowly raised to let her by.

She circled the complex, aiming toward the back and having to drive slower than she wanted to because of all the speed bumps spread throughout the large parking lot. She parked in a spot reserved for visitors between two buildings and turned off her car.

She looked around before exiting her vehicle, looking for both a particular car and for any possible troublemakers or delinquents lounging about before she was willing to step out. She saw neither.

She looked up at the balcony attached to Kristine's apartment, dismayed to see it dark. No car, no lights on. She checked her tracker one more time, preferring it to climbing to the third floor apartment. Why wasn't it showing her anything?

With a resigned sigh she got out of her car, locking it twice with her key fob, just to make sure. She made it almost all the way to the base of the staircase before a voice called to her in the dark.

"Hey lady, you seeking? My stuff is better than anything else you'll get around here. Whatcha need?"

She turned toward the voice and saw a tall, thin figure leaning against a wall in a walkway between the buildings. He was shadowed somewhat but she saw his face register her shape as she passed under a porch light. Before she could respond in any way he added, still looking at her belly, "Hey, I don't judge."

Wanting no trouble Brooklyn just said, "No, thank you."

"If you change your mind I'll be right here."

"Great," she mumbled to herself as she started up the stairs. On the top floor she aimed for the apartment furthest away on the left. She knocked, impatient for Kristine to answer before someone else came along and offered her drugs. Or worse.

She knocked again, harder and louder. While she waited she stepped to the side and cupped her hands to the window but the apartment was dark.

It didn't take her eyes long to adjust. Nothing looked amiss but it was hard to tell anything from the dark shapes of furniture. *Didn't she even leave a lamp on for when she'd return from wherever she was?*

She kept looking, but it was no use. No matter how much she squinted and readjusted her cupped hands on the window, she couldn't get Kristine to materialize.

Not wanting to go home without learning *something*, and under the guise of making sure she wasn't lying hurt somewhere inside unseen, she pulled out the key that Kristine had given her months before, for emergencies. She slid it into the lock on the door, knocking again as she went to turn the key. But the key didn't turn.

She used both hands this time, one to hold the knob and the other to wiggle and twist the key in the lock, but nothing happened. Surprised, she pulled out her phone and used its flashlight to get a better look at the lock. It looked brand new, not a scratch on the shiny metal surrounding the keyhole. Looking closer she also realized that the brand name on the key she kept on her key ring didn't even match the brand name stamped on the lock.

She'd changed the locks!

What the hell?

Chapter Four

The next morning was a Sunday and Brooklyn was at loose ends. She tried calling Kristine a hundred different times, but it immediately went to voice mail every single time. The tracker was equally useless and Brooklyn got more and more distraught as the day went on.

Where was she?

She thought about calling both the apartment office and the agency she'd found her through, but both were closed until Monday. Besides, what would she say?

Hey, have you seen Kristine lately? I've got no reason to think anything is wrong, really. I actually spoke to her yesterday morning before my fundraiser and all was well, but the tracker I have on her stopped reporting her whereabouts.

Yeah, that wouldn't look psycho at all.

She knew where she went to school and where she worked. Kristine had told her she worked for a call center and Brooklyn had often seen the tracker blinking at the work address she'd given but she had weekends off, so that was a no-go until Monday as well. So was trying to find her at the university she attended.

Where could she be? And why?

She'd originally wanted Kristine to move in with them. They had plenty of room, after all. What better way to keep track of her and her daily habits than to have her live under the same roof with them? But Kristine insisted on staying at her apartment, as it was close to both her school and her job.

Plus, Peter'd had a point. They couldn't exactly keep her a secret if she was living with them, could they? And no one knowing about her, including the staff, was one of the highest things on Brooklyn's list of priorities.

Although, right now, just finding her had leapt to the top of the priority list.

She knew there was nothing she could do until Monday, but what scared her most of all was the knowledge that even after Monday she could very easily come up empty handed. This was exactly why she'd put a tracker on her in the first place. She actually had two, one on her car as well as one on her phone, but neither were giving her anything anymore. Could Kristine have found them?

The one on the car could realistically have been found, if one had been looking. It was a physical device. But the phone one was a hidden app she used on her own phone to track a given phone number, so it wasn't like Kristine could have found anything on her own phone. It wasn't an app Brooklyn downloaded to it when Kristine wasn't looking, or anything that both phones had to acknowledge and allow. The only way for that tracker to go off-line was if the phone itself was turned off or dead.

For a moment she dared hope that was it. Maybe Kristine's phone was just off. But that was immediately dashed because she knew that if all was well and her phone had just died, the car tracker would still be working.

Had Kristine changed her mind and run?

Panic and fury filled Brooklyn at the thought. What if Kristine was trying to keep the baby as her own?

Stop! She told herself before she got too worked

up. *Now you're just getting hysterical for no reason. Why would she want to steal your baby? If she wanted a baby she could have her own. She wanted easy money to pay for school, not your baby.*

You just talked to her yesterday. If the whole brick thing hadn't happened, you probably wouldn't even know that the tracker wasn't working. You only looked at it because the brick thing did happen, and you had no information beyond a note saying 'I'm going to tell,' so you checked on your secret invest-ment. Like Peter said, it's not like Kristine would want to tell anyone, she's being paid handsomely for her silence.

She's not even missing, really. She just wasn't home. She's allowed to have a life. Maybe she went somewhere for the weekend, somewhere with no signal. Plus, trackers fail all the time. All of those possibilities make more sense than thinking she changed her mind or stole your baby. Why would she? I mean, it's not like she's carrying her own baby and getting cold feet about giving it up, this baby is 100% yours and Peter's DNA. I'm sure everything is fine.

She imagined Kristine being somewhere with no service, and then once she got back into signal range seeing how much Brooklyn had blown up her phone in worry. Kristine would call, and everything would be ok. She took a deep breath, trying to calm herself down. There was no reason to think that anything was wrong, she just had to wait until Kristine turned up, that's all.

Maybe I should go into the office for a bit? Peter's gone for the day golfing, and it's too quiet here with only my worrisome thoughts to keep me company.

Once she arrived at the complex that carried her name, she parked on the adoption side and let herself in. The adoption wing was where she usually spent most of her time and it was where she felt most comfortable, but it was as quiet and empty on a Sunday afternoon as her house had been.

She passed Peter and the other attorney's offices, half expecting one of them to be taking advantage of the quiet to get some work done, but she didn't see another soul. She made her way to her corner office and tried to make some headway on paperwork that had gone undone during the final days prepping for the fundraiser the night before, but it was pointless.

It was too easy for her mind to wander, too easy

to pull the tracker out every ten seconds in the hopes that she'd see something different each time.

No, she needed the activity in the other areas.

The entire complex was connected, so she could go anywhere in it without having to step outside. Each area was sealed off from the other areas so that no clients could wander freely from the adoption agency to the nursery, the delivery rooms or the maternity home, or vice versa, but some of the employees under her did have keys to everything. She, of course, had them all as well.

The nursery came first, being housed closest to the adoption arm for convenience. Brooklyn paused outside a large glass window that separated passersby like her from any actual babies kept inside. She saw one newborn, all bundled up and sleeping, while an on-duty nurse sat nearby, head down, doing paperwork.

The nurse, a newer hire named Ellen, must've sensed her presence because she looked up in surprise. Brooklyn acknowledged her with a nod and a quick smile. Ellen smiled back, then mimed holding and rocking a baby in her arms, her eyebrows raised in question.

Brooklyn shook her head no at the obvious invitation to come in and hold the newest arrival for a few minutes. No, another woman's baby held no interest for her since she came here to avoid thinking about the possible whereabouts of her own.

She waved in quick apology for disturbing the nurse and she continued on her way.

One newborn there likely meant one birth mother in recovery, and as she had even less interest in that at the moment than she'd had in the baby, she passed through both the recovery and delivery areas as quickly as possible, headed toward the maternity home.

The maternity home was in the oldest building in the complex. Everything else had been built out from it, over time, and it floored her that it was still used as often as it was.

She knew that as long as humanity existed there would likely always be adoption agencies around to help connect people who couldn't have children with people who could, but it was the need to still house and hide the women in a maternity home like hers while they did so that continually surprised her.

She guessed that even though the veneers of civilization seemed to get brighter and shinier as the centuries rolled on and picked up steam, some things apparently still hadn't changed all that much.

Especially for the poorer classes, in her experience. Even as birth control became both wider available and cheaper, and even though abortions were technically legal now in places, it seemed that insurance or lack thereof, money, religion and shame still limited the options of many, many women and girls.

Granted, it did keep her in business, which she was grateful for.

The door Brooklyn had to unlock to get to the maternity wing opened into the office and kitchen area, so anyone traveling between the wings could do so without disturbing any of the women in residence. As such, Carole, the cook in her first ramshackle version of a maternity home and who now, all these years later, practically ran this entire wing of the company single-handedly, was the first person she encountered.

"Hey! What are you doing here?" Carole asked when she noticed Brooklyn's arrival. "Why aren't you off celebrating your lifetime achievement award somewhere sinfully expensive?"

"I am. I'm here, aren't I? This is the most sinfully expensive place I know, just ask last night's donors," Brooklyn responded with a laugh.

"Oh, wasn't last night amazing?" Carole said. "I heard it broke records."

"It really was great, wasn't it? I can't believe you

guys were able to keep that award such a secret. Thank you for presenting it. And for all of your help planning the fundraiser itself, as usual."

"No thanks needed, it was my pleasure. But seriously, why are you here? You're not supposed to be here. I hardly ever see you on this end of the complex, and certainly not on such a beautiful Sunday afternoon. Is something wrong?"

"No, nothing is wrong. Peter is playing golf so I thought I'd come in and catch up on some work, but it was too quiet over there to concentrate."

"Well, if you're looking for the opposite of too quiet, this wing is always a safe bet. I'm finishing up some paperwork myself and was about to start prepping dinner for everyone. Oh, we got a new arrival yesterday. Her name is Sarah. She seems to be a cheerful one, especially for only being two weeks away from her due date. Seems like a true do-gooder, this one. She's ready to *get this birthing thing over with,* her words, and she's excited for her baby to go to someone who'll give it a great life."

"Hmmm, watch out for the do-gooders. She may crack last minute and change her mind."

"Very true. Lord knows we've seen that happen often enough. But I've got a good feeling about her."

"How many does she bring us to? I saw we had

one newborn in the nursery. You can't catch a break, huh? One leaves you for the hospital ward and another immediately takes her place. No rest for the wicked?"

"Thirteen women, from places as close as the next town over and as far away as Canada."

"Thirteen? Most people would consider that an unlucky number. Any of them giving you any trouble?"

"I don't believe in unlucky numbers; I just consider it a baker's dozen. Oh, that reminds me, I need to check on the biscuits. I started them early to free up that oven for dinner and they smell like they're just about ready. Do you want to eat with us tonight? It would definitely cure your *too quiet* issues," Carole said with a laugh.

"No, Peter will be home soon and our cook is making one of my favorite meals, but thanks for the offer. And don't think I didn't notice that you avoided my other question," Brooklyn said. "Who is giving you trouble?"

"What? No one. I wasn't avoiding the question," she said, looking back over her shoulder wide-eyed as she walked away from Brooklyn. She grabbed two oven mitts and turned her attention to the oven.

"Everything is fine here. I mean, there's always drama of some sort or another when you've got a house full of pregnant women and the hormones that go with them, you know how it is. But it's nothing I can't handle. I've been at this too long to put up with any trouble, you know that."

"Nothing I need to know about? Or deal with?"

"Not a thing," Carole reassured her. "It's the normal controlled chaos. Half the girls think it's the end of the world even being here and the other half can't wait for it all to be over so they can go back to their old lives. Nothing new under the sun."

"If you're sure..."

"I'm sure. The only thing pressing at the moment is the need to feed the horde. Are you sure you don't want to stay? I can put you to work..."

"I'd only get in your way. You know there's a reason we employ a cook at our house. If I was to let you put me to work, I'd turn your controlled chaos into actual chaos. And then you'd have a mutiny on your hands. Thirteen hormonal pregnant women would turn against the both of us, united in their distaste for their dinner being burnt to a crisp. Even your cheerful new arrival would turn against you, and we wouldn't want that."

"No, we certainly wouldn't," Carole said, smiling as she gingerly teased each biscuit off the tray and into a bread basket she proceeded to cover with a napkin.

"Then I will get out of your way before that happens."

Brooklyn let herself back out into the hall after a quick goodbye. She'd been looking for a distraction from her thoughts, but just the idea of spending the next hour or two helping cook for, as Carole had called them, a baker's dozen of hormonal pregnant women biding their time until their babies were birthed and adopted was not the distraction she was looking for.

Nope. Suddenly she couldn't get out of there fast enough.

As she headed to her car and then on home, she was accosted with memories of her own time in the home. Only she hadn't been forced to live in a maternity home, she'd been forced to live in a children's home. And then a string of foster homes.

She'd mentioned during her speech the night before that adoption was a cause close to her heart because she too had been put up for adoption, but what she didn't ever talk about was the fact that she'd never actually *been* adopted.

No one had wanted to adopt a six-year-old. They weren't as in demand as cute, fresh-slate, newborn babies were. Especially not six-year-olds who'd been rather un-ceremonially dropped off by their fathers after their mother had died.

Chapter Five

She remembered the day clearly. Like it was yesterday. It was some time after the bad car wreck that she and her mother had been in together. They'd both needed multiple surgeries and blood transfusions in the days and weeks after the accident, but only she'd ultimately lived.

Hurry up! Where are your shoes? Don't forget to brush your teeth. Come on, we've got to go!

Her father had been rushing her to get dressed for what she thought was to be her first day back at school after the accident. It was a damp, rainy day that invited lingering, not hurrying. She hadn't been out of the hospital very long and her mother's funeral had only been a few days before. She hadn't gotten to go.

She was excited to get to see her friends at school again but worried that it wouldn't be the same. That they'd treat her differently since her face looked different, the scar under her eye still relatively fresh. She'd gotten dressed and they'd headed off, only he didn't drop her off at school.

When he pulled up at a large, school-like building she'd never seen before, with angel wings carved into the woodwork that bracketed a large, foreboding, ornate, wooden front door, she'd thought he had an errand to do on the way. Maybe that was why he'd been in such a hurry.

She was really confused when he told her to get out. When she asked where they were, all he'd say was that it was her new school. But then he grabbed a suitcase from the trunk of the car and wheeled it in with them, seemingly unaware of the raindrops that were beginning to fall faster and faster. She'd had no warning that her entire life was about to change, again. Like losing her mother hadn't been enough.

She trailed behind him, the wheels of the suit-case making a humming noise on the concrete and leaving damp lines that outlined a new path she had no choice but to follow. He opened the large front door, ushering her in ahead of him before he let it close with a solid thud behind them, announcing their arrival with its echo.

"Here she is," he said to a woman who'd come out to the large foyer to meet them, her heels clicking a slow countdown as she neared. "I trust everything is in order? There should be nothing more for me to sign."

"Daddy, what's happening? Where are we?"

He turned to her then, kneeling down to meet her at eye level, rain dripping from his hair.

"I told you. It's your new school. It's also your new home. Apparently I'm not actually your daddy. Not according to your blood type, which I learned all about while you and your mommy were in the hospital. I learned many, many other things too, while she was in there. Apparently the combination of good drugs, being on death's doormat, and interesting bloodwork results loosens one's lips. Makes one feel the need to come clean and confess almost a decade's worth of sins."

She heard the words but she had no idea what any of them meant. All she knew was that the lady that had come out to meet them looked mean. Her mouth was circled in too bright of a red lipstick, and the building they were in smelled funny. Like a combination of the cleaning smells from the hospital and the sick smells that sometimes drifted out of the nurse's office at school. Or the kindergarten hall when someone didn't make the bathroom in time. She tried to ignore the woman completely, holding her breath against the smell as her dad kept talking.

"All I see when I look at you now is your mother. I loved her and she betrayed me..." He faded off, then jumped subjects and dove back in to try again.

"I can't support you anymore, anyway. Even if I could handle looking at you. We had no life insurance, I got fired for spending too much time at the hospital, and I'm going to have to declare bankruptcy to get out from under the medical bills that I'm already being hit with, so I've signed over my rights to you so I can start over somewhere far, far away."

He ran a hand through his hair, raking its wetness back. With his other hand he spun the suitcase away from him, toward the lady. She stopped its roll by sticking her foot out as he finished.

"I gave this nice lady all the information I have so maybe she can find your real daddy, but there isn't much to work with. Even so, you will have a much better shot at life with some other parents. Any other parents, really. So, good luck to you. As weird as this sounds I really do wish you all the best. I'm sorry."

And with that, he kissed her on the forehead,

said, "You can hate me if you want to, I do," shrugged, and left.

Over the next few years, as she'd been shuttled from the children's home to various foster homes and back to the children's home again, depending on the needs and whims of everyone else but her own, she'd developed ways to cope.

She'd learned a lot during those formative years between being dumped into the system at six and being spit back out of it at eighteen. She'd learned to expect people to fail her, to use her and abuse her, and most importantly she'd learned that ultimately everyone was out for themselves, and if she wanted to thrive, or even survive, she needed to be out for herself, too.

She'd never felt so confused, unlovable, worthless or out of control in her short little life as she had back then, after she'd lost both of her parents, one right after the other. And she'd never wanted to feel that way ever again.

But, on the plus side, she'd also learned how to spot opportunities to better her own conditions, and how to make sure she always came out ahead, no matter what it cost her. She'd learned how to turn other people's weaknesses, dirty secrets and tight situations to her advantage, and been able to turn those dirty little secrets into a very profitable business. All the while also being able to pair those dirty little secrets with loving adoptive parents, giving thousands of kids over the years a better life than she'd personally had.

But then... well look at her now, she thought as she rubbed her belly and tried to shake off her dark memories. She had it all, didn't she?

When people asked her how she'd done it, she liked to teasingly claim that she'd just been in the right place at the right time more often than not, but the truth was that she'd had to claw her way through the mud to reach each and every victory and accomplishment she'd ever received.

She had respect, money, and most importantly, control over her own life now. They were all things she'd had to earn, because they certainly weren't given to her. Neither as a child, nor as an adult.

But no one wanted to hear the truth, that she'd basically begged, borrowed and stolen to get here. No, they wanted to hear the sanitized, polished fairy-tale version of how she'd managed to build the company that proudly touted her name.

And she'd done it. Along the way she'd even found love. And the beginnings of the family she'd longed for all those nights she'd spent in the children's home, surrounded by people, and so very alone.

As she neared home, looking back on her past as unemotionally as she could, she realized that she'd come out on top. She was proud of herself. Instead of becoming a victim of the system, she now owned and ran the system. Or at least a very profitable piece of it. She'd earned her place in this world.

But, earned or not, clawing ones' way to the top left scars on both the climber and the climbed over. And not all scars healed cleanly.

She found herself tracing under her eye with a fingertip as she watched her gated neighborhood draw nearer. What a difference her opulent gated community was compared to Kristine's run-down, bars-on-the-windows kind of a gated complex, where drug dealers lurked inside the leaning and paint-peeled fences. She knew she easily could've ended up living just like Kristine if things had gone differently.

She couldn't help but shiver as a wave of imposter syndrome began to wash over her as she cruised down the street in front of such grand houses in her expensive car. She'd gone from dredging up old, painful memories to feeling satisfied and knowing she'd earned her place in the world right back to an irrational fear that the whole world could see straight through all of her pretenses, all in the stretch of a couple of heartbeats.

As she passed through the gates she only had one thought.

How dare someone like her think she deserved to be here, anyway?

She'd spent her entire adult life creating and building the security she so desperately longed for as a kid, and the sense of control that money and security would give her over her life.

Yet here she was, feeling very much insecure and out of control.

And then, as she turned the final corner toward home, she saw a police car sitting in front of her house.

Crap, I meant to look over the security footage before it went to the police. I'll have to make sure they leave me a copy, as they'll most likely want the original.

She parked her car in the garage and headed into the house. She hung her keys up on one of the hooks just inside the door out of habit and aimed for the back room they'd set aside for Charles and the rest of her private security team to use when they were on the property, along with their banks of video monitors and other equipment.

"Hello officer," she said, extending her hand out to shake his as she introduced herself. "I'm guessing you saw me coming? Not much happens around here that's not caught on camera, which is why we're so confused. It shouldn't be possible to throw a brick through our window and not be seen. I'm glad Charles was here to let you in, but I guess he would be. If he called you."

He shook her hand, introducing himself as Officer Sandage. He looked young, dark hair cut short like he'd gone from a stint in the military straight into the academy. He had a half-moon-shaped scar bracketing one eye that moved when he smiled, endearing him to her immediately. Obviously he'd been on the force long enough to see some kind of action.

Although, Brooklyn thought it could just as easily have been caused by a broken beer bottle during some youthful drunken bar mishap as anything in the line of duty. She knew well that one didn't have to be old to carry scars.

"Charles here was just filling me in on everything," Officer Sandage said.

"I was about to play the video for him," Charles said. "Not that there's much to see."

"Looks like my timing is perfect then, I'll watch it with you," Brooklyn said.

"Have you not seen it?" Officer Sandage asked her, looking surprised.

"Oh, I have," she reassured him, lying. "Peter

showed me after the fundraiser, but this time I get to watch it in the company of two experts."

He nodded at her and then signaled for Charles to hit play.

Boy, when they'd said there wasn't much on it, they weren't kidding. The quality was awful, like the camera was losing signal, or battery, or both. But it was wired in, so neither should have been an issue.

It kept jumping. Snowy bursts often covered the feed as well. She saw shadows move, but it could've been caused by a car, a person or even tree branches blowing in the wind. Even the audio sounded warped, like it was playing at quarter speed.

When it had struggled through the appropriate time period showing nothing useful, Charles stopped it. The officer watched him as he pulled what looked like a USB memory stick out of its dock and handed it over. The officer's eyes shot to Brooklyn's as he took it, and she could tell that he was thinking the same thing she was.

They'd called the police for this?

Granted, someone would've had to come to look around and do a report anyway, whether they'd had video or not. Although, since the glass had been replaced and the note touched and bagged, all without the police being called initially, the report was just a formality. They'd certainly get no prints off of the window, or anything else, now.

Speaking of prints, she remembered the note. She was about to bring it up to Officer Sandage when Charles spoke.

"I'm not sure what happened to the system as a whole, usually all our footage is top quality. But, as you just saw, this was not. That's the second reason I'm here working today," Charles said. "It certainly wasn't any footage we felt needed to be rushed to you last night after it happened, but I'm also here to diagnose everything and see what's going on. This is obviously unacceptable."

Unacceptable is right, Brooklyn thought. She'd seen better footage on the old VHS tapes the children's home used to use almost fifty years prior, tapes that had sticky fingerprints and spilled juice all over them. It was most certainly not the caliber of footage she expected to see.

"Well, it didn't get any better watching it with experts, that's for sure," Brooklyn said. "I was hoping that by watching it in here instead of on Peter's computer it would've been clearer, but it's pretty much crap, isn't it?"

She looked to Charles as she said that last bit, but he didn't meet her eyes. He was paying very close attention to the release form Officer Sandage had given him to fill out instead. Likely on purpose, she guessed. She wouldn't have wanted to meet her eyes if she was him, either. He was paid to do one thing and this was what he had to show for it?

Remembering the note, Brooklyn spoke up.

"Do you think you'll be able to get prints off the note attached to the brick?"

"The note?"

Confused, Brooklyn turned back to look at Charles. "You didn't mention that there was a note attached to the brick?"

Her tone was icy.

"We were just getting to that," Charles said. "He's only been here a minute longer than you."

"But you have it? To give him?"

"I..." he looked through nearby piles of paperwork. After lifting and replacing papers, opening and closing drawers, he finally said, "I don't think I do. It was here last night."

"When I saw it last night, Peter had it in his study. I'll go see if it's still there," she said, walking away from them, shaking her head.

Was he incompetent? He'd never seemed so before, but they hadn't actually had anything happen since he'd been hired on, either. It was all prep work and installation. Things done just in case something happened. Now that something happened, could he not handle it?

She made a mental note to discuss Charles and his security company with Peter later. She let herself into Peter's study and found the note still sitting on the desk where he'd laid it the night before, after she'd looked at it and handed it back to him.

She thought about making a copy of it before taking it to Officer Sandage, but she didn't think putting a plastic-enclosed paper on their copier-scanner would result in a quality image. The light from the copier would likely just reflect off the bag, giving them nothing.

She didn't dare risk taking it out of its plastic bag either. She didn't want to add her own fingerprints to whatever was already on it. She hoped that neither Peter nor Charles had handled it much in their removing it from the brick and bagging it, but now, doubting Charles' competence, she wasn't sure.

He's the one who told them what it said when he came to them at the fundraiser. If he'd bagged it then Peter's prints shouldn't be on it, but Charles' very well may be. Unless he'd worn gloves, which she'd hoped he'd done. She made another mental note to ask him when she got back to the men, and if it turned out that he did touch it, she'd add that to her discussion with Peter. Maybe it was time for a new security company.

Since she could think of no other way to make a copy, she took a picture with her phone, adjusting the angle for the glare off the bag, and headed back down the hall.

She handed it to Officer Sandage directly, mentioning that she'd personally only touched the bag it was currently nestled in and adding that it was her assumption that Peter hadn't touched it either, but that she wasn't sure about Charles or how it had gotten into the bag to begin with. Charles assured them both that it had been handled as minimally as possible and while gloved, but the officer shook his head.

"It likely won't matter," Officer Sandage said. "I highly doubt it'll be processed."

"Why not?" Brooklyn asked.

"It may be dusted for prints, but even that is iffy. At most those prints would be stored along with the note and the video, as part of the file, but I doubt they'll be run. What happened here basically amounts to vandalism, that's all. No one came in the house. Nothing was taken, no other damage was caused. Correct? Just a note on a brick through the window?"

"What about the message?" Brooklyn asked. "It sounds threatening."

"Or like kids being kids. *You can't get away with this. I'm going to tell?* Pretty generic. That brick could've landed inside any house in the city limits and stirred up a secret. It's very... what's that movie? *I Know What You Did Last Summer.*"

"You're older than you look if that's what this makes you think of," Brooklyn said, eyebrows raised at his reference.

"Not really. My girlfriend likes to watch old movies on YouTube and sometimes she makes me watch them with her. Poor man's Netflix."

"I don't remember how that ended, do you?" Charles asked.

"No sir, I slept through most of it, to be honest."

"I never actually saw it," Brooklyn admitted.

"Be that as it may, the point I was trying to make is that it was probably nothing. No cars seen, it was probably kids on foot, causing trouble. But I'll finish writing up the report, and if anything comes of it, I'll let you know. And if you guys have any more trouble, you should let me know. Otherwise..." Officer Sandage said, shrugging.

He pulled out a couple of business cards, wrote a report number on the back of both of them and handed them each one. As they finished up, Brooklyn was about to show herself out to check her tracker app for the thousandth time but something on one of the TV monitors off to the side caught her attention.

It looked like Kristine was on the news, but that couldn't be right. Could it?

Chapter Seven

The volume was off so she couldn't hear what was being said, but the picture being shown sure looked a lot like Kristine back when they'd first met her, before she'd gotten pregnant. The same long hair, the same facial structure. Though her face definitely looked a bit different now, with the added pregnancy weight softening everything.

The words *Missing College Student* graced the bottom of the screen while a reporter moved her mouth and hands soundlessly.

"Excuse me," Brooklyn said to the room at large as she left the men, not noticing or caring if they responded to her. She went upstairs to the bedroom, shut and locked the door, and turned the TV on. She flipped the channel to the one that had been on downstairs. This time with the volume up.

"We'll be keeping an eye on this story for you, and in the mean time we'll take you back to the studio for the weather report..."

Brooklyn searched the other local news channels but either she'd missed the story there too, or the first channel was running an exclusive. She turned the TV off and picked up her phone instead. Her heart raced as she typed words into the search bar. She was all thumbs, her hands shaking as she scrolled, looking for the station's online coverage.

There it was. Thank goodness for online simulcast, she thought as she clicked the ongoing feed and backed it up until she saw the words *Breaking News*.

"Police are reaching out in hopes of finding someone who knows something about missing college student Kristine Armstrong. According to Kristine's mother, who lives out of state, Kristine hasn't been heard from in over a month..."

"Wait, what?" Brooklyn asked the screen in her hand. "Over a month? I talked to her yesterday..."

"Her mother has told us that Kristine attends the university behind me, and has since classes started last fall. Kristine hasn't been home to see her mother since the summer, before classes began, but she says that they normally talk once a week. When Kristine missed a few phone calls her mother chalked it up to a busy school schedule, as the two did text back and forth more often than they talked.

"But when Kristine missed their standing phone call for the fourth week in a row her mother realized that it had been an entire month since she'd actually heard Kristine's voice instead of just responding to texts that her mother said 'anyone could be sending, really.'

"Her mother was under the impression that Kristine stayed on campus in one of the dorms," the reporter continued. "But according to campus police Kristine not only doesn't live in any of the dorms, she's not even a registered student."

"What?" Brooklyn asked again, of the empty room.

"Her mother is distraught, as you'd imagine. Though she freely admits that they have their problems, Mrs. Armstrong is most definitely worried about the safety of her daughter. She said even the texting has stopped as of a few days ago. She is asking that if anyone recognizes the woman in these photos, or knows the whereabouts of Kristine Armstrong, to please call the police."

As the reporter spoke, multiple pictures flashed up on the screen, but none were more recent than the summer before. Kristine wasn't pregnant in any of them and at no time during the broadcast did the reporter mention that Kristine was not only pregnant but very close to her due date. They also didn't mention knowing that Kristine lived in the apartments that could just barely be seen in the periphery of the camera, way back in the distance behind the reporter, nor that she held a job at the call center nearby.

Apparently the only thing they knew for sure about her was her name.

The broadcast ended again this time just like it had when Brooklyn had first turned on the bedroom TV, with, "We'll be keeping an eye on this story for you, and in the mean time we'll take you back to the studio for the weather report..."

Brooklyn stopped the playback and sat there on her bed, in shock. Confused, she backed it up and watched it all again, but none of her questions were answered by the second viewing.

The sense of foreboding that rooted itself in her stomach when she'd first seen Kristine on the silent monitor downstairs only grew. She felt herself grow warm and she was grateful to be sitting as worry spun with questions in her head, making her dizzy.

She's not registered at the university?

Her mother didn't mention that she was pregnant. Does she even know?

Yeah, Kristine had signed the non-disclosure agreement they'd required, which forbade her from revealing the name of the couple she was surrogating for, but she was allowed to say she was a surrogate. That way when there was no baby to show off after she gave birth she wouldn't have to lie and say she lost it or gave it up for adoption.

The only thing Kristine wasn't allowed to talk about was who the biological parents of the baby she was carrying were. The agency also signed the same NDA, on top of all their other promises of professionalism and confidentiality. It had been one of the requirements for getting Brooklyn's business. But she didn't even tell her own mother that she was pregnant?

Apparently I'm not the only one keeping this surrogacy a secret.

Maybe her mother wouldn't understand? It certainly didn't sound like the pair were close. And there was no mention of a Mr. Armstrong at all.

Did Kristine ever talk about her parents? Surely

she'd asked Kristine at the beginning of all this, "What do your parents think?"

But, Brooklyn couldn't remember.

At the very least the agency would have, in their surrogate application and vetting process.

Why did Kristine stop answering her mother's calls and texts? The easiest way to keep her secret surely would've been to not do anything different that would sound any alarms. Like *not* going no-contact and disappearing. Like *not* making the news as a missing person.

She's not even registered as a student? Does she live and work where she said she lives and works? Of course she does, I've been to her apartment. I've seen her car tracker at the call center. Although, come to think of it, I rarely saw it on the university campus.

So where is she?

"She is asking that if anyone recognizes the woman in these photos, or knows the whereabouts of Kristine Armstrong, to please call the police." The reporter's words rang in her ears.

Is Officer Sandage still here?

She stood up but didn't go downstairs to look. She didn't even look out a window to see if the offi-cer's car was still out front. Nope, instead she found herself in the nursery. It was next to the bedroom, through an adjoining door. So they could hear their baby when it cried at night.

It. She didn't even know if Kristine was carrying their daughter or their son. They hadn't wanted to know, so Kristine said she'd be surprised with them. She'd never learned the sex of her own either, she thought as she rubbed her belly and took in the nursery through worried eyes.

It was done in neutrals and pastels. Whites and sands, with accents in blue *and* pink, just in case. There were touches of soft yellow, lilac and mint green as well. The colors reminded her of a garden in early spring. Full of potential and possibility, with blooms just waiting to burst into life.

She walked around the room in a daze, touching the changing table, the stacks of blankets, diapers and burp rags. The stuffed bears and ducks. The child-sized rocking horse in front of the bookcase already stuffed with picture books.

Where was the baby Kristine held under her heart? The baby she was meant to be growing and keeping safe for them until it could be here, sleeping safe and sound under the mobile that would spin and soothe, as their newborn dreamed baby dreams of warm milk and cozy cuddles? Was it safe? Was Kristine? Had something bad happened to them?

Overcome with worry and fear, she dropped into an oversized rocking chair large enough to comfortably feed a hungry baby in during a future midnight feeding, and she placed both hands on her belly. She gave the floor a soft push, seeking to sooth herself in the moment where she had plans to soothe a baby in the very near future.

Where are you, Kristine? What's happened to you and my baby? Why won't you answer your phone?

Feeling confused and out of control, she tried to turn her thoughts toward something more productive. Something she could *do* to help find her baby, and Kristine of course, instead of sitting there feeling useless and vulnerable.

Like calling the police.

Her thoughts drifted, sorting through the pros and cons of calling the police to tell them that she'd talked to Kristine just the day before. All the questions they'd ask and the things they'd likely say bounced around in her brain, one after the other.

How do you know Kristine Armstrong? When did you last see her? What is your relationship? She's your surrogate? So, she's pregnant? Her mother never mentioned that. Hey, are you the same Brooklyn Taylor that runs The Brooklyn Taylor Center? Could you come in and give an official statement, putting your name and therefore your agency's name on offi-cial documents connecting you, your maternity home and adoption center to this missing pregnant woman who you say is having a baby for you even as you look ready to pop yourself?

No? We could send an officer to your agency instead, if you'd prefer. Or your house, for your convenience. Wait, wasn't there just an officer at your house taking a report on a different matter? A brick through a window with an interesting note attached, saying 'I'm going to tell?'

Brooklyn imagined the news crews beating the officers to her door. She imagined them sending multiple camera crews and reporters, to cover her home and her agency at the same time, and shivered. She imagined them beginning to dig through public records on her, her past, her husband and the agency, all for background chatter as they stood in front of both places, going on and on, just to have something to say to fill the air time since she had no idea where Kristine was any more than any of them did.

What a nightmare, she thought. Even imagining it was starting to give her a headache. Talk about feeling out of control, exposed and vulnerable.

No.

The fact that Kristine was carrying Brooklyn's

baby obviously made finding her a priority. She wanted them both found soon, safe and unharmed, probably even more than Kristine's obviously out-of-the-loop mother did. But, as worried and scared as she was, she also had a baker's dozen other pregnant women to look out for as well.

Women who may not appreciate their quiet time spent hiding themselves away inside the walls of her agency being so publicly forced into the spotlight any more than Brooklyn herself would.

Surely someone else will recognize Kristine from those photos, or by name. Someone from her apartment complex or from the call center. If someone else comes forward, *anyone else*, they'll let it be known that she hasn't actually been missing for a month.

Maybe they'll mention that she's pregnant, Brooklyn thought. *Because why wouldn't they? She's bigger than I am since my pregnancy followed hers. But that way, if someone else comes forward, there's at least still a chance that she won't be connected to me.*

Brooklyn didn't need any news crews hanging around the center. She didn't need them disturbing the current birth mothers and she certainly didn't need them scaring off any potential adoptive parents looking for a quiet, private adoption.

None of that had anything to do with Kristine and it certainly wouldn't help anyone find her. It would only complicate the search. Plus, she remembered one of the last times her agency had made the news, and she wasn't in any hurry to have it happen again.

Chapter Eight

Brooklyn felt like she was going crazy. Days had passed and there'd been no word from Kristine or updates on the news, even though she searched and scrolled and refreshed constantly. No change on the tracking app either, it still showed inactive and useless. Kristine hadn't answered any of her calls or texts, and the worst part was that the world seemed to be ok with all of this. Her baby was missing and everyone was just carrying on like it was a normal week.

Even Peter didn't seem overly worried. "I'm sure she'll turn up," he'd said on their way into the office together Monday. She'd agreed with him then, but by Wednesday morning she wasn't so sure.

"Do you think something has happened to her?" She asked him, yet again. "Something bad?"

"Well, we know she didn't go to her mother's for some downtime and a break from all her school stress," he replied. When he caught the look she sent his way he said, "What? Too soon? Sorry, I was just trying to lighten the mood, that's all."

"That's another thing I can't get over. Why did she tell everyone, from us to her mother, that she was going to school here if she wasn't? I mean, I kind of understand if she's hiding the surrogacy and needs an excuse to be away from her mom for almost a year, but us? Why tell us she's in school? Why would we care if she's enrolled versus just working or living nearby?"

"I don't know, Brook. I'm curious about that too, but we can't ask her until she shows up."

"I want to go by her apartment. See if she's there."

"I don't think that's a good idea. She was on the news. If her mother went to the news I'm sure she's also gone to the police. Who knows if one, or both, are there? You still want to keep us out of it, don't you? I mean, I don't care about that aspect. I never have. But how would we be able to stay out of it if you're caught on camera knocking on her door or peeking in her windows?"

She felt herself stiffen beside him as she remembered doing both of those things. Did he know? Her movement caught his attention and he took his eyes off the road to look at her.

"You don't exactly blend there; you know?" He asked, pointedly looking her over from top to bottom and back again, to prove his point.

Even without her pregnant belly she stood out at Kristine's apartment complex. Each and every article of clothing on her, separately, could likely pay for at least one month's rent. Her shoes alone would probably cover a year.

"Maybe I should've said that I want to go by her apartment *again*," she said, making her wishes known and confessing at the same time.

"Are you kidding me? You've already been by? When?"

"Saturday night."

"When Saturday night? After the fundraiser? With Jeff?"

Jeff was their fulltime gardener and sometimes driver they used for events like the fundraiser, or when one of them had a trip planned and they either wanted to work on the way to the airport or didn't want to park a car there until their return.

"No, not with Jeff. After I spoke with you in your study. I said I was going to bed but I couldn't sleep."

"You asked me that night if I thought *she* had anything to do with the brick. Then you went to her apartment? Do you know something I don't?"

"No, I just..." She didn't know how to finish. She'd just needed to do something that night.

"Well? Did you at least find anything out? Did you talk to her?"

"No. She wasn't there. That's why I want to go again, it's been days."

"At least you went before the news story. But I'm not taking you now, we'll be late. I've got a meeting with one of the other attorneys and like I said, I don't think it's a good idea."

"I don't think it's a good idea either. I just said that I wanted to, not that we should."

"Good, then we're on the same page."

She sighed, feeling dismissed, entirely uncomforted and invalidated. Brooklyn turned her attention out the window as he drove. Why wasn't he as worried as she was? It's his baby, too.

She felt alone sitting beside him. She didn't know why she expected him to understand how she felt, she knew very well that women usually carried the weight of most things emotionally on their own. Men did things, of course. They fixed things. And they thought things, but it's the women, at least in her experience, who *felt* things.

And she didn't like how any of this was making her feel now.

As he drove, her mind was free to wander. It wasn't long until she found herself in the past. Waiting at her doctor's office, in a room all alone.

She was naked but for the paper gown that always made her feel so exposed and vulnerable. She *hated* feeling exposed and vulnerable.

She heard the knock on the door and turned to watch it open. Her doctor started to greet her but stopped, looking confused.

"Why are you in a gown? This is a results appointment. I wanted to talk to you, not run more tests. Go ahead and get dressed while I go find my nurse. She's new, I apologize. I'll give you a minute and be right back."

"Can't you find her later? Just tell me. I can listen in a gown."

"Is your husband here? I can grab him out of the waiting room if so, and you can get dressed while I do. Then we'll talk."

"No, I'm alone. Like you said, no one mentioned that it was a results appointment. Besides, we know he's not the problem. I can get pregnant. It's staying pregnant that's the problem. Just... tell me. Will I ever be able to carry to full-term? These miscarriages are killing me."

Even in memory she felt every emotion those words hid. The shock and crushing disappointment of going from all is well to something is wrong. The guilt of wondering if she'd done something to cause it. The aching, lingering sadness and grief that never truly left, not really. Not even now.

She'd only been able to talk so blunt and unemotionally about it at the time by sheer force of will. One thing her time in the foster care system, and especially in the group home, had taught her was that no matter how you felt, you projected a tough, unaffected exterior or the world would eat you alive and then dance and gloat on your torn up remains.

She placed a hand on her belly in the now, resting it there as Peter drove on. She shook her head, dismissing the memory as best she could before it could dredge up old emotions. There was certainly no reason to dwell on her miscarriages now, was there? But the one that came next wasn't much better.

It was a happier one, but it didn't make her feel any less alone. The next memory put her smack in the middle of the IVF treatment, the day they took her eggs and Peter's sperm and mixed them.

The hormones they'd had her on up til then made her feel even crazier and out of control than she felt now, which was quite a feat.

She remembered swinging wildly between anger and desperation, joy and despondency, seemingly every five minutes or so. It had been like PMS on steroids, and she'd been glad the collection day had finally arrived.

"So, are we ready to harvest some eggs and make a baby?" The IVF doctor's words filled her mind like it had just happened yesterday and not months before. The words came in the door with the doctor, not even a *hello* or a *how have you been* preceding them.

"I'm beyond ready, to be honest," Brooklyn answered him. "These hormone shots to prepare my body for this whole thing are starting to get old, but beyond that they're making me want to cry one minute and want to kill people for no reason the next. I can't wait for these hormonal swings to be Kristine's alone, and not mine."

"Soon, soon," the doctor answered. "We have your husband's donation as well, yes?"

The question seemed rhetorical, as he was flipping through her medical chart before answering himself with a, "Yes, I see it. Let's get started, shall we? Is he here? To hold your hand for moral support? Or is he still in with all the videos and magazines?"

Brooklyn thought the last question was uncalled for and out of line, but she didn't want to piss off the guy who was about to be fishing around inside her body for the seeds to her future, so she didn't call him on it. She did answer to Peter's whereabouts, though.

"No, he just left. He was here long enough to do his part, but he had to go. It couldn't be helped, but it's fine."

"Are you sure?"

"What's the alternative? Timing is everything for these things, right? We can't reschedule, it'll throw everything off and the sooner I can stop taking these shots the better. Knowing that this will be over soon is all the moral support I need."

"Fair enough."

They'd mildly sedated her for the procedure, and she remembered wishing she could take some of that home and inject herself with it for a while after all the other shots she'd had to take. But thankfully the procedure was over about fifteen or twenty minutes later.

She'd had to call Jeff to come and get her, as they wouldn't let her drive after the sedation. But the in vitro office shared space with a large number of other offices, including their accountant's, so she just told him that she'd been there and lent her car to one of the girls in the office who was having a bit of car trouble. She figured Peter could figure out how to retrieve it later, since taking two cars and him needing to leave was the entire reason she'd had to call Jeff and then lie about it in the first place.

She'd been sore for days after, only reinforcing her wish that they'd sent her home with something stronger than a verbal recommendation that she take Tylenol til she felt better.

Brooklyn still swore they didn't get all the ripe and ready eggs they'd gone in there for, and that's how she ended up with her own positive pregnancy test so close to Kristine's. Or at least that's what she would say, if anyone even knew of Kristine's existence or questioned her timing.

She'd been thrilled about all of it, of course. Even if she was guarded at first, after all of her miscarriages. When Brooklyn finally told Kristine that she was pregnant too, at first Kristine seemed unsure.

Like she was expecting Brooklyn to tell her *Never mind! I don't want the baby you're carrying any more, now that I'm carrying one, too!*

But of course that wasn't the case. Both babies were Brooklyn and Peter's DNA, so there was no way Brooklyn would want to call a halt to anything. It was more like a surprise announcement of twins than any kind of complication that would change anything regarding Kristine. Once she'd been able to assure Kristine that nothing about their agreement was going to change, Kristine was at ease.

Overall the entire IVF experience had gone very well. Both her retrieval and then Kristine's implantation a few days later. Even the car issue ended up taking care of itself.

Peter was still out of town when she got the call saying that the fertilization had gone well and that they had multiple embryos ready for Kristine's implantation. Brooklyn had Jeff drive her back to the accountant's under the guise of getting her car back and going shopping, so she was able to be there for Kristine and then drive herself home.

She'd been surprised that Kristine actually wanted her in the room with her, but she'd been happy to be there. It wasn't until now that it dawned on her how odd it was that she didn't have someone closer to her, like her mother, in there with her instead.

Now though, she was thinking differently. Apparently Kristine hadn't wanted her mother to know about any of it.

Brooklyn's mind was pulled out of the past with a disorienting tug when Peter drove the car into the parking lot on the maternity home side of the center and turned off the car.

"Why are you parking over on this side?" She asked him.

"The other attorney wanted to meet somewhere more private than either of our glass-enclosed offices, so we're using one of the old offices in here since this building pre-dates open concept."

"What are you meeting about that has to be so secretive?"

"One of the birth mothers is making noises about wanting her baby back, even though the adoption has already gone through. We're just making sure all of our i's are dotted and our t's are crossed in case she gets serious and tries to sue. I prefer to do this sort of work away from the adoption wing. So many prospective adoptive parents come through on tours or come in to take possession of their brand new bundles of joy that I like to take no chances of any of this kind of stuff being accidentally overheard, that's all."

They let themselves in through the large, ornate, wing-bracketed front door of the maternity home, which opened into a warm and welcoming living-room-looking seating area. There was no TV here, as they preferred the ladies relax in the communal rooms further back in the building and away from the front door, where tours started and new arrivals entered. There was a large fireplace though, with overstuffed chairs, love seats and bookcases full of books. They were currently being dusted by Carole, who they both said hello to as they entered.

Brooklyn saw the back of a woman as she was walking away, down a hall that lead deeper into the center. She looked familiar. It took her a minute but she eventually realized that she looked like one of the attorneys from the adoption side, so she assumed that was the attorney who Peter was here to meet. When she said as much, pointing at the retreating figure, Peter said no. He was meeting one of the male attorneys, he didn't know why she was here on this side.

Carole saw who they were referring to right before the woman turned a corner and disappeared, and said that was Sarah, the newest addition to the home.

"Remember, I told you about her the other day. She's the gung-ho one who can't wait to deliver," Carole said, reminding Brooklyn.

"Oh," Brooklyn said. "The resemblance from behind is striking. Although, I guess she did look a little thicker at the waistline, but otherwise, it's rather uncanny. Same haircut and everything."

"Would you like to meet her?" Carole asked. "I can call her back, and you can marvel at the similarities up close. Although she doesn't resemble her near as much up close as she does from afar."

"No, that's ok," Brooklyn said.

"I don't have time myself," Peter added. "I need to get to my meeting. Here's the keys in case you want to go to lunch or something later, this meeting might take a while. Excuse me, ladies."

Peter gave Brooklyn a quick, dry kiss on the cheek and nodded his excuses again at Carole but she'd gone back to fluffing pillows and straightening up.

Instead of tucking the keys into her purse, Brooklyn decided to move the car to where they normally parked so she wouldn't have to walk to the other side. She made her own excuses to Carole after a few more minutes of small talk, then she headed off toward her office on the adoption side.

She had a full day planned herself. She had the final papers to sign on an adoption later in the day, with lots of refreshing the news to do in the meantime, interspersed with stalking Kristine's Facebook page and her trackers, in the hopes that something would update before she lost her mind.

Chapter Nine

One of Brooklyn's favorite aspects of her job was handing one of the babies who'd been born in the center that had her name emblazoned on the front to a happy, usually crying, adoptive couple and making their dreams of finally becoming parents a reality. It was why she'd started her company in the first place. And each successful adoption helped to heal a tiny wound inside her that had been torn apart the day she'd been given up for adoption herself.

But even as each child she helped get adopted did heal a piece of her, there was still that unhealed middle of her that she didn't think would ever be healed. At least not until her own child was born. Because if her father's actions had shown her anything it was that blood must be what mattered most. It had to be. Her father never would've given her up if she'd been of his blood, after all.

So when it didn't look like she'd be able to have her own, she'd turned to surrogacy instead of adopting from her own agency. Blood was best. But for others, obviously even second best was better than nothing. It was certainly better than going unadopted at all, wasn't it?

That's why she loved days like this so much. Because no one should have to live like that.

As she sat, smiling wide, across the desk from Mr. and Mrs. Cumby, her eyes dropped to the lifetime achievement award she'd been presented with. It took a place of pride between them as all three of them waited for nurse Anne to bring their bundle of joy in from the nursery.

She added her signature to theirs at the bottom of the very last document standing between them and parenthood. She then slid it over to their in-house notary to make it official.

That done, they continued to make joyous small talk with nothing left to do but wait for the baby's arrival.

When the phone on her desk chirped softly she said, "I bet this is her, saying she's got everything and she's headed our way. Here, let me put it on speaker."

Grinning, she hit the button. Opening her direct line to the room at large, she said, "Don't forget the diaper bag full of gifts that goes home with them, too. Baby Michael's new parents are waiting excitedly but impatiently to take their new little man home."

"Brooklyn?" The voice on the other end of the line filled the room.

"Yes, of course. Are you coming?" Her body reacted before her brain could, her head tilted and her eyebrows knitted together. There was something different about the voice on the line.

"Brooklyn Taylor?" The voice asked again, this time sounding even less like the nurse she'd been expecting.

"Who is this?" She asked, shaking her head and raising a shoulder at the couple in front of her in confusion but still full of anticipation.

"This is Kate Miller with KTYZ news, I was hoping to get a quote from you about the Kristine Armstrong case. I'm assuming you've seen it, apparently they haven't found her yet but they *did* find her..."

Brooklyn grabbed the receiver from the base,

cutting the voice off from broadcasting into the air and directing it into her ear instead.

"Oh, isn't that the name of that college student they were asking about on the news the other day?" Brooklyn heard Mrs. Cumby ask her husband at the same time that the end of the question the reporter was asking filled her ear.

"... do you have a comment about that?"

Brooklyn looked from Mrs. to Mr. Cumby, confused and in a panic. Why was a reporter asking her about Kristine? No one who hadn't signed an NDA even knew of their connection.

Maybe the fact that she was pregnant had gotten out and they were hoping to find a connection at the center? They had to be fishing.

"Mrs. Taylor, did you hear me?" The voice in her ear asked just as the door to Brooklyn's office opened and Anne stepped in, grinning. She had a diaper bag draped over her shoulder and a tightly wrapped baby in her arms. His tiny blue hat was all Brooklyn could see from her seated position as Anne began to transfer the warm bundle from the crook of her arm to the arms of his now-standing adoptive parents.

Their attentions were on each other, ignoring Brooklyn completely in their joy. Brooklyn looked over at the notary but she too was watching the scene before her. Mrs. Cumby started to cry as she took little Michael in her arms and kissed his downy forehead. The notary's eyes darted to Brooklyn in question, but she shook her head at her to say *it's all a misunderstanding, everything is fine.*

"How did you get this number?" She asked the voice. "This is a private line."

"Do you have a comment on the Kristine Armstrong case, Mrs. Taylor?" The reporter asked her again. "According to my sources Kristine hasn't been missing the month her mother had initially said, her whereabouts have been tracked to last Friday at least, for sure. But being as far along in her pregnancy as she is now known to be, and with her..."

"I'm sorry, no. I have no comment," Brooklyn said, interrupting her.

When her answer into the phone made every person in the room look at her, she smiled back at them and shrugged.

"I don't know any Kristine Armstrong," she added as her heart beat wildly in her throat and she fought the urge to throw up into the wastebasket beside her desk.

The voices continued all around her, from the questions in her ear to the cooing and celebrating in her office. She couldn't concentrate on either so she didn't quite hear anything the reporter was saying. She finally just repeated, "I'm sorry, but I can't speak to any of this. No comment."

"But..."

She hung up and the nurse asked her if everything was ok.

"Of course! I've no idea what that was all about, but it's over now whatever it was. The only thing happening in here right now is getting these two sent off right, with their brand new son."

'Her whereabouts have been tracked to last Friday...' The reporter's words echoed in her head.

I talked to her Saturday. Was I the last person to do so?

She plastered a smile on her face, making all the right noises and responses until she could reasonably shove everyone out of her office and shut the door. Once alone she searched online again but she saw nothing new about Kristine anywhere.

Hoping she was correct in her assumption that the phone call was just an overzealous reporter on a fishing mission, she closed up shop, told her receptionist that she could be reached on her cell, and she left. She headed home with a knot of dread beginning to bloom in her chest.

Once she got home she was dismayed to see a

police car in front of her house again. She caught a glimpse of the officer just before someone in the house let him in. It looked like Officer Sandage, so she let out a deep sigh of relief, assuming he'd come by to discuss something about the brick case with Peter or Charles.

After she hit the button to open the garage door she noticed that their other car was already inside. That was when she remembered that she and Peter had ridden to work together all that week. And she'd just left him stranded at work, without even telling him that she was leaving.

Apparently the reporter had spooked her even more than she realized.

She'd either have to send Jeff for him later or go back for him herself, but for the moment she had more important things on her mind.

Letting herself into the house she hung up her keys and went looking for Officer Sandage. She found him not in with the security feed but still standing just inside the front door. Apparently Charles had been the one to let him in and from the sounds of their conversation as she neared them, they were still exchanging pleasantries and just beginning to get down to business.

"No, nothing on the brick footage, I'm afraid,"

she heard the officer tell Charles. "I'm actually here to ask about Kristine Armstrong. They'd normally send a detective, but as I've already been here working an active case, and this is just a preliminary visit really, to gather some information..."

"Who?" Brooklyn asked, interrupting him before he could go into any detail. "Hello, Officer. Nice to see you again."

"Hello, Mrs. Taylor," he said, turning to address her as well as Charles. "Kristine Armstrong. Her mother has reported her missing and..."

"I just heard something about that earlier today. Someone said she'd just been seen a few days ago. Friday, was it? Doesn't sound like much of a missing person to me. Although I'd imagine that less than a week would feel like a month if it were my daughter, but still."

"Where did you hear that, Mrs. Taylor? As far as I know that hasn't been released publicly."

The look he gave her made her feel like a criminal.

"Well, it can't be too private. I heard it from a reporter." She didn't mention that the reporter had called her at work asking questions.

"Is she a pregnant woman, by chance?" Brooklyn asked him before he could ask any more questions in front of Charles. "Because I heard that bit as well, from the same reporter."

"She is."

"And you've been sent to us for your preliminary questioning? Cause all pregnant women must hang out together, right? Or, since her mother didn't appear to know about her pregnancy when she reported her missing, then she must be hiding it. And hiding it must mean that it has something to do with my maternity home or my adoption center? Maybe we should be having this discussion there," she said, trying to make this look like a routine business discussion so she could dismiss Charles from the conversation.

It wasn't until the suggestion left her lips that she realized that she didn't want any cops there any more than she wanted them here. But at the very least, she needed to move the officer to the other side of the house somehow, to Peter's study.

"If she is there, I could at least check for you, but the name doesn't ring any bells. She isn't a minor, is she? I mean, minors can give their babies up for adoption too, even without their parents knowing in most states. It's just that we keep those records separate. But the news mentioned that she's college age.

Wasn't she also lying to her mother about being in college?"

He didn't rise to her pointedly mentioning Kristine's apparent history of hiding or lying, but he did answer her about her age.

"No ma'am, she isn't a minor. She's in her early twenties. But her mother mentioned you by name. Brooklyn Taylor. She said that Kristine was..."

"Well, that's also the name of the center," she said, purposely interrupting him again while wondering how Kristine's mother knew to send anyone to her when she didn't seem to know anything about anything else.

"The Brooklyn Taylor center is where we... actually come with me. I should be able to access some records from my husband's study. You can ask me about her in there. I'm guessing you're done with Charles? Surely he didn't know anything about a missing Kristine Something? We'll let him get back to work."

She led him away, grateful that there were no cameras, or recording devices, inside the house. Once inside the study, she shut the door. He didn't waste any time.

"Her mother said she works for you personally, ma'am. As your surrogate."

His eyes pointedly dropped to her stomach, and then came to meet her gaze again, eyebrows raised.

Before Brooklyn could ask how in the world she could possibly know *that*, he added, "She also mentioned that it was supposed to be a secret. I didn't realize that she meant a secret even inside these walls. I'm assuming that's why you couldn't get me away from Charles fast enough?"

"You're good! They should make you a cop," she said, laughing. "I don't suppose you happened to say any of that to Charles? We try to keep our employees out of our personal business. At least as much as possible. I'm sure you understand."

"Yes, ma'am. No, we hadn't gotten that far. He assumed I was here with an update on your brick situation. You've certainly got a lot on your plate at the moment, don't you, Mrs. Taylor?"

"You have no idea."

"Is Ms. Armstrong correct? Have you hired her daughter as a surrogate?"

Chapter Ten

Brooklyn's first instinct was to deny it. But this wasn't a nosy reporter, this was a police officer. And if Kristine truly was missing, that meant her baby was as well. If her baby was missing, or if something bad had happened to them... well, she couldn't bear to even think about it.

"Yes," she finally answered. "Yes, Kristine is my surrogate."

"You said this is your husband's study? Is he here? I'd like to speak with him as well."

"No, he's still at the center."

"Does he know you've hired a surrogate? Or is this a secret from him, too?"

The look she gave him could've melted ice. She

was grateful he had his head down, writing in a little notepad he'd pulled out of his pocket.

"Of course he knows. His... input... was required."

When he looked up at her again, a questioning look on his face and his pen poised, she filled him in. Simply and bluntly.

"They took his sperm and my egg, mixed them together and put them in Kristine. His participation was important, so he definitely knows. The baby she's carrying is ours. One hundred percent our DNA. She's just... the oven our baby is baking in, so to speak."

"I see. So, what is baking in your oven, then? To continue this rather interesting metaphor."

"Proof of God's sense of humor," she said with a laugh. "Everyone said that once we relaxed and stopped trying, we'd get pregnant. We didn't relax until the IVF with Kristine was successful."

"A literal brother from another mother, huh?"

He laughed at the look she gave him and said, "Never mind. You said you own an adoption center. Why didn't you just adopt?"

Why is that any of your business? Why do you have to ask so many questions? What does that have to do with finding Kristine?

Instead of saying what she was thinking, she said, "I know it probably sounds bad for me to say, but I wanted to have my own child. Maybe not wanting to adopt makes me a hypocrite, but it's the truth. It's also the reason we kept the surrogacy a secret. I didn't want to field questions at work, or in my personal life, about why I wasn't using my own agency to have a child. We are privileged to have the money to be able to do it the way I wanted, so we did. End of story."

"So what were you planning on telling people?"

"What do you mean?"

"Well, if you're keeping a surrogate a secret because you don't want to field questions, and then suddenly you have a baby, but you didn't adopt... don't you think there would still be questions? A lot more questions?"

"We were planning on figuring that out after the IVF took. If it didn't work, we didn't want endless people asking us all the time how it was going. My fertility isn't anyone's business."

"And now?" He asked her.

"And now, *what?*" Her patience with his questions was wearing thin.

"Once Kristine gives birth ahead of you, or at

least near you giving birth, how are you planning to explain that? Twins? Twins born a month apart?"

"I don't... we haven't..."

"Or now that you're nearing your own due date with all apparently going well, maybe you decided that your secret surrogate wasn't needed anymore?"

His insinuation that she was the reason Kristine was nowhere to be found infuriated her.

"You think I'd do something to my own baby? Or to Kristine? That's insane! Why would I...?"

"You said it yourself, you wanted to have your own child. Maybe as your own due date neared, you figured that the best way to avoid answering questions about extra babies and secret surrogates was not to have either."

She wanted to tell him to leave, to get the hell out, but she knew she couldn't. Rage and indignation were rolling through her. She was more concerned about Kristine and her baby than anyone, and the very idea that she'd do something to harm her own child, or the woman who carried it, was unbelievable.

But it also shifted something inside her.

Up until now she'd been trying to hold onto rationality. It was rational to think that Kristine had just gone out of cell service, maybe spending a week with a friend in a remote cabin or something. It had only been four days since she last talked to Kristine, it was rational to think that calling her a missing person was a huge overreaction.

It was rational to assume a woman who obviously didn't want her mother to know how she was earning extra income could think that a job that would take nine months to complete could be hidden by saying she was away at college. Women hid stripper jobs and cam girl jobs all the time, why wouldn't one think she could hide a surrogacy job for a few months, especially if she wasn't particularly close to her family?

Many of the women in her maternity home over the years had pretended to be away at school, or visiting relatives out of state or overseas, or any other variation of cover stories to hide what they were really doing.

Those were just some of the very rational things Brooklyn had been telling herself over the past few days to keep the panic at bay, trusting that any minute now a text message from Kristine would pop up on her phone apologizing for being incommunicado for a few relaxing days.

But this officer was at her home. Asking her the kinds of questions he was asking her, after a reporter had called her at work. Both of them separately connecting her with Kristine somehow, when no one should've been able to connect them.

Everything keeping Brooklyn rational and sane was starting to give way.

Her anger and indignation morphed into true fear and she found herself asking him, wide eyed, "Has something happened to her? Is she truly missing? You wouldn't be saying things like that, insinuating things like that, if you didn't know something."

But all he did was ask her more questions.

"How did you connect with Kristine? To hire her?"

Brooklyn answered him. Honestly and directly. She was too numb, and too scared, to beat around the bush or do anything but try to help him find her baby.

"Through a service. A very discreet service, if you want them to be."

"And the name of this very discreet service?"

"The Surrogacy And Fertility Agency."

"And how did you find them? Cause everyone in the baby business knows each other?"

He smiled after saying that, referring back to her joke before, about all pregnant women liking to hang out together. He was obviously trying to put her at ease and smooth over his previous insinuations. Or maybe he wanted to keep her on edge, playing both good cop and bad cop. Either way, it was working. She was definitely on edge.

"It is a small world, but no," she said, smiling back and allowing him to think she was soothed. She started explaining things she never thought she'd have to explain. "I'd had no interaction with them, or any other surrogacy agency, before we housed one of their surrogates. At the center. That generally isn't what we do, but we made an exception because her case was rather tragic."

"Tragic how?"

"The couple that hired her died. They were involved in some kind of mugging gone bad. But since they were dead, and the surrogate had no connection to the baby she was carrying, nor did she want to adopt it as surrogating was just a job to her, the agency and her both decided that adoption was for the best. And since that *is* what we do, and since she wanted to give birth somewhere private where the news reporters couldn't find her as her case was rather unique, she gave birth at the center under an assumed name. Like a lot of the girls do. And the baby was adopted through us. So, when I found myself entertaining the idea of a surrogate, I turned to them."

"A lot of women who give their babies up for adoption through you do so under assumed names? Is that legal? Assumed names can't be listed on a birth certificate, can they?"

"No, of course not. They only go by those assumed names while they're living in the maternity home. So if someone calls for them, fishing for information, if they don't know the name they've chosen to call themselves we don't patch them through. Like how celebrities will register at hotels under fake names. After birth, when it comes time to sign the adoption papers, that's all done with their legal names. Though we still refer to them by their assumed names until they leave us. And not everyone uses assumed names. Not everyone feels the need to."

"I see. OK, back to Kristine. What can you tell me about her? Why did you choose her?"

"She was new in town, which was a plus for me. She didn't know anyone. I figured that would make keeping her a secret easier. She also mentioned that she wouldn't be living here long either, which was another perk.

"She *said* she transferred up here to our local university to finish her degree. That she'd started back home at a community college and had knocked out her first two years there, transferring up here to finish.

"She said it was the perfect time to apply, begin the sometimes long surrogacy application and pre-screening process, and complete a pregnancy to help her pay for college. Then, after graduation and giving birth, she'd be gone. Off to start her next adventure.

"She seemed perfect," Brooklyn finished up with a shrug. "When we interviewed her she also said she'd just started working at a call center near both her apartment and the university, but that she'd prefer to work as a surrogate. She said if we chose her she'd likely quit at the call center, especially if we wanted her to. So she could concentrate on school and not have to work a stressful job, too.

"But as far as I know she never did quit. We never asked her to, because she said she liked it there and it didn't turn out to be stressful once she learned the ropes. You may want to talk to them as well if you haven't already, but now I'm wondering if her call center job was even real since school wasn't. As you can tell, she said a lot of things. If I didn't have a key to her apartment I'd wonder if that was a lie, too."

"You have a key?"

"For emergencies, yes. I've never used it. And

now I'm wondering why she needed two jobs. Us and the call center. If she wasn't putting it toward college, I mean."

"How much are you paying her?"

"Ten thousand dollars a month, which is more than the average. My understanding is that the average going rate is two to five thousand a month for ten months, once the surrogate becomes pregnant. With bonuses for each procedure until she became pregnant. But, with our privacy clause and NDA there's a rather large additional monthly bonus added."

"An NDA?"

"A non-disclosure agreement. We're paying her extra to not say who she's surrogating for. A lot extra. Though she is free to admit that she's a surrogate in general. So that people are prepared when she has no baby to show off afterward.

"Which reminds me, you said it was her mother who sent you here with the knowledge that she was our surrogate. Doesn't that seem odd? I mean, since she didn't seem to know anything else about her daughter. How did she know that? You should've had to go to the agency with a warrant for that information."

His jaw tightened then, but he didn't answer her question. He asked her another one instead.

"And when is the last time you spoke with or saw her?"

She narrowed her eyes at his avoidance. She'd definitely come back to it.

"I talked to her on the phone Saturday."

"Do you talk often?"

"At least once a week, sometimes more. Sometimes less."

"How often do you see her?"

"Once a month initially. Or thereabouts. More often as she got closer to her due date."

"When you spoke to her Saturday, how did she sound?"

"Fine, I guess. Normal," she said, shrugging again.

"What did you talk about?"

"Just how she was doing, if she needed anything. Nothing out of the ordinary."

"What time was that?"

"Sometime in the morning. I can look at my phone and give you an exact time."

"Please, yes."

As she dug her phone out of her purse and found the time of her call on it, she asked, "If she was just seen Friday, and I talked to her Saturday, is she even still considered missing? And who saw her Friday?"

"I'm not at liberty to say."

"I'm assuming you've been by her apartment? Talked to the office there?"

"I'm not at liberty to say."

"What are you at liberty to say? Can you at least tell me how her mother knew she was a surrogate when she didn't seem to know anything at all before?"

"Your reporter friend didn't give you that information? When she told you the other things that aren't public knowledge yet?"

"I said I heard it from a reporter. I didn't say it was a friend. How do you know it wasn't from the TV?"

"It wasn't. Not yet. My guess is it'll be everywhere soon though. I'm also guessing then, that if it wasn't a friend, someone called you for a comment. Did you give them one?"

"I denied even knowing her name."

He went still at that, his eyes probing hers before asking, "Why?"

"She caught me in the middle of signing adoption papers. She called my private line at the center and mentioned knowing that Kristine was pregnant.

I assumed she was fishing on the pregnancy angle. I did what I'd do if anyone called asking about someone through unofficial channels. I denied any knowledge and said no comment. But I told you the truth. You're all that matters."

He nodded, but it wasn't reassuring. She felt the knot in her stomach draw tighter.

"Why? What does it matter if I denied knowing her?"

She could practically see the words *I'm not at liberty to say* forming automatically on his lips, but that wasn't what came out. Instead, after looking silently at her for a long moment, he replied.

"Kristine's mother sent us to you because after she managed to get herself into Kristine's apartment, where she found Kristine's phone and purse but no sign of Kristine, she started tearing the place apart. She found Kristine's diary. If I had to guess, I'd say the police were her second call, her first being the press."

Chapter Eleven

I didn't think it would be this hard to do this alone, or to hide it all from my mother. I miss her a lot more than I ever expected to. At first it was kind of fun. I felt like I was handling my problems like a grown up, you know? Figuring it out. Standing on my own two feet and making it work. Adulting.

All of mom's hopes for me hinged on me going to college, being the first in our family to get a degree. To get a good job. To make something of myself.

She grew up near here, before life took her out of state. She used to tell me stories of when she was a little girl, watching all the college kids around town. How much fun their lives looked, how important they seemed. How smart and worldly. And how she never got to go but hoped I could. How she hoped that my life would be better, that she could give me the life she'd wanted.

It was the only university I even applied to and I was sure I'd get in. I mean, it's not like it's Harvard or anything. It's just a state school that happened to be important to my mother. I didn't even apply as an incoming freshman, I applied as a transfer student. Someone who already proved they could do two years of college coursework and had decent, if not great, grades.

I didn't expect the rejection letter. When it came, and I opened it in front of her, I didn't have the heart to tell her. I hadn't applied anywhere else, so I couldn't even say 'Welp, not the one we really wanted, Mom. But I did get in locally instead, so I'll still get to graduate and I can stay close!'

So... I panicked and did something stupid. I told her I got in. I told her there was a scholarship and grants, that I'd be living in the dorms, and that a food plan was even included. Her dream. The dream she'd wanted for herself and then for me.

I decided I'd go down and figure it out somehow. I'd use the money I'd saved up for school to live near the school instead. Maybe I'd get a job at the university. Anything would work, even as a janitor or in the food hall. I'd meet people. Get known around campus. Workers got a free education, so I knew the jobs would be hard to come by, but surely something would be open. I just had to be close. Be available.

But there was nothing. I got a job at a call center nearby instead, to pay for my apartment. I talked to mom every week, telling her how much fun I was having and how my nonexistent classes were going. We'd text while I was on breaks at work, like I was between classes.

I'll just reapply when the application window rolls back around, that's all. It's common for two years of school to take three years, no big deal. And this time I'll apply to more schools. Schools closer to home. I've probably got a better chance of getting in back home anyway, plus then it would even be cheaper. In-state tuition is always cheaper.

Plus, this way, if I do get accepted here next year, having an apartment here for a year already would give me in-state status here as well, making next year cheaper. And if I don't, surely I'll get in somewhere. I could use mom's address if I get accepted there and this one for other schools close to here. And wherever I get accepted to, I'll go next year. I'll just tell mom that the new school is better for some reason. Closer to her, better for my degree, something. And if I get accepted here, so much the better. Only one year lost, right?

And then I saw the ad.

It was for The Surrogacy And Fertility Agency. They were looking for surrogates and they were willing to pay fifty thousand dollars for them.

Fifty thousand dollars! Five thousand dollars a month for ten months just to be pregnant. To do something some of my friends' back home were accidentally doing for free. The ad said they were a full service agency that matched women who could get pregnant with people who couldn't. They paid for travel and other stuff too but that wouldn't apply to me, they were local.

And, according to the ad, they were desperate. Apparently a lot of people want babies and can't have them, so they were promising fast matches and the best benefits in the market.

Who knew there even was a market? But the ad stuck with me. It gnawed at me.

My call center job pays ten dollars an hour. At forty hours that was four hundred dollars a week. Sixteen hundred a month, before taxes. My apartment took half of that. Do you know how much college five thousand dollars a month could pay for? I could put it all back while living on the pay from the call center.

So I did it. I applied. And this time I did get accepted, lol!

And boy did I hit the jackpot. The couple I got paired with, Peter and Brooklyn Taylor, they wanted one thing above all else. Secrecy. And they were willing to pay big for it, too! Twice as much, which is insane, but who am I to turn my nose up at twice the money I was already ecstatic about, just to keep their secret?

I mean, I wanted to keep it a secret, too.

I could just see me telling my mother that instead of being in school like I told her, prepping to become somebody, I was selling the use of my body for ten grand a month. Wouldn't she be proud? I imagine her introducing me, her very pregnant daughter, like 'This is Kristine, she's carrying some stranger's baby for money to pay for college. At least she's not a stripper?'

Lol, nope. I mean, what's one more secret at this point, right? It just means that I have to be 'too busy with school and work to come home' until after the birth.

So, the Taylors'. Apparently they run some local adoption center, so I guess I could see why they wouldn't want it getting around that they were looking for a surrogate instead of just adopting.

They're an interesting couple. When they first interviewed me they came off as having the perfect lives. She's kind of petite, but she came off as larger than life. 'Large and in charge' comes to mind, even though she really is kind of a little thing. I think it's her presence. Plus, she smells of money, of course. Reeks of it. They both do. Apparently there's a lot of money in the baby brokering business.

Even in heels she's shorter than her husband. He's really tall. Like basketball tall, which just makes her look shorter. He's charming, though. Kind of intense, but charismatic to her take-no-prisoners' attitude. They say if you're going to partner with someone, especially in business, that you should complement each other. Have one be strong were the other is weak and vice versa. They definitely seem to be that.

Anyway, all I came away with after that first meeting was that they seemed nice, looked like they'd definitely have no problem being able to pay what they were offering, and that secrecy was a high priority. As was not waiting. They were past ready to get things underway. I was past ready to start banking 10k a month myself, so that worked for me.

Brooklyn seemed happy that I asked her to be in

the room with me during the implantation. I figured they'd both like to be there when their baby batter mini me's were put in my oven to bake, an expression that Brooklyn seemed to get a kick out of, so I offered that to them. I'm not shy about body stuff so I didn't mind two virtual strangers being there. The whole situation is rather strange, after all. Why not let them share in the weirdness, right?

But only Brooklyn came. She said Peter was out of town. Apparently he travels a lot. I wonder if he'll keep that up once the baby is born, but really, it's not any of my business. A couple like that will likely have a nanny helping out anyway.

I do wonder if Brooklyn gets lonely though. Maybe that's why she wants a baby come hell or high water? But still, why not adopt, ya know? I'm sure a couple like them could adopt a lot of kids. They could Daddy Warbucks the crap out of themselves, couldn't they? But then, could they keep running their business? Oh well, again... none of my business. I'm just the womb for rent. I know jack about the lives of rich people, after all.

But, so far everything has gone really well. The pregnancy has progressed normally, according to the doctors who know about such things. And the money keeps hitting my account like clockwork, so that's a huge plus.

Still though. I didn't expect it to be so hard. Keeping secrets. Staying away from my family back home. Not telling my mother about any of it. I've no one to talk to, really.

I think Peter gets it though. He comes by my apartment sometimes. Calls me and texts me, asking how I'm doing. Brooklyn does, too. Well, she calls and texts, she doesn't come by.

She seems a bit colder though, like I mentioned. All business. Transactional but friendly enough. Like, when she checks up on me she asks me if I've been remembering to take my prenatal vitamins or if I'm able to put my feet up when I'm at work.

But when Peter checks on me he asks if I've been eating well. If I hesitate at all, even slightly, he offers to swing by and drop off either some take out or some of the leftovers their chef made. He doesn't stay long or anything. Or offer to take me out to dinner. Nothing like that. Nothing creepy or out of line. Just warmer, that's all. His checking on me feels more personal, less transactional.

Especially once I started to show. It's like the whole thing got more real then, you know? I mean, the morning sickness was real enough for me, as was the first trimester sonogram. But once I started to pop, once others could tell, once the evidence was visual and he could see that this was really happening, he seemed to check up on me more.

Maybe traveling so much and not seeing the progression happen like Brooklyn did when she'd meet me at my appointments made each time he'd see me seem like everything was happening faster? Maybe the reaction of 'Wow, you're really starting to show' is more shocking when it's been two or three months since he'd seen me, when Brooklyn sees me at every appointment? I don't know.

I just know that once I had a bump to rub, the checkups from them doubled from just hearing from Brooklyn to Peter taking more interest as well. That's gotta be a good thing though, right? Having both parents involved is always best for the baby, after all. And if he gets drawn in, if he ends up really taking to fatherhood, maybe Brooklyn won't give off that cold and lonely vibe quite so much anymore.

Helping them become a family feels good. Watching them take interest in the baby feels good. And boy, let me tell you what, watching that ten grand hit my bank account every month feels really, really good, lol.

And, speaking of money, I need to get to work. It

doesn't pay what renting out my womb pays, by any means. But it does help me pass the time. And every day that passes means I make more money and get closer to getting to go home, see my mom, and putting this whole, weird, amazing adventure behind me.

Chapter Twelve

A knock on the door to Peter's study interrupted the last few words of Brooklyn's conversation with Officer Sandage. She opened it to find their housekeeper, Lana, who asked if she should come back later to clean since the study was currently occupied.

Brooklyn jumped at the chance to ask her to show the officer out so she could stay and fire up Peter's computer to see if everything Officer Sandage had just told her was being broadcast to the world yet. Brooklyn told Lana that she needed a few minutes, and that she'd leave the study door open when she was finished, so that Lana would know when it was ready to be cleaned.

She finished the last, polite closing words with

Officer Sandage, asking him to please keep her informed if he learned anything about what they'd been discussing and he assured her that he'd be in touch before following the housekeeper out.

Once alone, Brooklyn shut the office door again. She leaned her back against its solid weight and closed her eyes in despair. Kristine truly was missing, wasn't she? Her phone and purse had been found, no one had heard from her, and both the police and the press were involved. This couldn't be a good sign. Where was Kristine? What had happened to her?

What's happened to my baby?

With a sinking feeling she opened her eyes, took a deep breath and crossed the room. She let herself drop into Peter's leather ergonomic desk chair. She put her elbows on the desk, planted her face in her hands and thought briefly and wistfully about the bottle she knew was hiding just to the right of her knee, in the drawer. Then, with a shake of her head, she pulled herself together.

The most important thing was finding Kristine. She knew that. She felt that truth in every cell of her body. Her gut was a knot of fear and pain, but her mind refused to go there. If she looked into the abyss of the possible things that could've happened to, or could currently be happening to, either Kristine or her baby, an abyss of possibilities that ranged from a car accident to foul play, an abyss that her mind was opening wider and wider for her to fall into, she didn't think she'd ever be able to come back out of it.

She forcibly turned her attention instead to the phone call she'd gotten from the reporter. What all had she said? Why hadn't she excused herself to talk more to her, to drill the reporter with questions?

"...Apparently they haven't found her yet but they did find her..."

She must've been talking about Kristine's cell, purse and diary.

"...As far along in her pregnancy as she is now known to be..."

Brooklyn assumed she'd written about everything, including the surrogacy, in her diary. That was how they'd found her. They weren't fishing, they knew.

"I don't know any Kristine Armstrong," she'd told the reporter. This wasn't going to go well; she knew that from experience. She knew what happened when the press got hold of things that already didn't look good. They made them look worse. They made them look... evil.

The last thing she needed right now was the press digging around, looking for ways to make everything look sordid, and twisting everything until all her secrets were flapping around like clothes on a clothesline when none of it would help anyone find Kristine. How could it? Neither she nor the center had anything to do with Kristine going missing.

But she knew it wouldn't matter.

And Peter being in closed meetings about one of the birth mothers wanting her baby back even though the adoption has already gone through wasn't going to help matters in the slightest.

It wasn't the first time a birth mom changed her mind and it wouldn't be the last, but she remembered all too well the one time such a thing went public, so the timing of news crews targeting her center for *anything* couldn't be worse.

Many birth mothers had taken them to court over the years but only once had the court case escaped the privacy of the courtroom to play out in the public eye, and Brooklyn did not want a repeat of that fiasco. Their numbers had crashed during and after, in both the number of birth mothers and adoptive parents, and it had taken them years to get back to where they'd been before that.

She didn't want that to happen again, not when Kristine wasn't a birth mom changing her mind about adoption. Finding Kristine had nothing to do with her center at all, not like last time. Last time it made sense for the center to come under fire.

To be honest, back then there had been some grounds for that birth mother to stand on. The court decision could have gone either way, since that birth mother's case worker even admitted on the stand that she'd misled the woman, even going so far as to admit outright lying to her.

According to the law, that didn't matter. Whether the birth mother was lied to or not, the adoption itself was still legal and couldn't be undone once what happened had come out. She couldn't legally get her baby back even though that particular baby shouldn't have been adopted out to begin with. It was too late by then. The papers had been signed by all parties, the time period to fight it passed.

Plus, the adoptive parents fought even harder to keep their new baby than the birth mother did. Or could. They'd out-lawyered the girl, and out-moneyed her. And in the end they'd won. But it had been a spectacle of a case, shining a spotlight on the agency that Brooklyn did not want to see happen again.

Granted, so far being able to point back to that very public case kept any other birth mothers with similar cases and aspirations of getting their babies back from trying too hard. Birth mothers who'd just changed their minds a few hours, days or weeks after the ink dried were told to look that case up. It was public information after all, and the news footage was easily found just by a quick internet search.

But that case, and the public scrutiny it brought, almost put her out of business and it's what drove Brooklyn's almost irrational fear of reporters, news cameras and bad publicity. It's why she wanted to keep her personal business out of the public eye so desperately. Business was one thing, but this wasn't about business. This was about a missing person who had no connection to her center.

But that wouldn't matter and Brooklyn knew it. It would become a witch hunt or smear campaign against her and her center instead of a concerned search for Kristine.

When something bad happened to a woman, especially a pregnant woman, it was always the ones closest to her who were looked at hardest, relationships questioned, secrets exposed. Kristine didn't have a man in her life, as far as anyone knew, and she was states away from her family. *Those closest to her* automatically defaulted to Brooklyn and Peter and Brooklyn knew it.

She hated that all she could do was hope that the

press kept their reporting to the search for Kristine, but she knew that it was likely her denial of Kristine and her wanting to keep everything a secret that would ironically end up being what inevitably turned the press against her, it was just a matter of time.

Speaking of, she wiggled Peter's mouse to see if the sharks were already circling. When his computer woke, it came to life with a paused video on the screen instead of the desktop she was expecting. She maneuvered the mouse to the corner of it, meaning to minimize it before opening an internet tab to search for information about Kristine, but something about the still image showing in the video gave her pause.

It looked like it was a feed from one of their video cameras out front.

Now, it was natural for Peter to be able to view any of the camera feeds from his computer, as it would be silly for the only viewing access available to be down in the monitor room set up for their security personnel. It was also normal for Peter to sometimes check the footage when the security guys weren't on the property, or even for the grid showing all of the cameras at the same time to be running in real time on his screen while he was in here doing paperwork or talking on the phone and not using the computer for something else at the time. He often used it sort of as a background or a screensaver while he was doing other things.

None of that was odd in and of itself, but this frame was frozen as the camera was focused clearly on a person. And it was the time and date stamp in the corner of the feed that caught Brooklyn's attention.

The stamp was of the exact date and time that they'd been at the fundraiser. The date and time that someone had thrown a brick through their window. So why was it showing a woman, plain as day, when the footage they'd given the police was a fuzzy, useless mess?

Brooklyn clicked '*play.*'

Chapter Thirteen

Today was interesting, to say the least. Peter called right as I was getting off work. My back was aching, my feet were as swollen as my belly, and he said he happened to have a crapton of leftovers with him from some dinner meeting he'd attended and wanted to know if I'd be interested in them.

I was. Any day that I don't have to cook after work is a good day in my book, so I gave him the go ahead to bring them by. That wasn't the interesting part though, as it's not entirely uncommon. I've actually quite enjoyed the times he's dropped food off for me.

The kinds of places he frequents are a world away from my normal, read that as cheap, places to eat. And

I am definitely not above accepting leftovers from places that would likely not even let me wait tables for them, let alone serve me, without some serious upgrades to my dress code. I swear I've eaten better since he and Brooklyn have come into my life than I ever have before.

No, the interesting part was that this time he ended up staying a while and eating with me, although I'm still not fully sure how it happened. I remember him handing me a bag that was still quite warm, and as I caught a whiff of its contents I asked him if it tasted as heavenly as it smelled.

He laughed and said, "I've no idea, I was too busy with words coming out of my mouth to be able to put any food in." He went on to say that the meeting had kept him so busy talking that he was actually hungrier leaving his dinner meeting than he'd been when he'd arrived.

He'd handed everything off to me at that point, but my upbringing had me asking him to join me before I could think to stop the words. He said no at first, thanking me for the offer, but his stomach growled its protests right then, just like you see happen on TV shows or in books, so I insisted he stay, even as I more than half expected him to refuse again.

After a longing sigh, which I took as a yes, I just

pulled him the rest of the way into the apartment and shut the door behind him. "You always make sure I'm well fed," I told him when he still seemed unsure. "It's only right that I do the same. Even if it is technically with your food."

He laughed and accepted and before I knew it we were crowded around my tiny little café-style kitchen table that, until then, had only seen single serving plates atop it before.

We were largely silent at first, as often happens when two starving people are initially diving in to quiet their hungers. But it didn't take long until our polite grunts and exclamations of how good everything tasted slowly changed over to somewhat painful attempts at small talk.

Even the small talk grew larger once we'd unboxed the sinfully decadent desserts that had been included. There was just something about the rich sweetness topping off our full stomachs that invited lingering and savoring. And there was just something about lingering and savoring that invited deeper conversation. If I could've added a glass of wine it would've been a perfect meal, although the decaf I brewed us instead was a close second.

I told him stories about growing up back home that made him laugh and he countered them with his own, which surprisingly weren't much different than mine. Apparently he hadn't always carried his silver spoon. Neither had Brooklyn, according to the few things he let slip about her upbringing, as well.

He didn't talk much about her, saying instead that her story was hers to tell, not his. But he did imply that nothing had been handed to either one of them, and that everything they'd built they built together.

He was more open about his own story, though. He hadn't been born wealthy, like I'd just kind of assumed. But he hadn't been poor, either. Not like he hinted that Brooklyn had. His situation seemed somewhat similar to mine, actually. Not exact, but enough that I could relate.

His parents had wanted more for him than they'd had, and though it was often a struggle, he did, obviously, make his way through law school. He'd done his internship in family law, which is what initially got him into the orbit of adoptions, and of Brooklyn and her ideas for what eventually became The Brooklyn Taylor Center.

I think he was just about to launch into the story of how they met when his phone broke the spell. He said it was nothing, just a notification that he'd attend to later, but it was just enough of an intrusion to remind us of where we were, who we were, and what we were doing.

Not that we were doing anything wrong, it was just that we'd almost forgotten for a moment that we weren't old friends catching up, or new ones feeling each other out. We weren't colleagues, or even equals. We were employee and employer of a sort, with its implied power imbalance. And... well, it was rather an intimate moment, was it not? Us, sharing this decadent meal, alone together.

I was carrying his child. His and Brooklyn's. And we'd forgotten that for a bit, but also not really, so the interruption was probably for the best. We both had lives we should get back to now that our impromptu dinner and subsequent lingering was done.

If we'd been a couple, the next likely step would've been to rinse the dishes together and either adjourn to the couch to cuddle up and watch a movie or to instead move to the bedroom for a little...

Nope, that's too weird to even imagine, let alone write down.

I scooped up the minimal dishes, basically silverware and coffee mugs, and made myself busy. I thanked him again for feeding me. I made sure to tell him to thank Brooklyn as well. I wanted to keep her presence very much at the forefront, to normalize the day and to anchor her here with us somehow.

He went with it, awkward small talk reinserting itself again perfectly where it was needed, as he couldn't really even pretend to offer to help me clean up. That largely meant throwing containers in the trash, so he was free to accept my thanks and move on, with nothing left to say but goodbye.

At the front door though, he stopped. He turned back toward me, looking like he wanted to say something else, but was unsure if he should.

"What is it? What's wrong?" I asked, when he stared too long, deliberating.

"Nothing's wrong, it's just..."

"Just what?"

"I want to touch you," he said, finally. And then he got flustered when he realized what he said. He corrected himself, explaining. "The baby, I mean. Your belly. I've been watching it move, all during dinner. I'd like to feel it, that's all."

It was such a natural, reasonable thing to want to do, wasn't it? So why did it make me feel so... I don't even know what, honestly. But my first instinct was to deny him. To say no.

But it was his child; so didn't he have every right? It made perfect sense that he'd want to, that was his baby in there. But it was also my body. I had every right to refuse him, as well.

So, whose rights took priority in a case like this?

I'd have no issues letting Brooklyn do it, if she asked. I've often let her, actually. Anytime she'd wanted to. But those times were at one of the doctor's visits she attended with me, as we didn't see each other anywhere else.

There were no public celebratory lunches after. It probably wasn't too unusual to see her out with some pregnant woman or another in the course of her day, but it wasn't common, either. Especially not the same woman all the time. People would ask who I was.

I'd never been to their house either, again because of the secrecy. She'd said that she didn't want anyone to know, even her staff there.

"I know Brooklyn has, touched you, I mean," he continued. He seemed as unsure as I was. "But, I didn't want to assume I could. It feels forward to ask, really. Like I should attend your next appointment instead, and touch it there. It would seem more official there."

His thoughts were mirroring my own.

"More natural, less creepy," he said.

I laughed. It wasn't that it felt creepy, it just felt... intimate.

"Yes! That's it, that's the word. It seems intimate. To even ask," he said.

It surprised me because I didn't think I'd said it out loud.

"Brooklyn hates it when strangers try to touch her belly," he continued. "But...?"

"But you're not a stranger," I said, trying to reassure him. Or myself. "You're the father."

"Yes, exactly. Only..." His words lingered there.

This was unchartered territory, but so was him staying for dinner. And that had gone well. Quite enjoyable, really. So, what do I do?

What did I want to do?

I realized that I wanted to give him this. I wanted to give this to myself, even. To allow myself to be touched outside of a clinical environment, by someone who cared. Cared about the baby if not really about me. But I could pretend, right?

Not that he cared about me instead of the baby, but that he, that someone, cared about me in addition to the baby. I was more than a walking incubator, after all. Wasn't I?

I had feelings, and hormones. And this whole situation was so much harder than I'd ever imagined it would be. I was so alone in this, really. So lonely.

It's not like I wanted him, per say. Or wanted to

keep their baby, or any of the things that the psych interviews screen for. It wasn't anything like that, nothing devious or untoward.

It was just... human. Human to want connection during a difficult time, that's all.

I knew if I was in his shoes I'd want to touch me. To touch my belly. To feel my baby roll under my palm. So I let him. Of course I did.

And it was fine. Still a bit awkward and weird, but it seemed that way for both of us so I wasn't alone in that, I don't think. And it was nice to feel not-alone in something again.

But now, hours later as I write this, I just can't help feeling that this whole night, innocent as it was, was a terrible, terrible mistake.

Chapter Fourteen

Brooklyn watched the woman throw a brick through her window, again and again. She kept rewinding it, hoping one of the viewings would trigger something besides rage and confusion.

The video was crystal clear. This was exactly the quality she'd expected to see when she'd watched the other footage, standing side by side with Officer Sandage, as Charles hit play the first time. This was why she and Peter had both been so confused the night of the fundraiser, when Charles first told them that he didn't know anything and hadn't been able to identify anyone from what they had.

The video showed *nothing identifying*, he'd said, when he came and took Peter back with him, leaving her alone at the fundraiser. But the only thing *not identifying* about it was that Brooklyn hadn't ever seen the woman before to be able to identify her.

She had red, almost auburn, hair pulled back in a messy ponytail with tendrils hanging and swinging wildly as she moved and threw. Her face was lightly freckled and her eyes were pinched with anger and the effort of the destruction she was caught in the middle of.

She looked to be in her mid-twenties, curvy but not in a pregnant way. More like in a swimsuit model way. She was nothing but hips, breasts and fire, but she wasn't anyone Brooklyn knew.

But, why was this on Peter's computer? Obviously he'd seen it. Why hadn't he told her?

Had he discovered somehow that Charles was being less than truthful? Was Charles the one hiding this? Was the brick and its note meant for him? Had Charles given the police tampered with and unusable footage to cover someone *he* knew? Someone *he* recognized?

Or was Charles just following orders given to him by Peter?

When the twentieth viewing didn't answer any of her questions, she emailed herself a copy of the video for her own safekeeping. Then she opened a new internet tab, like she'd woken his computer up to do originally, and she started her search for the newest information on Kristine.

She didn't have to search very hard. She clicked on the first headline that populated her search results, recognizing the name attached to it as the reporter who'd called her office. She must've had the article ready to print when she'd called.

ALLEGED SURROGATE KRISTINE ARMSTRONG STILL MISSING

FIRST LISTED AS A MISSING COLLEGE STUDENT, TWENTY-YEAR-OLD KRISTINE ARMSTRONG WAS FIRST REPORTED MISSING BY HER MOTHER, JANINE ARMSTRONG. IT HAS SINCE BEEN DISCOVERED THAT KRISTINE IS NOT A COLLEGE STUDENT ATTENDING THE LOCAL UNIVERSITY BUT SHE IS INSTEAD ALLEGEDLY A SURROGATE MOTHER FOR LOCAL COUPLE PETER AND BROOKLYN TAYLOR.

THE TAYLORS' OWN AND OPERATE THE BROOKLYN TAYLOR CENTER, A LOCAL GROUP HOME AND ADOPTION CENTER KNOWN NATIONWIDE.

Kristine's mother first reached out to reporters when she realized that it had been an entire month since she'd last spoken to her daughter on the phone, even though text conversations continued, until they too stopped last Saturday. That was almost a week ago.

Janine Armstrong has since reached out to us again, seeking our help in finding her daughter. According to her, police haven't been as helpful to her as our viewers have been.

"Some people contacted me through Facebook after the newscast," Armstrong said. "They were the ones who told me where Kristine has been living and working, not the police. So, I went down there myself and broke in through a window beside her front door. Don't judge me, any mother would've done the same."

Armstrong then told us what she saw. Kristine was nowhere to be found but her

PURSE AND PHONE WERE LOCATED ON A TABLE INSIDE THE APARTMENT. AFTER A THOROUGH SEARCH SHE ALSO FOUND WHAT SHE SAID IS KRISTINE'S DIARY.

IT WAS OUR REPORTING THAT FIRST BROKE THE NEWS THAT KRISTINE WAS NOT A STUDENT AFTER ALL, BUT IT WAS THE DIARY SHE FOUND THAT LEAD ARMSTRONG TO BELIEVE THAT HER DAUGHTER WAS INSTEAD A SURROGATE MOTHER FOR THE TAYLORS'. ARMSTRONG HAS STATED THAT SHE'D BE RELEASING MORE OF THE DIARY'S CONTENTS TO US SOON AND SHE'D ALSO BE TURNING THE DIARY IN FULL OVER TO THE POLICE AS WELL.

GOING ON THE INFORMATION THAT ARMSTRONG HAS ALREADY SHARED, WE DID REACH OUT TO THE TAYLORS' FOR COMMENT.

PETER TAYLOR DID NOT IMMEDIATELY GET BACK TO US WHEN WE ATTEMPTED TO CONNECT WITH HIM BUT HIS WIFE BROOKLYN TAYLOR, WHO IS ALSO PREGNANT AND CLOSE TO HER OWN DUE DATE, DENIED KNOWING ANYONE NAMED KRISTINE ARMSTRONG. ONCE WE

PRESSED HER AGAIN SHE STATED, "I'M SORRY, BUT I CAN'T SPEAK TO ANY OF THIS. NO COMMENT."

POLICE SAY NEITHER OF THE TAYLORS' ARE YET BEING CONSIDERED PERSONS OF INTEREST, BUT THEY ARE, AND WILL BE, LOOKING AT EVERYONE WHO HAS ANY CONNECTION WITH KRISTINE ARMSTRONG. THEY ARE ALSO ONCE AGAIN ASKING ANYONE WHO KNOWS KRISTINE, OR WHO MAY HAVE ANY INFORMATION ON HER CURRENT WHEREABOUTS, TO PLEASE COME FORWARD.

A half-dozen more articles and newscast videos just like that one followed, one after another. They all said the same basic thing, just in a different arrangement of words. Brooklyn exited out of everything and sat with her head in her hands again, thinking.

She fought the urge to get up and go to Kristine's apartment, like there would be anything there for her to see. Maybe the window her mother had broken would still be broken and she could get in and look around.

And find what? Do you think her mom left the

diary there so you could read it, too? Or maybe Kristine left multiple copies of it spread around the apartment just in case two different people wanted a copy? Or maybe no one looked under the bed yet and Kristine's hiding under there, waiting for you to find her?

She rolled her eyes at her own reaction, willing herself to calm down and think. She wanted to move, to do something, but she didn't know what. She didn't want to go back to work, she'd just left there. She didn't want to stay in Peter's study, not with everything she'd just learned closing in on her, plus Lana would be keeping an eye on the door, wanting to keep to her cleaning schedule so she could go home.

Even though she didn't want to stay where she was, she couldn't think of any other place in or out of the house that she wanted or needed to go to. What she wanted was to go find Kristine, but she didn't know where or how.

Think, think, think!

"Some people contacted me through Facebook after the newscast," Kristine's mom's words from the article surfaced in Brooklyn's mind. She opened a browser window on Peter's computer again and went to Facebook. What was her mom's name again? Janine. Janine Armstrong.

While Facebook loaded and Brooklyn signed in she eyed the minimized security footage again. She wanted to ask Peter about it but Kristine took priority and Peter wasn't here to ask.

That thought reminded her that he probably didn't know she'd left work, so she popped off a quick text telling him that she had the car and to let her know when he was done so she or Jeff could pick him up. She didn't expect an immediate answer since he was likely still in his meeting, so she wasn't surprised when she didn't get one.

She turned her attention back to finding Janine online, assuming she'd be easiest to find through Kristine's friend list instead of by searching for Janine Armstrong by name. Once she found her she clicked on her name and was glad her account was set to public so she didn't have to 'friend' her to see her postings.

Brooklyn was surprised to see that her last few postings seemed to suggest that she was posting from Kristine's apartment. Was she staying there instead of at a hotel? And the police were letting her? She'd just admitted to the world by way of that reporter that she'd broken in. And if she'd found Kristine's purse, cell and diary there but not Kristine, didn't that make her apartment a possible crime scene?

Before she could think better of it Brooklyn decided to go there, too. She had no idea what she'd say or do once she got there, but she'd figure that out when the time came. She shut the computer down again and headed out, leaving the study door open for Lana.

She grabbed her keys, backed the car out and headed for the gate only to turn around once she got near it and saw the news van already parked and waiting just outside of it. She could see the gate guard having a heated discussion with the van's driver, but Brooklyn didn't want to risk driving by them to exit so she u-turned and headed for one of the lesser used back exits from the neighborhood, hoping none of the other gates had anyone lying in wait.

As she weaved her way toward the back exit her phone rang. It was Peter. She answered it, putting it on speaker.

"Hey, I got your text. Don't worry about picking me up, I'm going to catch a ride home from Wes. We're cutting out early today."

Wes was one of the other attorneys, likely the one he'd been meeting with, so she nodded along as he spoke. She was about to warn him about the main gate but he kept going.

"There is a news crew here," he said. "Apparently the word is out about us and Kristine so I'm waiting near the exit in the hospital wing for Wes to bring his car around for me. I thought this would be a quiet door to meet him at, but I was wrong. I guess the new girl in the maternity home went into labor early so there is more activity here than I expected, but that may work in my favor. I can slip out in the chaos. Either way, I'll be home soon."

Brooklyn told him what awaited him at home, unless the guard was successful in chasing them off. Peter said that at least Wes' car wouldn't be known to them and had a dark tint, then they hung up.

Brooklyn aborted her journey to the back gate and went home to wait for Peter instead. Thinking that he likely saved her from an ill-advised trip to Kristine's apartment, she parked in the garage and hit the button that closed the garage door after her. She turned the car off and sat, thinking. Not able to come up with anything more productive to do, she pulled Janine up on Facebook again, on her phone this time, to see if she'd posted anything else.

Janine's latest post was that the police were there now, kicking her out and making her go find a hotel. Apparently, even though it was Officer Sandage who told her about Janine 'finding her way into Kristine's apartment and tearing it apart' they'd learned that she was back there again and intending to stay there at the same time the rest of Facebook did, and were putting a stop to it.

She toggled over to Kristine's page to check on it, but there were no postings from her, just comments from well-wishers. Feeling desperate, antsy and stymied she finally let herself back into the house intent on getting to the bottom of at least one issue once Peter got home.

The redhead on the security footage.

Chapter Fifteen

We really shouldn't be doing this. It's not right. I know it's not right. So, why can't I help myself?

Am I that starved for love that I'll settle for clandestine moments and stolen kisses from a man who doesn't belong to me? A man who'll never leave his wife, and who's told me so in no uncertain terms?

This is crazy! She's as much a part of me as he is. I'm carrying their child. I'm meeting up with her at doctor's appointments where she smiles at me and caresses my belly and then later, after, I meet up with him here. In secret. Where he kisses me and caresses my... well, everything.

It's an unholy trinity, the three of us. I know he says that she doesn't mind, or wouldn't if she knew. I *know he says they have an open relationship and have for a long time. I know he assures me that these stolen weekends where he tells her that he's out of town are some kind of code for them, but it's all so new to me. It's all so... sordid!*

But at the same time, it's all so exciting!

I feel like I'm in a soap opera. One of those super-dramatic, unrealistic ones where there are murders and twins and comas and secret relationships and fights are more common than meals but it's so weird to be living in one. I feel like I had a walk-on part in Real Desperate Rich House Husbands of Surrogate County and ended up staying on for the season.

I mean, come on. Anyone reading or watching this season of my life would say it's too unrealistic. And yet, here I am. Being paid an obscene amount of money to carry their child, making nice with the wife during the day and making very, very nice with the husband at night.

Not every night, of course. But quite a few of them since that first night that he stayed for dinner. The night that he shyly and rather awkwardly said that he wanted to touch me. I thought then that it was possible that it had been a mistake to eat dinner with him, and maybe it was, but somehow, even now, I don't regret it.

It's just one more secret to keep, right? One more thing to hide. One more interesting twist to my life and the year that, once it's over and I'm back home, well paid and empty wombed, will become nothing more than a memory to pull out when I'm in the old folk's home and my life is boring and married and divorced and my own kids are grown and gone and don't come visit me.

They say what doesn't kill you makes you stronger so maybe I'll be the strongest woman in that old folks' home when my time comes, hmmm? Because as long as nothing goes wrong, as long as I don't do something even more stupid and fall for him or something insane like that, then one day this whole sordid, surreal situation really will just be a memory. And if so, I might as well make it one heck of a memory, right?

And so far, I am well on my way.

He lets himself in with their emergency key. The first time he did that it took me by surprise because I thought Brooklyn was the one holding it for safe keeping. So, when I heard the key in the lock, and I knew that only me, the apartment office and Brooklyn had one, I thought for sure it was over for us.

I thought she was coming to scare me and confront me, but when the door finally opened and it was Peter standing there, with his arms full of dinner and flowers, I was so relieved. He said that anything standing between him and me, even just my locked front door, was an emergency situation when he'd been missing me as much as he had been, and I had to laugh at his inventiveness.

Speaking of his inventiveness, wow. That man has taught me quite a few new moves. I can't lie flat on my back much anymore, the weight of the baby squishes some important nerves and blocks blood flow when I spend too much time on my back, but he's taken that well in stride. I've learned some positions that will serve me well even after all this is over and we've broken ties and gone back to our real lives.

That's what this all feels like, actually. That none of this is really real. That it's some kind of odd, surreal break from real life and that real life wont commence again until after this affair is over, this baby is born and handed over, and I'm back home with nothing to show for any of it but fat stacks of cash, this diary, and a whole lot of surreal memories.

This whole year has felt like that, if I'm being honest. From the moment I got my rejection letter from the university and the lie that I'd been accepted came out, until right now, ruminating on new positions with my rich, married lover, invented to accommodate his and his wife's baby inside me. Surreal, right?

Even the fact that I've become 'the other woman' doesn't feel real, because that is so unlike me. In my real life, my life before, I'd never even imagine being willing to do any such thing, but it's the surreality of this whole situation that's even allowed any of this to happen.

Being so far from home, all alone with no real connections to my own life except lying contact with my mother, contact during which I'm telling her about classes that don't exist and friends that don't exist, that's what set the stage, I think. Then the secrecy and surrealness of the entire surrogacy situation, hiding more secrets, pretending more and more things that just aren't true, that's what allowed this newest twist of becoming his personal secret to even have a chance at happening.

Back home, in my real life, the real me, the boring me, would never have allowed myself to become someone's secret, and now that seems to be my entire identity. I'm Brooklyn's secret. I'm Peter's secret. I'm even becoming a secret from myself, if that makes sense.

I'm becoming something that even I won't acknowledge to myself, once this is all over and I'm back home and back in my own real, boring life. But, I'll let you in on another little secret...

I think Brooklyn knows about us. I've seen her car in the parking lot. And one of the times I swear I saw it was one of the nights Peter was here. He had me in the dark, up against one of my open windows, when I saw her car out there in the shadows.

She was in the perfect place to watch, at the perfect time. What are the odds that that wasn't set up beforehand, huh? But then again, if they've got an open relationship, maybe she's open too, about how her thing is to watch from the shadows? Maybe they're both playing me to get what they want in all this, too?

But again, what goes on with them is none of my business, is it? It's almost at the end for the three of us now, anyway. My due date is getting closer, I'll hand them their baby at the end and we'll never see each other again.

If Brooklyn hadn't gotten pregnant herself right after I did I'd wonder if there might not be a second round with them in my future. Maybe a few years from now, if they decided to go the surrogate route again later, to give this baby a little brother or sister. But, since Brooklyn's already got that in the works, I highly doubt that'll happen.

So, most likely, I'll ever see either one of them

again once this one is born. And I'm good with that. As interesting as this whole experience has been, I mean them and their relationship no harm. I am looking forward to washing my hands of this whole year and putting the surrealness behind me. We're getting close, too.

I'm looking forward to getting my old, boring, real life back. As fun as it's been, I miss the simplicity of my old life. The honesty of it.

Oh, well. Soon enough.

Chapter Sixteen

rooklyn stared out from her office window, killing time until Mr. and Mrs. Williams were to arrive to sign their final adoption papers and take their newborn daughter home, by watching as a few straggling but hopeful reporters milled about, sipping coffees and hoping to catch someone from the center outside.

She was glad that her windows were mirrored, allowing her to watch them even though they couldn't watch her in return. She thought it was only fair, since they, and by extension the whole world, had been voyeuristically watching her and Peter for almost a week now.

Brooklyn couldn't believe it had been almost a week since Kristine's diary was released. Almost a week since Brooklyn's name, and of course Peter's, good lord Peter's, had been forever entwined with Kristine's. All three of their names had been the only thing on anyone's lips ever since. It had also been almost a week since Brooklyn had confronted Peter about the redhead on the security footage and almost a week since she'd fired Charles and his entire company, against Peter's wishes, and had hired a new security company to take their place.

And in all that time, there'd still been no word on Kristine.

It definitely wasn't for lack of trying, as the police had questioned them almost daily and had installed a special tip line just for information on the whereabouts of Kristine Armstrong. But, despite everything including the diary, the case had gone nowhere.

Brooklyn and Peter had been presenting a united front, at least in public. They'd tried to add a reward offer to the police tip line, but as she and Peter were considered persons of interest if not full out being named as possible suspects, the police wouldn't cooperate on the reward. They said they had their own crime stoppers reward attached, using money that came from funds other than from an overflowing pot attached to people who possibly have a conflict of interest.

Brooklyn tried to tell them that their interests were the same, finding Kristine, no matter where the fingers finally pointed. But they'd still rejected their offer, so she and Peter had instead offered their reward money separately from the crime stoppers reward.

And still they heard nothing.

Brooklyn sighed, her eyes following the reporters' every movements while her thoughts were everywhere but. She tried to direct those thoughts to preparing for the adoption signing that was due to happen shortly, but she found herself instead wondering if any of this would still be happening if her past had been different. If she herself had turned out differently.

If she'd never been dropped off at the steps of the children's home would she have ever opened this center? She highly doubted it. So, if she'd never opened this center, would she have had the money to hire a surrogate? Would Kristine be going about her life entirely unaware of her, or of Peter, and therefore be safe and accounted for now, or at least not be carrying their child wherever she was?

Because Brooklyn wished she was anywhere but

here and was anyone but herself. Who would she have married, what line of work would she have gone into, if she hadn't ended up here?

She'd thought that pairing kids with families, helping them get adopted, like with this signing today that was usually her favorite part of her job, would heal something inside of her that had splintered more and more with the passing of each year during which she'd lived at the home and no one had chosen her. And it had, to an extent. But it only helped heal the fractures that spread out from the initial break. Nothing had been able to heal the cause, the fact that she'd been given up in the first place.

So who would she have been if her mother had never died?

She'd certainly never have been unceremoniously dropped off on the front steps of the building on the other side of this complex.

The building that now housed the maternity ward was actually the very same building that had been her group home back in the day, complete with the angel wings that still bracketed and embraced the ornate front door.

It was one of the reasons she didn't spend much time on the maternity side, or with the women there.

The memories of living there always hid behind every rehabbed and repainted corner.

Brooklyn remembered the day she signed the papers, buying the building she'd grown up in. Symbolically it had been important to her that she'd been dropped off just inside its front door, unwanted, with nothing. Then, years later and all grown up, she'd bought it. She'd repaired it, added on to it, expanded it and turned it from the worst memory of her entire life, a place that initially brought her nothing but pain as a child, into a fresh start.

She'd built a business of hope and joy from a crumbling remnant of her childhood, and made a new life for herself in the process. One where she'd been *this close* to finally having everything she'd ever wanted.

And now it looked like it was all going to be taken from her again. Kristine, Peter and maybe even her center, too.

The news crews still blanketed the grounds both here and at home. The publicity and suspicion cast on her and Peter personally had of course spread like a cancer to cut off the successful center. Their numbers of interested adoptive parents had dropped dramatically and their maternity ward tours and reservations died completely.

It still floored Brooklyn how many pregnant women were looking for not just shelter but a secretive shelter away from prying eyes. And the attention focused here with Kristine's disappearance was a far cry from that.

It was actually kind of amazing that the adoption today and its associated paper signing was even still on the books. So many people had bailed on her and her company in the wake of Kristine's diary being made public that she was half convinced that today's signing, the adoption of Sarah's baby, would be canceled at any minute.

It was ironic, really. Sarah, their newest maternity client, the one who'd brought Carole up to her baker's dozen, might very well be their last incoming mother to ever enter under those ornate angel wings, if things carried on as they were.

It was funny though that the newest one had jumped the line and given birth ahead of all the others, although they did have two more women in labor in the hospital wing at the moment. But that just went to show the unreliable and unexpected nature, of not only pregnancy and birth, but of the business itself. In the space of a week the maternity home had dropped from thirteen women to ten, with no one lined up to take their places.

Even the babies can't get out of here fast enough.

Brooklyn laughed at her own moroseness on a day that usually brought her so much joy. Today would likely be bittersweet. Who knew how many more adoptions this place would even see?

She knew that missing person cases like Kristine's were hard on everyone involved. Even the ones with the most joyful outcomes, like she still held out hope that Kristine's would be, could be catastrophic. Investigations like it tore families apart, bankrupted businesses and livelihoods. Would theirs survive? Their business or their marriage?

When she'd asked Peter about the footage of the redhead, Kristine's diary hadn't been released yet.

He'd denied knowing anything about her at first. He said he'd only discovered that same original footage that morning, when he'd been randomly clicking around in the system, looking for something else. He'd pulled the clip aside to look closer at it later, because it was time to leave for his meeting, only Brooklyn got to it first.

He said he was as confused about it, and its time stamp, as she was. He even trotted out the unoriginal *why would I leave it there to be so easily found if I was the one trying to hide her to begin with?*

So Brooklyn called Charles in.

The look on his face when confronted was so guilt-ridden that she initially thought Peter was telling the truth. But then he looked to Peter and he said, "I told you I wasn't comfortable doing this..."

Brooklyn fired him on the spot and when Peter tried to defend him by saying that he was only following orders, she obviously knew the truth. The whole thing had scented of *woman scorned* from the beginning.

Then the diary came out.

Of course he denied everything in it as well. He said none of it was true, not the food deliveries nor him ever using our emergency key to go over there for anything. He especially swore that they haven't had sex anywhere, let alone in her window in full view of anyone who might be watching.

Brooklyn may have been tempted to believe him there, since the diary had also said that Brooklyn was there watching them through that window as they had sex, and she knew that definitely wasn't true. But he'd just denied screwing the scorned redhead too, and Brooklyn had seen the aftermath of him breaking that off firsthand.

Granted, he did finally come clean about the redhead, so why continue to lie about Kristine? Because of the press? Deny your lying eyes and all that? But if he and Kristine weren't sleeping together, why would she say they were, in a diary not meant to be seen by anyone? So one of them is obviously lying, but who?

No matter what he may or may not have told Kristine, Brooklyn knew they didn't have any kind of an open marriage. Not unless you counted Brooklyn opening herself up to being hurt every time he did this to her.

Why do I continually have to deal with the fallout from his indiscretions?

But it had been years, *years*, since his last indiscretion. Or so she thought, until the diary and the redhead.

Two at once now? How does he find the time?

Of course only one of them was currently missing and unable to explain themselves. That certainly didn't look good. Brooklyn had seen what the redhead was capable of when Peter supposedly ended things with her. But what if he and Kristine had ended things as well?

Maybe that hadn't resulted in a brick but in a missing woman and unborn child instead? Had Peter done something to her? If he was capable of getting Charles to alter footage going to the police, could he have been capable of doing something to Kristine, even as she carried his and Brooklyn's baby? Or had Kristine maybe removed herself from the entire situation?

But surely she'd have come forward by now, if that was the case.

Unless she couldn't.

Because with every page released from Kristine's diary, the hits just kept coming.

Chapter Seventeen

*B*rooklyn is seriously starting to freak me out. I swear she knows and I think she's watching us. I keep thinking I see her everywhere. Little glimpses of someone who looks just like her turning the corner ahead of me at the grocery store, only there's no one there when I investigate. Cars that look like hers a few cars behind mine in traffic. I'll lose that car by driving around, but then there it is again. It's almost like she can track me somehow.

Once, I came out to a flat tire when I was headed to work. Now none of these things prove anything, and they can all be explained away as innocent coincidences, but still. I just get this feeling sometimes that maybe it's her. But I don't understand why that would be. What would be the point?

If they've got an open marriage, and I've no reason to doubt that they do, because it fits with her whole 'secrecy and keeping up public appearances' vibe, why would she follow me or Peter, or care about what he's doing at all? Or who he's doing it with? Doesn't an open marriage imply that she's free to see whoever she wants, too? So why would she care who he's seeing?

I mean, it is possible that he's lying to me and he's actually cheating on her, I guess. Though it would be a lot easier to tell that if they weren't hiding the surrogacy. If they weren't keeping me hidden for other reasons, I'd wonder why he only comes here. Why he never takes me out, or even to a hotel, if they both discreetly see other people.

Unless it's not him that she's interested in. Maybe it's me specifically.

I know that she's reassured me, from the very beginning of her own pregnancy, that it wouldn't change a thing between us, but now I'm starting to wonder. The further along we both get, the weirder she gets. At my last doctor's appointment, she said something I can't get out of my mind.

I'm so close to delivering that they were checking the baby's positioning. The doctor mentioned that it looked like I'd dropped, and he said that the reason the baby was making me pee constantly again was because its head was putting pressure on my bladder. He said that was a good sign that things were progressing right along, because instead of being up under my ribs like the little bugger had been, it was getting ready to be born by positioning itself to head-butt its way down the birth canal.

And that's when Brooklyn said, kind of out of the blue, "Wouldn't it be a shame if, after all this time, something bad were to happen to either one of you?"

What the hell did that mean? It was such an odd thing to say.

Now, I've been known to say awkward and inappropriate things in my time. And sometimes my sense of humor runs to the dry or morbid side, so I almost laughed. Like when you get the giggles during a funeral service, but there was just something in her tone that gave me chills.

There was something cold and calculating to it. When I looked at her in surprise, her eyes got wide. Like she hadn't realized that she'd said it out loud.

I remember thinking at the time, 'Either one of us? As in me and the baby? Or as in me and Peter?'

I did ask for clarification. I said, "Something bad? Like what?"

She tried to wave it off, saying something like, "Oh,

don't mind me. I'm just getting nervous about everything going right. I meant that to come out more like in a throwing salt over your shoulder, preventative, superstitious way. Not in a creepy way. It's just me trying to manage my expectations, that's all. We're just so close, aren't we? This is really happening, isn't it? All of it."

But still, it was that tone again. The way she looked at me when she asked if 'all of it' was really happening made my blood run cold. And when she said 'We're just so close, aren't we?' I couldn't breathe.

Was she talking about the baby, like the timing was getting close? Or was she referring to Peter and how she knew we were sharing him?

I tried to laugh it off with her, but neither of us were at ease after that. In fact, that was the first day that I thought I saw her again. Hours later, when I was taking my break at the call center, I slipped outside to where the others sit to smoke sometimes.

There wasn't anyone there, so no dangers of anything second-hand, but it was a quiet spot to sit and I was enjoying the feel of the sun on my face as I had my lunch. But then I had the oddest feeling that I was being watched.

I looked up, my eyes searching. I cupped my hand

and put it to my forehead to see better and that was the first time I thought I saw her car. It was across the street in another parking lot. I couldn't tell for sure but it looked like it had someone in it. Someone looking my way.

Then the door behind me opened and more employees came out. When I looked back, the car was gone. I took the rest of my lunch inside since the new arrivals were digging for cigarettes and lighters, but that was just the first time I started to feel like I was being watched.

It started happening all the time, but I don't remember having that feeling before that day. Before she'd said what she'd said. But maybe that's just when I got more cautious. Or maybe that's just when I started paying attention to my surroundings more, I don't know.

I felt like I needed to be more careful somehow. But that was just silly, wasn't it? It's not like she'd meant me any harm. Why would she? And I'm sure she'd meant her baby no harm. Like she'd said, we're so close. It's almost over.

If I'd ever had doubts about her regarding this baby, surely those had passed long before. I mean, yeah, I'd been a little worried way back at the begin-

ning of all this. Especially when she'd first gotten pregnant, too.

That would've been the time for her to change her mind about me if she was going to, wouldn't it? I'd had to sign something saying that I'd allow them to 'reduce' the numbers of embryos inside me if more than one or two took, and if Brooklyn ever wanted me to. They said it was a standard part of the contract, but if she'd wanted me to reduce the number of babies I was carrying to zero, and stop paying me because she didn't need me anymore, well wouldn't the first trimester have been the ideal time to do that?

When she didn't, I was happy, of course. But my understanding is that she'd gotten pregnant before. Her issue seemed to be carrying to term. So, I could see her expecting to possibly lose her own baby at some point, and therefore keeping me 'unreduced' would allow us all some time to see if either one of us had any problems later on in our pregnancies.

And now that we are both well past the time where even an early birth would be a problem, I've got to wonder if she isn't regretting me. She wanted her own baby above all, and now she's looking at two.

Does she see me as being a problem now? A redundancy she hadn't expected to have to deal with?

Is she wishing she'd reduced me from her life long ago, and therefore also from Peter's?

Or maybe I'm just paranoid.

I'm sure these are just the odd ramblings of a pregnant woman. I've heard that pregnancy hormones can really do a number on a woman's paranoia. Makes you see things that aren't really there. Not like hallucinations, but like connecting dots that don't exist.

But then again, Peter has said some things. Let things slip on occasion. Nothing I can quite put my finger on or point to, but just things about her past. Things that leave me uneasy about her. And maybe that center they run, too. Peter mentioned something about how some of their adoptions have been questionable.

I tried to pin him down on what that meant exactly, but he wouldn't elaborate. All he'd say was that things weren't always what they seemed, but then he was quick to change the subject. With his tongue. And I forgot all about it after that, until just now, writing all this out.

The other day though, after having that followed feeling again, I finally asked him if he'd told Brooklyn about us. Were they that open? Did she know we were seeing each other?

He said no. He said that he'd learned a long time ago that knowing the who hadn't worked out very well for them in the past. I don't remember the exact words but they'd included 'rubbing her face in it makes her jealous in a way that not knowing the who does not.'

Since I was more than half convinced that she was very well aware of his current who, his answer didn't sit well with me. The last thing I needed was for Brooklyn to feel jealous of a relationship I was only in for the fun, and that I knew wouldn't be continuing much longer anyway. But his rather unemotional statement that her knowing hadn't worked out very well for them in the past made me wary. There was something he wasn't telling me.

He soothed my concerns as best he could, but they still linger, even though I'm sure I'm probably just being paranoid. I mean, it's not like I expect anything bad to actually happen. We're too close to the end. What could possibly happen when we're this close?

Chapter Eighteen

"**Y**ou never told her we had an open marriage, that's what you're saying?" Brooklyn asked Peter. "Why don't I believe you?"

"Of course I never told her that. First of all, it isn't true. And second, I never told her anything. We've literally never been alone together. I've never seen her without you present, I've never taken food to her apartment, and I've most certainly never slept with her."

"You were never with her when you were supposedly out of town?"

"No."

"Were you ever with the redhead when you were supposedly out of town?"

"Shari? I..."

"Don't say her name."

"Yes," Peter said with a sigh. "Sometimes I was with the redhead when I said I was out of town. But only a couple times."

"Did you tell her that we had an open marriage? The redhead. Is that your line?"

"No. I don't have a line. I don't make a habit of cheating on you. It was just this one time."

When she shot him a look, he sighed and amended his reply. "Other than that time. That was decades ago, Brooklyn. We weren't even married then."

She didn't reply with words, just with another look. A look that told him exactly what she still thought, all these years later, about that excuse.

"Twice. Twice I've been unfaithful in all the years we've been together. You know about both of them, I'm obviously not polished enough to get away with it well. And I'd already ended it with Shari, sorry, *the redhead.* That's why she threw the brick. It was already over."

When Brooklyn just kept looking at him he said, "But I've never touched our surrogate. She's lying in that diary. None of that ever happened."

"Why would she lie in her private diary?"

"I don't know. Maybe it wasn't so much a diary of things that happened that she wanted to remember forever but a diary of her fantasies or something. What about the stuff she says in there about you? Did you spend your days following her around, tracking her car?"

"I did not follow her around, no."

He zeroed in on what she hadn't said. "But...?"

"But what?"

"Damn it, Brooklyn. You tracked her car? How? Why?"

Sometimes Brooklyn wished two decades together weren't so telling. That he couldn't read her quite so easily.

"It was just an app."

"An app would work on her phone but to track her car you'd have to put something on it. Or in it. Which was it, were you tracking her phone or her car?"

Seeing no need to deny it now, and needing someone to talk about all this stuff with, she answered him honestly. They were pariahs at the moment. All they really had was each other, better or worse.

"Both. I liked knowing that if anything ever

happened I could find her. I was just keeping an eye on our investment, that's all."

"So that part in her diary was true? You *were* following her."

"I was not," Brooklyn said. "I never physically followed her. I never went to her work. I never shopped at her grocery store. All I did was occasionally see where she was on the app."

"And that thing she said that you said? Did you really tell her that it would be a shame if something happened to her? To them?"

"Maybe? I don't remember exactly. I'm sure I didn't mean it like that though. And I definitely didn't do anything to her. Not like the news is making it out to look. And we're suing Charles, by the way. Don't think I won't. Him selling that footage of the redhead to the news stations is what got them to really turn on us. To get so nasty about all their accusations and insinuations. That added to that damned diary."

Peter nodded his agreement and added, "Yes, that was not only unprofessional, it violated the NDA all the staff signs. We'll kill him and his business, legally. He won't get away with that."

Peter had been the one to tell Brooklyn about that before she'd had a chance to see it on the news.

Charles had apparently jumped at his chance to get back at them for firing him for, as he'd put it, *doing what he'd been told to do by his employer* in replacing the footage of that night.

The footage of the redhead throwing the brick played on a loop for days in the background of every newscast, her angry face highlighting all the snippets from Kristine's diary as every newscaster in the state, and likely beyond, salivated over every sentence that told the tale of Peter being a cheater and of him and Brooklyn's *'obviously unhappy and troubled marriage'* that allegedly seemed to include tracking, harassing and seducing their poor, young surrogate.

Brooklyn had been waiting in dread for the redhead, Shari she'd learned her name was, to come forward for her fifteen minutes of fame and give interviews about her affair with Peter, but so far she hadn't. Instead what had set off an entirely new round of frenzy for the news cycle was the stuff that Kristine's mother Janine was just now coming forward with.

Brooklyn and Peter took a break from their arguing as the promised interview they'd been waiting to see cued up on the TV. The reporter who'd called Brooklyn's office the week before, Kate Miller, was gearing up to interview Janine in one of those one-on-one exclusives that newsrooms couldn't get enough of.

Brooklyn watched in a daze as basic introductions were made yet again, like there was someone watching who'd just climbed out from under their rock and was learning about this case for the first time.

She noticed how well they'd cleaned Janine up. Not that she'd needed cleaning, she'd always come across well before as a concerned-if-struggling mother, but apparently she'd gotten the whole treatment of hair and makeup for the bright studio lights anyway. She looked more like a news anchor in training with all the high-def makeup caked on than a stressed out mom concerned for her missing adult child.

The reporter covered old ground, repeating things Brooklyn had wondered about before but had only recently learned herself, like how Kristine's father had died years ago and that was why there was no father figure seen with Janine any time she made one of these appeals to the public. But finally, after making sure everyone was caught up, she pounced.

"You're coming forward today with new information that you've said you've kept quiet about thus far because it was information that even Kristine herself hadn't been aware of before she went missing, is this correct?" Kate Miller asked as Janine seemed to steel herself to open a closet door that would expose at least one dancing skeleton.

"Yes, that's correct."

When Janine remained quiet instead of bursting out with whatever she'd come to say Kate prodded her with, "And you've decided to come forward with it now because it connects Kristine to the Taylors' in a way that they hadn't been known to be connected before?"

Brooklyn could hear the unspoken words she'd left out. *Like having their baby and sleeping with Mr. Taylor while being tracked and followed and threatened by Mrs. Taylor wasn't connection enough...?*

Brooklyn closed her eyes against the unsaid but implied accusations and took a deep breath, in and out, waiting.

"Yes," Brooklyn heard Janine say, eyes still closed in defense of whatever was coming. "We'd never actually told Kristine, but she was adopted. We adopted her from the Brooklyn Taylor center twenty years ago."

Brooklyn's eyes popped open and found Peter's.

"That's it? That's the big secret?"

"Apparently," he answered.

"Oh, thank God. I thought it was something important."

The interview carried on but Brooklyn watched it relieved. She'd been expecting the equivalent of a sex tape, or doctored footage of her and Peter throwing a body into the river.

"...so you're saying that the connection between Kristine and the Taylors' goes back at least twenty years then. And yet Kristine never knew. Is there a reason you never told her she was adopted?..."

"They're acting like this matters," Brooklyn muttered, confused. "Good Lord, I thought they were going to say that Kristine was carrying your child or something. I mean, yours and hers, not yours and mine."

The relief had her rambling.

"Like that's a *'connection,'*" Brooklyn continued, making air quotes with her fingers as she spoke. "Kristine didn't know, and even if she did, she applied to an agency. She had no way of knowing ahead of time she'd be assigned to us. She didn't come knocking on our door asking to have the baby of the couple that ran the agency she didn't even know she'd been adopted from. This is stupid. And it's not helping anything or anyone."

Brooklyn flicked the TV off once it became

apparent that there would be no new revelations and they were just using the time with Janine to go over old ground.

"I'm going to work before I don't have a company to work at anymore. Are you coming, too?" Brooklyn asked Peter, as she gathered her things in a cloud of irritation that masked anger at the news cycle, rage at her husband for helping feed them and, above all else, a desperate fear for Kristine and her baby.

Wrapping herself in the routine of working was the only way she'd been able to get through the day without breaking down in a puddled mess thus far, and she clung to it ferociously, no matter how it looked to the press. Because she didn't think she'd ever be able to claw her way out of the looming, bottomless pit of despair if she actually gave into it.

"Why can't they use their time to actually find her instead of dragging us through the mud every chance they get? We didn't do anything to her. She isn't chained in our basement for goodness sake."

Chapter Nineteen

I had to have the locks changed today, Peter's been scaring me. Sometimes it's like he's a whole different person. It took me a while to pinpoint when he started to change though, but I finally did. It was when I started talking about ending things and about how we wouldn't be together for much longer so we needed to enjoy the times we had before they were over.

He doesn't like that kind of talk at all.

He gets so angry. Irrationally so. And he's not someone I enjoy being around when he's acting like that. It changes everything about him. All the lines of his face get harder. Harsher. And his eyes... His eyes get this almost cruel glint to them.

It's kind of spooky actually, when I'm able to look

at it with a sense of detachment. It's like he becomes his own twin or something. I don't mean like in some multiple personality disorder way, it's more like that he unleashes something that's always there inside him, just under the surface. But that something is usually more hidden. Or at least usually under more control.

He stands a little taller but his muscles get stiffer, more tense. His chest gets puffier, more bowed. He stands closer, hovering. No. Looming. He looms over me, in my space, like he knows that just being bigger than me, stronger than me and standing right there is going to be enough to intimidate me or something.

And it does, a little. His brows draw together and he looks down on me, and him being so tall, it makes me step away from him. Instinctively, you know? Just to put some space to move between us.

I think the first time it happened was when I asked him in passing if I was the only one he was currently seeing on the side, and oh boy, he did not like that.

I didn't even mean anything by it, I know what we are. I know they've got that whole open marriage thing going on. And I know our days are numbered, I was just genuinely curious if I was the only one he was 'out of town' with on occasion or if he had a menagerie of us, that's all.

He never did say, now that I think about it.

Mentioning a menagerie just now reminded me. Another time I was teasing him. I forget how it started but it started innocently enough and I said something about how convenient it was that he usually had a dozen women to choose from at any time, sequestered there just on the other side of the building where his office is, and how at any time he could go fishing in that pond if he wanted to.

I mean, some wouldn't take well to it, but surely some would. It would alleviate either the drama or the boredom of living with a bunch of other women, wouldn't it? To have this tall, handsome man giving them some attention. A rich lawyer to boot. The hotness of sneaking around, catching forbidden moments in empty, old rooms, hoping not to get caught. Plus, there would be the added perk for both of them that the women wouldn't go and get pregnant and cause him any trouble, would they?

I thought it was funny, but he did not. It made me glad that I bit my tongue and didn't ask him if he ever wondered if Brooklyn would've liked to have watched. I'm not sure now how he would've reacted to that teasing question.

He did tell me once that he was breaking one of their rules in being with me. It was the same day that he told me that Brooklyn didn't like knowing who he was seeing at any given time and that he'd learned long ago that she saw them knowing the who of their relationships as rubbing each other's faces in it, or one upping each other in some sort of competition, or something. Instead of just getting their needs met outside of the relationship impersonally, I guess.

Such an odd situation, those two. But anyway, he said their only other rule, besides not naming names, was that they couldn't see anyone they both knew. So basically strangers were fair game but as I'm definitely not just some stranger, I was supposed to be off limits.

I told him I was fine with breaking it off early if he thought that being with me might cause him problems, especially since I was going to have the baby soon anyway, but he kind of went crazy. He said he's the one who gets to decide, not 'the woman.'

When he saw my face after he said that, he backpedaled. He said he was just playing around, and it happened so early on in our relationship that I let him. I didn't really think any more of it, but that was before I knew better.

And things have just gotten worse, really.

He started letting himself in at odd hours, when I wasn't expecting him to even visit at all. I think he was trying to catch me seeing someone else because sometimes it would be two or three in the morning when hearing the front door open and close would wake me out of a dead sleep. Talk about giving a girl a heart attack.

He'd come into the bedroom almost defensive, looking around like he was going to see feet sticking out from under the bed or find someone hiding in my closet. When he didn't, he'd slide into bed beside me, telling me that he'd missed me so much he just couldn't stand not to come and see me. Touch me.

But sometimes I think he also came when I wasn't home. I'd come home from work and things would just be off. Like they'd been riffled through, or picked up, looked over and set back down. Though once he did leave a huge bouquet of flowers right in the middle of the table we first ate at together. That was early on though. All the later visits just seemed... searched.

And lately they seem ominous. When I come in from work sometimes there are little notes he leaves. They almost look, on the surface, like love notes. Can't wait to see you. Can't wait to get my hands on you. But something about them creeps me out. My skin crawls when I see them in random locations when I know they weren't there when I left.

I've asked him to stop, under the guise of him just being here so often and so randomly now, in broad daylight. He's tempting fate that we'll be seen. Caught. But he tells me I'm being silly or over dramatic.

Don't you like knowing how much I care about you? He asks. Don't you enjoy knowing what you do to me? The thrill of being caught is half the fun. Besides, I like surprising you. I like being in your space. Smelling the scent of you when you're not there. Some days that's all I get of you and some days that's just not enough for me.

He told me he likes to lay in my bed when I'm gone. He lifts the covers and climbs inside. He said he pleasures himself in my bed, his head on my pillow, thinking of me while I'm at work.

I've obviously got to end this. I can't wait until the baby is born to do so, either. So, I had a locksmith come out and change the locks. I had to give a key to the apartment office of course, but I've got the only other key now.

He's supposed to come over tonight, so I'll be ready. When his key doesn't work I'll tell him why, and I'll end it. I'm getting so close to my due date that

I could go into labor at any minute anyway. I'm only ending it a little bit sooner than planned. A week, maybe two.

I'm a little scared though. I keep remembering his words, from before. 'I'm the one who decides when it's over, not the woman.' So I guess if there are no diary entries after this one and I'm never seen or heard from again after tonight that'll mean it didn't go well at all.

I'm kidding, of course. It's not like he's ever really been violent or anything. Not really. I'm sure it'll be fine.

Chapter Twenty

If she's ok, if she's still alive somewhere, has she had my baby yet? Thoughts of Kristine, and the baby she carried, were the only thoughts occupying Brooklyn's mind at any given time.

Yes, she'd read all the diary entries the press printed. Yes, her marriage and her business were suffering, she wasn't sure either would survive this and she wasn't sure she even wanted them to. Yes, she dealt with swarms of reporters and police officers now on a daily basis, but all that was ever running through her mind was *Is my baby ok? Is my baby ok? Where is Kristine? What happened to them? Is my baby ok?*

There were no more entries in Kristine's diary

and the entire country was blaming Peter for her disappearance because of it, but Brooklyn had never known Peter to be violent. That, and the other things written in the diary that Brooklyn knew not to be true, gave her pause. She'd never followed Kristine, not once.

It did explain why Brooklyn's emergency key hadn't worked, she'd noticed that the locks had been changed way back on the night of the fundraiser. Had Kristine really been missing for over two weeks now? It seemed like just yesterday she'd gone out there and tried her key, and yet it also felt like it had been two years ago. Time stood still and rushed by all at the same time.

The last diary entry, the one that mentioned having the locks changed, also mentioned how close Kristine was to her due date. She'd been expecting to go into labor at any time. Had she?

The brand new key Kristine had made had been found inside, on her keyring with other keys, including her car keys. Also found inside when Janine broke in was Kristine's phone and purse. All that, together with the diary, painted a vivid and dire picture of what may have happened to Kristine.

But none of the diary entries were dated, so no one could pin down the when behind any of them.

All Brooklyn knew was that the last one mentioned the new locks and she'd seen the evidence of new locks the night of the fundraiser. But how long before that had they been changed?

She'd spoken with Kristine that morning, so if they'd been changed days before, that meant she'd talked to Kristine after she'd supposedly ended things with Peter, and all had been well. Or that she hadn't actually gone through with ending things after all.

If she'd had them changed that morning, that meant she'd been planning on seeing Peter that night, likely after the fundraiser. But she'd already disappeared by the time of the fundraiser. Hadn't she?

That was the first time the tracker had shown nothing. And she hadn't driven out to check on Kristine until after Peter had gone silent in his office, likely passed out and sleeping off his liquor.

His car had been there when she'd left, it was there when she'd returned, and she'd had Kristine's unknowingly useless key with her. Unless of course Peter had made himself his own copy. It would've been easy enough to do, since she always left her keys hanging in the same place at home, on the hook by the garage door. But he couldn't have gone to see her that night. Could he have? After she'd returned?

Surely not. And that was assuming anything in the diary was even true.

She recalled the diary mentioning that a spare key was given to the apartment office. She assumed the police would check with them and they'd get a date for that final entry soon, but so far they weren't being very forthcoming with any information considering that she, and more specifically Peter, were considered suspects.

Likely the only thing keeping Peter from being arrested was the inconsistency of the supposed facts. That and the lack of a body. Or the lack of *any* actual proof, really.

Kristine's car still hadn't been located. There had been no sign of a struggle at the apartment. No overturned furniture, no blood. No semen was found in her bed. The police had dusted for Peter's prints and even done the luminol thing where they checked for cleaned up blood. They'd found neither.

Peter's prints were not found anywhere inside Kristine's apartment, but Kristine's were. So it wasn't like someone had wiped the place clean of all prints while resetting the upturned evidence of a struggle.

The only prints had come back to Kristine, Janine and apartment staff.

And, of course, Brooklyn's. Her prints were partials, obscured some by Janine's, on the outside of Kristine's apartment from the night of the fundraiser. Those raised some eyebrows at the police station, but neither her prints nor Peter's were found anywhere inside.

That supported Peter's claims that he'd never set foot in there and that everything Kristine had written about him was a lie. With no proof that anything written in the diary was even real, no evidence of any foul play and no body, they couldn't arrest him.

And Brooklyn wasn't sure if they should, although the entire rest of the country playing armchair detective from their computer screens seemed to think he was guilty.

Granted, Brooklyn knew for a fact that Peter cheated. She thought there might even be something to the whole 'fishing from the maternity home pond' thing, even though Kristine had only touched on it in the diary herself in passing. But Brooklyn had never known Peter to be abusive, not in all the years she'd known him.

At least not physically.

She couldn't deny that there might have been

some abuse of power going on over the years. She'd had her moments of concern regarding Peter and the women in the maternity home, because of how she and Peter had first met and gotten together, and because of the time he'd cheated before they got married, but she'd never really let her mind go there, even to wonder. She didn't want to know either way, not really.

She liked to think that she'd been special, that the way they'd met wasn't indicative of how he normally operated but was instead proof of his instant longing for and loving of her in particular. Because otherwise... well.

Otherwise he once again looked guilty of something shady and untoward.

He was quite a bit older than Brooklyn and had been working in family law when she met him. She'd technically been a minor, about to be released from the foster system and therefore the group home setting when they first got together, but she never saw it as him taking advantage. At least not back then, when she was living it.

To her the age number tied to her birthdate meant less than nothing. She'd had to grow up long before the number caught up and reflected that. To her he represented stability. With him on her side, she began to feel secure for the first time. Secure, taken care of, and finally loved.

It was with his help and support that she'd even thought herself capable of taking on a business like hers. It was his money and his education, connections and knowledge of the law, mixed with her sheer determination, that got it off the ground.

He'd always humbly backed away from taking any credit, saying he'd never had the money or connections she apparently thought he did, but she wouldn't hear of it. He had some, and she'd had less than none, so to her way of thinking his help with any of it was what had made it all possible.

She'd thought she'd found love with Peter, but over the years she'd had her suspicions about his fidelity. Or lack thereof, really.

A few years into them seeing each other, when their business was just starting to take off but before they were married, she'd found out he'd been seeing someone else. It was a huge blowout, of course, but he'd ended it. He'd chosen her when she'd given him the ultimatum, but she'd be stupid to think there hadn't been any others in twenty plus years, no matter what he was saying now.

Back then she'd stayed because she was young, stupid, and entwined with him in a business she didn't think she could continue without him. She made some bad choices herself back then, same as him. Choices she'd have made entirely differently now, with more experience under her belt.

But most of all she'd stayed for the same reason anyone does. She thought she loved him and that he loved her and that they could move past it, stronger for it. So they'd gotten married to cement their new and improved relationship.

Looking back on everything from where she was now, she still didn't know where she would've ended up without him but she almost wished she'd gone it alone. Almost. But not quite.

She'd made something of herself. She'd helped a countless number of woman and families, making herself wealthy and powerful in the process. She could leave it all behind now and be ok, but back then?

If given another chance to start over she knew she'd do it all the same. Even the bad things. Even the things she tried not to think about.

But she did recognize that over the years she'd become jaded. With the business, with him. With the things she chose not to see. She stayed because of her own damaged self. She'd been unwanted, unloved, and over the years had gotten more and more desperate for a baby.

Because with her history and in this marriage, she fully believed the only way she could have someone to truly love, and who'd finally truly love her, was to have a baby of her own.

Maybe it was stupid, but there it was.

She rubbed her belly as her thoughts tumbled and twirled.

There are a few things I would change, though. A few key choices that might've made all the difference. But here we are, aren't we?

Tired of her own thoughts, Brooklyn looked around at her empty, quiet office. Business was so slow now it was almost nonexistent. She had no signings. No one else had given birth since the two that had gone into labor on the same day a few days before, on the day of her last signing. She wasn't even sure why'd she'd come in.

She needed something to do. She thought about stalking Kristine's and Janine's Facebook pages but the thought of reading all the well-wishes posted there again, especially on Janine's page, made her feel ill. People were going out of their way to support Janine on social media, strangers from around the world were posting their thoughts and prayers for her missing child, but no one was posting anything in support of Brooklyn's missing child, were they?

Brooklyn's child was missing too, and the fact that she and Peter were getting crucified while Janine was being supported was salt in Brooklyn's wounds. Everyone was also still going on and on about what a coincidence it was, or wasn't, that Kristine had been adopted from the center, their conspiracy theories growing wilder with each moment.

Instead of stalking Facebook, Brooklyn started pulling up records. Kristine had been adopted twenty years before. They'd digitized some of the old records but some were still paper files stored in their storeroom. It didn't take her too long to find it though, and soon she was opening the Armstrong's file.

Robert and Janine Armstrong had adopted a baby they'd named Kristine Armstrong just over twenty years before. And as Brooklyn read further, her heart began to beat faster. Her stomach dropped, then the contents of her lunch rose back up and she lunged for the trash can beside her desk. Her blood pounded so hard in her ears that she couldn't even hear herself puke.

Kristine had been born here, all right. But her

birthmother had named her Sarah. Sarah Scott. Kristine wasn't missing, she was Sarah.

Sarah, their newest maternity ward client. Sarah, the one who'd looked so familiar when Brooklyn had caught sight of the back of her the day Peter had his meeting. Sarah, the one that Carole said was a cheerful do-gooder who couldn't wait to *get this birthing thing over with* and who was *excited for her baby to go to someone who'd give it a great life.* Sarah, the woman whose baby Brooklyn had most recently signed adoption papers for.

Sarah was Kristine and Kristine was Sarah.

Brooklyn's mind was whirling and her body wanted to be sick again. As she dry-heaved over her trash can all the bits began to fit themselves together in her head. She felt her heart shatter into pieces. Her soul ached with the unfairness of it all. The cruel deviousness of it all.

Her surrogate had purposely given away her baby. Her baby wasn't missing, or in danger. It wasn't somewhere out there still unborn. Her child had not only been born, it had been born right here in her center. And it was a girl!

She had a daughter and she'd been right here in this very room with her!

And she'd had no idea.

She finally knew where her baby was and yet she still couldn't have her. Hold her. Love her. Because she'd handed her daughter over to strangers to take home with them.

But now she knew.

And she knew just where to find her.

Part Two

Kristine sat painfully erect, spine stiffened and chin raised, in what probably looked to everyone watching as defiance. Defiance was part of it, she couldn't deny that. But it was also from fear. Everything was about to change.

Her eyes closed, she counted each and every slow breath, trying to ground herself in what she was about to do. Controlled chaos reigned around her. She felt her hair and makeup being finished, she heard the busyness of the scurried prep work taking place as she concentrated on breathing in deeply, and then breathing out. It was too late to back out now, even if she'd wanted to. It was time for phase two.

She'd called Kate Miller, the reporter who

seemed to be everywhere on the news talking about her, just two hours before. In that two hours Kristine had gotten the reporter to agree to, and set up, this exclusive story with two conditions. First, this interview had to be done live on air, and second, Kate couldn't let it be known outside of whatever absolutely essential skeleton crew was needed to pull this off that Kristine was no longer 'missing' but was coming forward to speak to the world on live TV.

No prerecording it for editing before airing, no scheduling any *Kristine Armstrong has been found and will only talk to us, live at 6!* promotional teasers ahead of time, and no contacting the police before the interview.

"Are you ready?" She heard Kate ask from the seat across from her as the room quieted and someone yelled, "Here we go!"

A male voice at the news desk nearby started his spiel, breaking into people's scheduled TV programs and interrupting them with a system that was usually only utilized during severe weather or mass casualties.

Kristine took one last deep breath, muttered, "No, not really," and then opened her eyes as the desk anchor wrapped up with, "And here is our own Kate Miller with this exclusive interview. Kate?"

Kate turned to the camera as it zoomed in tight on her. She apologized for interrupting the regularly scheduled programming, announcing the fact that she was doing so to bring the viewing public breaking news in the Kristine Armstrong case, and then she paused dramatically before turning to Kristine as the camera pulled back to include her in the shot.

"As you can see, Kristine Armstrong is alive and well. She contacted me earlier today saying that she wanted to come forward and tell her story. If you've been following this story at all you know that Kristine was first reported missing by her mother. As new information came out over time it was also reported that Kristine was allegedly pregnant, as a surrogate for the Taylor family."

The camera moved in closer again as Kate continued speaking. It switched from a wide shot of Kate and Kristine sitting side by side to zoom in on Kristine alone, up close.

"As you can also plainly see," Kate said. "Kristine looks very different here now than she looked in any of the photos previously shared by the press during the search. Her hair is much shorter and a different color, but most striking to me personally is the fact that Ms. Armstrong is not visibly pregnant at this time.

"We have verified Ms. Armstrong's identity prior to going live with this interview, but that is all that she'd allow us to verify ahead of time. Was she a surrogate? The diary entries we've previously shared were all we had to go by before today in the search for Kristine, but now she says she's here to tell us everything. Has she had the baby? Was she ever really pregnant? Where has she been all this time and why is she coming forward now?"

The camera pulled back again, until both women were seen on screen once more.

"Kristine," Kate began, switching from introduction mode and turning from the camera to face her interviewee. "I have so many questions. I'm sure everyone watching does, as well. But my first one is why come forward like this? Why contact me first and not the police? Or your mother, if you haven't already? Does Janine know you're OK?"

"No, she doesn't know. No one does. I came to you first because I wanted to tell my story myself. I don't want anyone else to tell it and I don't want it coming out filtered through her, or through anyone else, before I have the chance to say everything I want to say. And I didn't go to the police because I fully expect them to arrest me, likely as soon as this interview is over. Or maybe even before we finish, depending on how fast they get here as we're speaking."

"I must admit," Kate said. "That response was the last thing I expected to hear. Why in the world would they want to arrest you? They've been doing everything they can just to find you."

"Janine sped up my timeline when she announced to the world that I'd been adopted from The Brooklyn Taylor Center," Kristine said. "Whether or not the police decided to look into that angle right away, pulling my adoption record to be thorough, I figured that Brooklyn would. And while the police will have questions when they see those records, Brooklyn won't. She'll *know*. She'll know exactly who I am and what I did. She'll know it's over. And my guess is she'll run."

"Wait a minute. I don't understand," Kate said. "What did you do? It sounds like you're saying that... I'm not entirely sure, actually."

"I'm saying that nothing happened to me. I wasn't missing, but I let the world believe I was. I checked my pregnant self into The Brooklyn Taylor Center, had the baby, and signed it over for adoption."

"But..."

Kristine watched the reporter sort through her words. Confusion showed first, then disbelief dawned.

Kate shook her head like she couldn't believe what she thought she was beginning to understand, so the confusion came back as she tentatively asked, "So, you weren't actually their surrogate, then? Or... Oh, my God! You *were?* And you purposely...? But why?"

Kristine reveled in making the reporter lose her professional demeanor. It proved to her that the plan was perfection. But what good was the ultimate revenge if no one knew?

Tit for tat was only the beginning. That aspect had gone perfectly, but now it was time to initiate the public destruction. Even if she destroyed herself and her own future in the process, it would be worth it; a suicide bomber whose weapon was an explosion of truth.

"I purposely gave Brooklyn and Peter's baby up for adoption, yes. I'm guessing that you understand now why I assume I'll be arrested shortly. As confessions go, this one is as public and un-coerced as they get. I'm here of my own free will and I want to tell my story before the police and any lawyers are involved."

"I guess the next obvious question then is why."

"Oh, I'll get to that. But first I'd like to suggest that the police seek Brooklyn Taylor out before they come here for me. I'll be here for a while, telling my story. I don't plan on going anywhere, but I wouldn't assume that the same could be said of Brooklyn."

"What do you mean? What makes you say that?"

"Because I'm assuming that as soon as word got out that I'd been adopted from her center that she'd pull my file, like I already said. Even thinking it had to be a coincidence, it's the first thing I'd do if I was her. Wouldn't you? Pull the records on the adoption of Kristine Armstrong by Robert and Janine Armstrong?"

"Yes, I probably would. Out of sheer curiosity. But that had to have been about twenty years ago. What does an old adoption have to do with anything now?"

"Just *everything*," Kristine said. "When Brooklyn opens my adoption record she'll know where to find her baby. Most women would turn to the police at that point, but I don't think she will. Calling the police would do her more harm than good and there's a decent chance that she'd never get her baby back that way anyway.

"Either the adoption of the baby I carried for her would be overturned for fraud, since it obviously wasn't my baby to give. Or, the adoption would be upheld, like has been the case with many adoptions that shouldn't have happened out of that center over the years. But, if Brooklyn calls the police, the truth of everything would have to come out either way, in court, before her baby's fate is decided."

"What truth are you talking about?"

"I don't think Brooklyn will turn to the police after she opens my adoption record because," Kristine continued, ignoring the reporter's question. "Not only will she know where to find her baby, she'll also know that it's about to be over for her no matter what. This case, my case, is already too public.

"I think she'll do some quick money-transfer magic, if she can. I think she'll go try to get her baby back before anyone is the wiser, and then I think she'll disappear into a non-extradition country. Maybe with her husband, but maybe not. After all, the press hasn't been too kind to him lately, have they?"

"Those are some very serious allegations," Kate

said, her reporter facade firmly back in place. "Have you brought any proof of anything with you today or are you just using this venue to..."

"Before we dive into me more fully," Kristine said, interrupting again as she turned from Kate to face the cameras before continuing. "I'd just like to say something to two people first. To the police, before you come for me, find Brooklyn. And to anyone who has adopted a baby girl from the Brooklyn Taylor center in the past couple of weeks, if you see her anywhere near your new baby, don't hand her that baby back or you'll never see it again. Maybe your adoption will be overturned and maybe it won't, but make sure you go through the courts. If she's at your house now with some kind of story, she's about to take your baby, *her* baby, and run."

With that said, Kristine turned to face Kate again. "Ok. Now you can ask me anything. What do you want to know?"

Chapter Twenty-Two

"You said that when Brooklyn opens your twenty-year-old adoption record she'll know where to find her baby. How is that possible? Do you know where the baby is?" Kate asked.

"No, I don't know who adopted her. The center only does closed adoptions from the maternity home. We don't get to choose the people who adopt our babies, or even know their names."

Kristine saw the reporter's eyebrow cock at adopt *our babies* but Kate didn't press the point that the baby Kristine signed over wasn't hers to give. But that was the beauty of the whole plan, wasn't it? Who watches a woman go through labor and give birth to a child and then doesn't just assume that the child is hers?

"When Brooklyn opens my record," Kristine continued, explaining everything in clear terms for the viewing public as well as for Kate. "She'll of course see that I was placed with the Armstrongs', but she'll also see the names of my birth parents on my original birth certificate.

"My birth mom named me Sarah, Sarah Scott, before my adoptive parents renamed me Kristine Armstrong. Sarah Scott is also the name I used when I checked myself into Brooklyn's center, although once you enter the maternity home you're only known by the first name of your choosing. I chose to be known as Sarah there, but no one there knew my last name or if the name Sarah was an alias or not. Turns out it was, and it wasn't.

"I have a copy of my old, original birth certificate and had an ID made from it to cover me in all the legal paperwork. It was an alias, since I'd been named Kristine for most of my life, but it also wasn't an alias, since that was technically my name at birth. But Sarah is all anyone at the center knew me by.

"Since a Sarah Scott recently delivered there and even more recently signed her baby over for adoption, all Brooklyn has to do is look to the adoptive parents of Sarah Scott's baby to find her and Peter's baby. The baby I gave birth to."

"Ok, but you made it sound even bigger than that. You said she'd know the why of all of this too, from pulling your record."

"She will. She'll recognize my birth mother's name, and she'll know everything."

Kate opened her mouth to ask another question but Kristine didn't give her time to speak before carrying on.

"I'm not going to say her name here, that's one piece I'll leave for the police to announce, or not, as they see fit. Because everything I did, I did for her. But not with her. She had no part of any of this, she doesn't even know who I am, so I won't say her name here. I'm sure I won't be able to keep her out of it for much longer, but for now I still can."

"You gave Brooklyn's baby up for adoption for your birth mother, who had no part of this and doesn't know who you are? Can you elaborate on that more? Explain why? Because none of this makes any sense, so far."

"I can. Somewhat. See, I only found out I was adopted a couple of years ago. Once I turned eighteen and..."

"Janine waited until you were eighteen to tell you that you were adopted?"

"No," Kristine said. "Janine never said a word. That's why I was so surprised when she said it publically, forcing my hand to come forward today. She had no problem announcing that to the world at large, but she kept it from me my entire life."

"So if Janine didn't tell you, who did?"

"My birth mother did. I know, I just said that she doesn't know who I am. What I meant is that we hadn't officially met in person when she told me. We met online. She was able to get ahold of the closed adoption records somehow, and though she'd known where I was placed and how to find me for a long while, she waited until I turned eighteen to contact me."

"So, out of the blue," Kate said. "Some woman contacts you online at eighteen and she tells you that she's your birth mother? And until then you had no idea you were even adopted. And you believed her?"

"Of course not, not at first. But Janine and I didn't have a great relationship, so even though I was doubtful, it did tug on something deep inside me. I started digging into the file Janine kept on me. The file where she stored my birth certificate, my shot records and my baby book. Stuff like that. I won't go into every little thing here, I know our time is limited and it's the story highlights people are interested in. We can leave the paper trail details to the police for now, but suffice it to say that it didn't take me real long to verify everything this woman, my supposed birth mother, was saying."

"Ok. So, then what happened? You verified it, you were adopted. Then what?"

"You know the general story of the Titanic, right?"

"The ship?" Kate asked, her brows punctuated her confusion at the seemingly sudden change in topic.

"Yeah. How it was just plugging along until it hits this chunk of ice in the middle of the ocean, but at first no one has any idea of the actual extent of the damage? Cause all you can see on top of the water, as huge and hard hitting as it was, was the literal tip of the iceberg? How you couldn't see everything that lay hidden just under the surface? How no one was at all prepared for the sheer size of the thing still largely hidden underwater and certainly no one would've imagined the reality of the depth and scale of the damage that had just occurred quite yet?"

"Yeah?"

"Yeah. It was like that. I was the Titanic. I was just cruising along in life and finding out I was adopted was the chunk of the iceberg that hit first, out of the blue. But until I started digging and talking to my birth mother online, I had no idea the size of everything still to come that was lurking there just under the surface."

"How do you mean?"

"I soon learned that my birthmother didn't give me up for adoption at all. I was stolen from her. She never signed a single paper and, in fact, she'd left me in the care of people she trusted for what was supposed to be just a few days, while she went to see her sick and dying mother. When she came back home, fully expecting me to be where she'd left me, she was instead told I'd been adopted and there wasn't a thing she could do to get me back."

"That... sounds horrific," Kate said. "But, it also sounds implausible. Like something out of a fictional Lifetime movie. How was that possible? To be given up for adoption like that? And how do you know that what she told you was true? It almost seems just as likely that it's the kind of story one would tell themselves to help them sleep at night in the years following a decision that they regret."

Kristine nodded and then said, "I can see where it would seem like that. And, I'll be honest, I didn't believe it at first, either. At first, I thought maybe this was some kind of scam. A way to get money out of adopted children seeking their birth parents, or something like that, even though I hadn't been seeking any birth parents. Because I didn't know I had any, as I didn't know I was adopted.

"But, as time went by and I dug further and talked to my birth mother more, it became obvious that everything she was telling me was the truth. And why would someone lie about that? It was twenty years ago, like you said. Why not just say, *I gave you up, cause reasons, but now I've found you again?* I won't go into every detail here, like I already said, because to do so would give up her identity. But let me assure you, I would not have done what I did if I was at all unsure of the truth of these allegations. Brooklyn and her center straight up stole me from my birth mother and then sold me to the Armstrong's, and everyone called it an adoption."

Kate then said, "That brings us back to what you did then, doesn't it?"

"It does," Kristine agreed. "What I did was partly out of revenge, I admit that fully. Revenge for myself and the possible life I could have had that was stolen from me. I also did it out of revenge for my birth mother, and everything I now know about her story.

"But it's more than just revenge. It's also about justice.

"I know that people claim that revenge and justice should never go hand in hand, but I've learned that that's an idealized vision of the world. Real life doesn't happen the way we wish it would. In real life, evil often prevails, and the bad guys often win. Especially when there are vast amounts of money involved. Money has a tendency to make people turn a blind eye to what is right. They say that justice is blind, but we all know that that is often not the case. But what does make people turned a blind eye to justice is usually cold hard cash. And a lot of it.

"So, yes, what I have done up until now was purely based on my own selfish need for revenge. That part is over, and I got away with it, too. It is done. I could've stayed disappeared and lived as Sarah Scott somewhere and no one would've been the wiser, with Brooklyn's baby adopted out to someone else, against Brooklyn's will. Just like I was, just like what Brooklyn did to my birthmother, stealing me from her.

"And if this case is treated the same way that

they have treated every other adoption that should never have happened that's come out of that center, then this adoption will also be upheld. Like mine was. Her baby is gone. Karma is a bitch, isn't it? Oh, sorry. Can I say that on TV?"

Kate shrugged and Kristine continued on.

"But the second part of my plan is just beginning," Kristine said, warming to everything she was saying, speaking faster. "It's where I shift my focus away from my own revenge and turn instead to justice. I plan on bringing everything I have against Brooklyn. In court, in public, even if I have to fight this fight from a jail cell, I am determined to prove every claim I make against her and her center. I intend to back it up with records, and I am hopeful that everyone that watches this story play out in the near future, everyone that has been harmed by the Brooklyn Taylor center, will come forward and tell their stories, as well.

"It's my intention that this, my story, my birth mother's story, is just the beginning. If others come forward and bring their proof, their court papers, their stories, this will snowball into an avalanche against Brooklyn Taylor and her center."

Kristine turned to face the cameras again as Kate looked on, shocked.

"Brooklyn, I am coming for you. Giving your baby away was just the beginning. The beginning of the end of you. You will pay for what you've done and you know as well as I do that you've done a lot that still needs to be paid for. Soon everyone else will know it, too."

arole stood frozen. She'd been making lunch for the half dozen women still left in her care when the small TV she'd had on for background noise switched over rather abruptly from mindless soaps to a special announcement on the Kristine Armstrong case.

She couldn't believe what she was seeing. The woman she knew as Sarah, who had recently been one of her charges and who was calling herself Kristine Armstrong on the TV in front of her, was being interviewed.

And what an explosive interview it was! There she was, on live TV, admitting that she'd checked herself in here purposely to exact her revenge on

Brooklyn by giving Brooklyn's baby up for adoption. She looked straight into the camera and told everyone to watch out for Brooklyn, as she was likely out trying to steal her own baby on her way out of the country. All that before straight up accusing Brooklyn and the center of stealing babies and running an unethical center.

Holy cow!

Carole watched wide eyed and open mouthed as Sarah stared right at her from the TV, saying she was doing it all for a birth mother she refused to identify, adding an ominous *I'm coming for you, Brooklyn,* and then being hauled off and arrested by two police officers.

She continued to watch as Sarah let herself be lead to a patrol car waiting out front with the cameraman following. She'd said she'd been expecting it to happen, to be arrested mid-interview, so she didn't resist and didn't seem surprised.

Carole was though.

The TV went back to regularly scheduled programming and Carole found herself still staring at the screen, but the soap opera that resumed playing mid-scene about one twin killing another for the love of some rich dude in a coma at the nearby hospital had nothing on what had just played out live on air for the whole world to see.

No longer aware of anything that was being broadcast on her TV, Carole instead found herself suddenly transported twenty years into the past. Back to the time that Sarah had just been talking about on-air, when she'd said she'd been adopted from here. Although, she called it being stolen.

Carole had worked here back then, too. She'd been with the center from its very beginning.

Brooklyn started it as a small, one building operation with only three other people, total. Peter had been their only attorney, one nurse worked in labor and delivery while also covering the nursery and Carole had been the cook and housekeeper, long before she'd been put in charge of the entire maternity wing.

A lot about the place had changed since then, Carole knew. She'd watched it grow over the years. But much had stayed the same. And a lot of the things that Sarah just said in her interview were true. At least, they were rumored to be.

She'd been around long enough to see a lot of things nobody knew she'd seen, and she knew where a lot of the proverbial bodies were buried. She just hadn't expected all their dirty laundry to be aired so publicly after so much time had passed.

Times were different back then and although a lot of the adoptions held here over the past twenty years were exactly what they seemed, in fact most of them were legitimate, not all of them were. Not by a long shot.

The sheer number of women living here over the years, each one of them carrying a baby, sometimes two, with most of them being unwanted but some of them being very much wanted just not allowed to be kept, was greater than one would think.

Add to that the even larger numbers of hopeful adoptive parents waiting in the wings that far surpassed even the large amounts of available babies, with all of those potential adoptive parents having in common a dangerous combination of desperation mixed with vast amounts of money they were willing to trade and outbid each other over just to hold a baby in their arms when they couldn't have their own was staggering.

The whole operation had been ripe and ready for exploitation, especially when you factor in its matriarch coming of age and arising from the ashes of her own desperate childhood situation with a determination to succeed at all costs and an *I'll come out on top no matter what* mentality paired with an attorney husband eager to please and willing to stretch every loophole in the law into a shape that fit their goals and it was easy to see how things had eventually gotten to a place where a woman fresh out of her teens was bent on revenge and seeking her own brand of justice on live TV.

It was all understandable on a logical level, at least in hindsight. Carole just never thought she'd actually see the day. Not after everything else she'd seen over the years.

Things that wouldn't be allowed nowadays, like the center running lots of ads in the back of the various teen magazines. Ads that said things like, *Pregnant? Alone? Confused? Do your parents not understand, or are you afraid to tell them about your predicament? Are you being kicked out? We can help!*

She remembered recruitment videos being made that showed happy pregnant women being treated like royalty. Their smiling faces around tables laden with food or lounging on their beds, bellies bulging, looking like they hadn't a care in the world. The videos had voice-overs added, compelling young women who were in delicate conditions to call for more information about the center.

The videos would be played on a loop at high

schools in booths manned by salespeople during the same job fairs as the various colleges. Booths spread out between the military recruiters, beauty schools and the airlines seeking flight attendants. Often a few of the current maternity home residents would join them, always the largest women closest to giving birth, but never any of the ones who'd let it slip that they were having second thoughts.

She remembered too, hearing about some of the large bonuses given to people who could get women in the doors. Like a bounty. No matter what they had to tell them to get them there.

And those were the above-board-for-the-times memories.

There were also the overheard fights. The desperate, tearful voices begging to hold their babies. The firmer, often cruel voices telling them that their babies were better off this way, with couples who could afford to give them better lives than they could. And the threats that if they changed their minds they'd have to pay the center back for all the overnight stays, the private rooms, the food and medical care that was paid by the adoptive parents expecting to take their newborn babies home.

You can't afford to raise this baby, they'd say.

You're not responsible enough, are you? Or else you never would've wound up here in the first place.

She remembered hearing vaguely of court cases. They were rare though, because it was rare that any of the birth mothers actually had the means to take the center to court. Add to that the rumors of bribery of police officers, lawyers, even the occasional judge.

Over the years she'd heard Brooklyn and her center snidely compared to Georgia Tann and her Tennessee children's home in overheard comments sometimes out in public, and when the movie *Butterbox Babies* came out she couldn't bring herself to see it.

She knew the center she worked at was nothing like that, certainly no babies died or were even ever in danger. The birthmothers never were, either. In fact, Carole prided herself on being there for the birth mothers, especially. She was always nice to them, never disrespectful or anything of the sort. Because she knew personally how easily one could find themselves in such a compromising situation.

She remembered being pregnant and giving birth herself in the early days of the center. She remembered how her baby's father acted when she told him that she had every intention of keeping and raising their baby, no matter that she worked at the center and had access to an easy way to *get rid of it*.

She hadn't been sure how she was going to make it work either, so she could relate to the women she cooked for. She could've moved back home, even with her baby, unlike most of her charges. But she'd wanted to stay where she was.

She had friends here and her job cooking at the Brooklyn Taylor center had been a godsend. It included room and board plus a salary, just for making breakfast, lunch and dinner for a houseful of other pregnant women and cleaning up after them.

She had been grateful when Brooklyn had suggested that she just keep her baby with her once she'd given birth, even though her situation was rather complicated. The center was small but growing, and it had been pointed out to her that they were fully prepared to keep a newborn on premises. At least for a while.

They were not equipped to have a toddler running around by any means. But being able to stay here and continue working with an infant while she figured it all out was a lifesaver.

Diapers, formula if needed, even newborn clothes were plentiful, and there was even the full time, live-in nurse on staff at all times.

So when she was told that she could continue to live on site, and while she worked they could move a bassinet and eventually a playpen into the kitchen for her, she was grateful. And if needed, she could always drop her baby off in the nursery to be minded as well.

The center wasn't perfect by any means, but she had good memories here, too. Memories of having the bassinet beside her bed in her room. Getting to wake up with her baby beside her, feed her, change her, wear her in a sling attached to her front while she made her way into the center's kitchen to prepare breakfast for not only herself, but whoever was staying at the maternity center at the time.

Back then, they were so small. There usually weren't many women in-house, making breakfast for herself and a couple of other women was the routine, and it wasn't long before Carole had grown just as adept at making breakfast with a papoose attached to her as she had been used to cooking with a big belly instead, just weeks previous.

The women she cooked for sometimes cooed over her baby and would help hold her while Carole worked, and sometimes Carole kept her hidden and wrapped up more closely because a well-loved and taken care of infant wasn't always a welcome sight to some of the inhabitants of the maternity home who we're planning on giving their babies up for adoption, so she played it by ear with who was in-house that week on how she handled everything.

When there were women in-house that wanted nothing to do with even the idea of an infant being nearby, Carole, on those days, would leave her daughter in the nursery since her job was to feed the girls, but not antagonize them and stress them out even more during this stressful time.

It truly was a different time back then, she knew. Women didn't have the choices then that they did now. They had to do things that people now just wouldn't understand. Couldn't understand. Society as a whole was just different. Sometimes your choices were made for you.

But nowadays, with the Internet, the MeToo Movement, and all the rest, fighting back was becoming more and more normal. Like Sarah's appearance on live TV and her subsequent arrest.

Carole didn't think that Sarah could fathom a time before, how different things were. She couldn't understand, not really. She'd publicly said she was doing what she was doing for revenge. Revenge and justice, for herself and her unnamed birthmother, two very different women born in very different times.

But both women could agree on some things, Carole thought. She could agree that everything Sarah said in her interview was correct. And that things were likely to be very different around here after that interview.

Chapter Twenty-Four

Kristine looked around at the other women sharing the same cell with her. There were only four others, although the large intake cell looked like it could hold quite a few more. The officer who booked her in said this was where everyone went at first, as a holding cell, until some sort of sorting occurred.

His wording reminded her of the sorting hat in Harry Potter and she'd been unable to suppress her giggle when she asked him how the cell would decide. Or did it automatically just sort anyone arrested into Slytherin? But he didn't seem to get her joke, which only made her laugh harder. Apparently getting arrested made her inappropriately giddy, like laughing at a funeral. Though she figured that getting arrested was kind of like being at her own funeral, as her life was probably over.

At least it wasn't likely that any of the other women waiting to be sorted with her would harass her, she thought. Since all of the prison movies she'd ever seen usually showed even the toughest inmates largely avoiding the batshit crazy ones, and cackling as she still was over her own sorting cell joke, she figured she probably looked as certifiable as they come.

Although none of the others seemed to be all that interested in giving her any attention at all, let alone any of the negative variety. Apparently all the *attack the toughest one you see so they'll all leave you alone* advice she'd ever heard bandied around in the very few actual prison movies she'd ever bothered to watch was just as fake as most everything else coming out of Hollywood. But as this wasn't a prison, just the local city jail, she decided to keep the advice in mind for later, though. Just in case.

No one really even looked up as she'd found a seat on an uncomfortable bench near the door the officer had opened for her, and then locked behind her, when she'd entered the cell. She, of course, wondered what they were in for, but she most certainly didn't plan on asking.

She'd been processed in, her fingerprints and her mugshot taken, before she'd been shown to the large cell. They'd even swabbed her cheek for DNA. She hadn't been in there long when the guard came back for one of the other women, telling her that her transport to the county jail had arrived.

Kristine was surprised when the next time the officer came it was for her. After all, there were three other women who'd gotten arrested first who she assumed would be sorted before her.

When the guard called her name he told her she had a visitor, an attorney. The three women still in the cell with her all looked up at that and gave her the evil eye. Apparently having an attorney show up this fast was an abnormality. It got her the negative attention she'd been able to avoid up until then.

The guard led her down a hall and through a room that looked like it was set up for visitors. Signs posted all throughout reminded anyone looking that all visits were recorded with both audio and video. It made her wish she'd had more notice that an attorney was coming, so she could have planned this better, knowing that it would be recorded.

She would have to be careful and only say and do things that she wanted on the public record. Things that would help her case, not hinder it. And by helping her case, she didn't mean that she had to be careful not to implicate herself or make herself look guilty. She didn't care about that. She knew she was guilty. But she had to be careful what she said, all the same.

And hopefully she could use these publicly recorded sessions in a way that would help her cause. Taking Brooklyn down.

Instead of sitting her down in the larger visitor's room, her guard kept going. She wondered where he was taking her, surely he was on the up and up, wasn't he? This wasn't one of those evil guards you hear about that take prisoners aside and make them do things for better treatment, was he?

Did she even have an attorney waiting for her? She hadn't contacted one. They'd offered her a phone call but she didn't use it. She didn't have anyone to call.

He opened a door off the hall and motioned her in. A man in a suit was already inside. He stood up when she stepped in, introducing himself as Mr. West.

"Call me Dennis," he said. "I'm not much on formalities."

Kristine hoped that didn't mean he was a bad

lawyer, since formalities were pretty much what law was all about.

"Kristine Armstrong. And Sarah Scott. Depending," she said, shaking his hand. "But I didn't call a lawyer. I don't know any, besides Peter Taylor. And I doubt he'd defend me, or send anyone else to."

"Which name do you prefer to be called?"

"I get to choose? They booked me under the name Kristine."

"You get to choose. With me, anyway. We'll see when it comes to the court proceedings."

"In that case, I'd prefer to be called Sarah. I want to be what my birth mother intended me to be," Sarah said. "I'm proud of what I did. I'm not ashamed and I don't want to hide behind the adoptive name Janine gave me any longer. I want the world to know who I was meant to be. Who I really am. And why I did what I did. She needs to be taken down. Brooklyn, I mean. So does he. And that center does, too. Is everything we discuss here on the record? We're being recorded, right?"

"No, it's illegal to record an attorney client meeting. Only the non-attorney visits are recorded, there is no equipment in this room."

"Oh, ok. I see."

"Do you still want me to call you Sarah or was all

that for show?"

"Both," Sarah said, smiling. "But why are you here? Are you court appointed or something?"

"No. I saw you on TV. That was quite the interview you gave."

"Thanks?"

"You have quite the array of charges pending against you already too, likely thrown in there by someone friendly with the center. You've made quite an enemy, you know."

Sarah wondered if he'd say *quite* as much in the courtroom as he had in the past three sentences, but she said instead, "I'm not sure I can pay you. I don't..."

"There will be no charge. I'm doing this for personal reasons."

"Oh? Did they steal your baby, too? Or are you one of the stolen ones, like me?"

"Neither. But, I've faced The Brooklyn Taylor Center in a lawsuit once before. It came about as suddenly as you have. That is, if you'll allow me to represent you?"

"That depends. How'd it go with your last center client?"

"Not well. Not well at all, to be honest. And I can't say that it'll go any better for you."

"Yeah, I figured as much. Kind of hard to defend someone who goes on live TV and says *I did it, I'm not sorry, and I'm not done,* isn't it?"

He laughed, and as odd as the whole situation she'd gotten herself into was, she trusted him already.

"Is that why you're offering me your services for free? Because you don't think we can win? Why take my case at all then?"

"On principle."

Sarah sighed. So much had been said in just those two words. On principle. The center obviously touched many lives, and not all of them in a good way.

"I was in court one day for something else," he said. "And this woman was walking up and down the hall asking anyone in a suit if they were a lawyer. When I said I was, she asked me for help.

"She'd given a coworker of hers that she hardly knew a ride to the courthouse and in the drive over she found out that the other woman had a court date to try and get her baby back. She offered to stay for moral support and to drive her home again afterward, but when they got inside the courtroom she saw that her coworker was all alone.

"She didn't even have an attorney meeting her there; she was going to plead her own case. But the other side, The Brooklyn Taylor Center, they'd sent three or four attorneys. She didn't think that seemed right, so she prowled the halls until she found someone willing to represent her coworker. Me.

"So I walked in there. You should have seen the judge's face and the faces on all the attorneys on the center's side. They were shocked that she had an attorney, that was the last thing they were expecting.

"I was able to get myself appointed, but it didn't do her any good. They had her signature on the adoption papers, but she claimed that they lied to her. Told her she was signing something else. She was still groggy from giving birth and they shoved this paperwork in her face and told her she was signing something about pain relief... She got railroaded.

"I was eventually able to show that her signature was coerced. I even got the social worker assigned to her case to admit on the stand that she'd flat out lied to my client. *I needed the money,* she'd said, admitting everything. *I didn't get paid if she didn't give up this baby.*

"As surprised as they were that she had an attorney, and as well as her case did end up getting presented, it didn't matter. They upheld the adoption.

"The whole thing was a travesty. It offended my sense of morality. I know, I know, insert lawyer joke here. But that combination of seeing the look on their faces when she had an attorney, and the way it all went down, it just didn't sit right with me.

"So, when I saw you on TV I knew it was highly probable that what you were saying was true. And here I am. Got here as soon as I could. I can't guarantee you will win, you likely won't. But I'm willing to do this for free, on principle, like I said. But also because of selfish reasons.

"The publicity on a case like this is going to be great. And I'll be as upfront with you as I want you to be with me, no matter how this goes, I'm going to win. It's going to bring me a lot of paying clients, especially if you've got the proof you say you do. It may not matter in your case any more than it mattered in hers, but there is a high probability that the truth will get out. And who knows what that can lead to."

Sarah didn't have time to do much more than shake her head at his story before he was launching into her case as quickly as it sounded like he'd launched into that other poor woman's.

"They'll be swabbing you for DNA, of course, if they haven't already," he said. "Once as part of your arrest, but the Taylors' attorneys will want a second one done by someone of their choosing. They'll swab the baby, too. And the Taylors' themselves. To prove who the biological parents are once and for all, so it's not a 'he said, she said' situation. Surrogates are supposed to abstain from sex during crucial times, but it wouldn't be the first time that a surrogate's baby doesn't come back to the parentage it is assumed to be.

"But, it's gonna take some time, DNA takes time. If the baby's DNA comes back to where you happen to be the parent, then you're within your rights to give up your own baby..."

"It won't," Sarah said. "There's no way it's going to be related to me, genetically, unless it's immaculate conception. Because I'm not seeing anyone. And I haven't had sex in any of this surrogate window."

"Be that as it may, it still has to be proven. But that will help me mount my defense, if I know as much as I can upfront. So I will work under the assumption then that the baby is the genetic offspring of Brooklyn and Peter. In which case, this likely isn't going to go well for you, like I said."

"That depends on what the definition of *going well for me* is, doesn't it? Since my entire intent is to get every eyeball I can on this case. I want to take them down, and I know that the only way to do that is for this to go viral. And I can't think of a more viral click-bait headline than *Surrogate Intentionally Gives Baby Up For Adoption*, can you?"

"Well, there is that."

"Have there been any updates on the baby? Did the police take my advice and find her, in case Brooklyn was planning on going after her, like I thought?"

"I haven't heard anything, but I'll check on it. There's a lot I'm going to have to get started on if we're going to do this. You haven't actually said if you'll accept me as your attorney..."

"I accept."

"Ok. Then I need some information from you so I can get started as soon as I leave here. I'll get a subpoena for your adoption records. Both of them, the one from twenty years ago and the papers you just recently signed. For the first one, can you give me any more information? I know you were adopted by Robert and Janine Armstrong, but what were your birth parents' names? Scott was the last name, right? Who was your birth mother? What's her first name?"

"It's Carole."

Chapter Twenty-Five

Sarah was only a few months old when she was stolen by people Carole Scott thought she could trust.

Everything had been going swimmingly. Carole very much enjoyed waking up in the morning with her daughter in her room at the center. Keeping her close. Taking her into the kitchens and having an occasional built-in baby sitter in the center's nursery.

Right up until the day her father called to tell her that her mother had taken a turn for the worse and Carole needed to come home and say her goodbyes.

It was Brooklyn who convinced her to leave the baby.

"You were just there pretty recently on your vacation slash maternity leave," Brooklyn had said.

"They've met their granddaughter. Your mom has dementia and your dad is trying to take care of your mom. He's got his hands full. Why don't you go ahead and take a weekend, or a week, or take as much time as you need, really. Go back down there and get things in order. Leave Sarah here. We can handle her for a while. Go. Deal with everything and come back, we'll keep her safe."

So she did. And it was the worst decision Carole ever made.

The whole time she was gone Brooklyn kept saying that everything was fine. *Take your time.*

When she got back, it was late. She showed up in the middle of the night, letting herself in. She went straight to the nursery first thing, to see her baby. Only she wasn't there. The nursery was empty and the nurse who'd been with them from the beginning was gone, too. Brooklyn had fired the original nurse and the new nurse had no idea what she was talking about.

Carole called the police when she couldn't get ahold of Brooklyn or Peter quickly. The police were finally able to get ahold of them and they all convened at the center, together.

When everyone arrived, Brooklyn went into apology mode. She apologized for wasting the police officers' time. She apologized for Carole's hysterics. She told the police that Carole had signed over her daughter for adoption before she left to deal with her parents. That she was a good employee who was just overwrought with being a parent. That it was all too much and although Carole had tried to keep her baby and juggle motherhood with work, she just couldn't handle it all.

And then when her mom got sick and her dad needed her help, it pushed her over the edge she was already on. She realized that she just couldn't do it all. And above that, didn't want to do it all.

They tried to make an exhausted and grieving Carole doubt herself.

Brooklyn told the police again and again that Carole signed over her daughter, went to visit her parents and came back, just like she'd been expecting her to, because of course her job still stood. She was a great cook who'd just found herself overwhelmed with parenthood, that's all.

They did the responsible thing, Brooklyn told the officers. The kind thing. They got Sarah adopted as soon as possible so that by the time Carole came back, all traces of her would be gone. They did Carole a favor doing it so quickly even, since Sarah wasn't a newborn anymore. Like her being a few months old by then made her less wanted or harder to place or something.

Carole adamantly denied all of it, of course.

But then Brooklyn pulled out paperwork.

It had Carole's signature on it. Peter backed Brooklyn up, saying that he drew up the contract himself, and that Carole signed it before she left. It was two against one. The old nurse who watched Sarah on occasion wasn't even still employed there to contradict them, conveniently.

They had their story straight, with paperwork on their side, and in their eyes, Carole was just a hysterical woman who either regretted her decision or, after the trauma of *both* of her parents actually dying while she was gone, Carole somehow didn't remember that she had given her daughter up for adoption.

Like someone could just forget signing their daughter away.

But the police accepted their story like it was something that could've actually happened that way. Like they'd heard it a million times before.

Maybe they had, Carole thought. Maybe the stories she'd always heard were actually true and the police really were owned by the Taylors'. Maybe they'd heard some version of what Brooklyn was trying to pass off as the truth many times already by then.

But it broke Carole.

She was inconsolable. Sobbing and yelling and arguing with all of them. She never would've given her baby up for adoption. She tried to tell them that it was Brooklyn who talked her into leaving Sarah there while she dealt with her parents and it took longer than planned because while she was down there her dad got in a car wreck taking her mom home while Carole had taken another car to go to the store to stock their house up with the stuff they'd need to let her mom finish her last days at home, like she'd wanted.

Carole lost everything almost at once. Both parents, in such a surprising and traumatic way, and then once she came home after missing her daughter terribly and being away from her for far too long, far longer than planned, she came home to her daughter being stolen from her by the very people she'd left her with to care for her while she was gone.

She lost it to the point that the new nurse, the one Carole was convinced had been hired to replace the only other person who knew the truth, had to sedate Carole with the stuff they sometimes had to give the struggling, birthing mothers when they become too inconsolable.

But, in the back of Carole's mind, as her entire world was splintering, breaking apart and falling down around her, a couple things happened.

One, it verified the rumors. Yes, she'd seen a lot of legit adoptions go through the center in those first couple of years. But there had been enough questionable ones that she'd been uninvolved in, but had heard about from the girls she cooked for, to make her wonder. But until it happened to her, she hadn't been sure. It had been easier to accept the same stories that the police were accepting about her now. *She changed her mind, the hormones had gotten to her, it was too late to overturn an adoption.* And she'd been willing to overlook the doubts, because until then they had been so good to her.

The other thing that happened in the back of her mind was the beginnings of the planting of seeds for revenge.

Even in her drug-addled brain, foggy from being sedated, she knew her options were limited. And in the days after, when she could think more clearly, she could still only see a few, sad, imperfect options available to her.

She could quit and move away a broken woman,

which is probably what they'd hoped she'd do, and what a lot of the women she'd heard about likely did do. But she knew she would never get Sarah back by quitting and going away, and she knew if she quit, her chances would be even worse. At least staying there, she had access to the building, to the records.

Her second option was that she could fight it. But she knew she couldn't, even if she could find proof. She didn't have the resources or money to take them to court. Even the few who had couldn't convince the bought and paid for judge to overturn any of the adoptions when the proof had been on their side. No, as much as Carole wanted to go public, to stand toe to toe with them and fight for her daughter back then, she couldn't do it. She knew she'd never win.

Twitter and Facebook didn't exist back then, or viral posts or social media warriors. All there was back then was the local news and a corrupt system. She couldn't even afford to try to pay to play. She couldn't fight them. And she hadn't been willing to just go away.

So the only other option she could see was to stay. To make them think they won, and to work in the background to take them down. To take care of the women who came through the doors as best she could, while also starting to gather proof. To listen to them more. To watch and to learn.

Plus, staying was the only way she could think of to find out who they'd given her baby to. She needed to stay close, to get into the records, or she'd never even know who had her Sarah. If she could find her file, she could find who adopted her. She could gain access to the money the center had somehow too, and she could steal her baby back and run.

So she decided to stay. She decided to keep her friends close and her enemies closer.

And now, so many years later and looking back on it all, she thought it was darkly, ironically, morbidly funny what Sarah had said about Brooklyn on live TV. Accusing Brooklyn of planning on subverting funds from the center, grabbing her own baby from its adoptive parents and running. Cause that had been her plan too, twenty years before.

Apparently the apple really didn't fall far from the biological tree.

Chapter Twenty-Six

Brooklyn eyed Peter as their two attorneys talked to each other across the highly polished table. She watched him as the lawyers' voices droned on in the background, words like *arraignment* and *test results* and *pre-trial hearing* swam by her as she wondered what was going on behind her husband's eyes, since he wouldn't look at her.

This is all your fault. She aimed her thoughts in his direction but he showed no response.

She turned her attention back to the attorneys. Only two were here today to discuss what would happen next, where they stood, but this was only the first of what would be many strategy sessions. If, or when, they went to court there'd be even more attorneys at their side, but for now it was just these two.

Forest Hill had been their family court attorney for many years. Despite his unfortunate hippy name, he'd always come through for them in the past when one of the girls tried to take the center to court and Peter found himself a defendant instead of their defender. Forest knew where all their proverbial bodies were buried, as it was his job to handle the shovel.

The other attorney, Dee Thomas, had been brought in by Forest. He said that they needed to add a criminal law firm to their roster, and her firm was the best one in the area.

"We need a firm with experience both defending and prosecuting criminal cases," he'd said. "Yes, Kristine is the one who's been arrested, so we need someone good to prosecute her, but if her entire defense really is going to be basically saying that wanting revenge against you made her do it, we need to be prepared for that as well. Since she's openly declared her intent to come after you, we need someone that can both prosecute her and defend you at the same time."

So here they were. Kristine Armstrong, or Sarah Scott, as she was preferring to be addressed, had been arraigned, according to the brain trust across the table. That meant that charges were officially filed and announced, and Sarah had to officially state the plea that they'd all go forward based upon.

She'd pled not guilty, which angered Brooklyn to no end.

"How could she plead not guilty when she just went on live TV and admitted everything? Doesn't that make it a confession?" Brooklyn asked, interrupting the conversation between the two attorneys that was bringing Dee up to speed.

"Almost everyone pleads not guilty at the arraignment stage," Dee said. "And it makes sense to me why she would, based on that live interview. If she pleaded guilty, the judge would give her a sentencing, and it would be done. Over."

"As it should be," Peter said.

"But, if she pleads not guilty," Dee said, raising her pointer finger and continuing. "She gets a trial. And it's apparently a trial that she wants, because her intent was only partially to take your baby. She said she wants to take you down with her. And if she admits to what she did by pleading guilty and she is sentenced, she can't. But with a trial, that's when you, and the center, become witnesses. With testimony. And that's when any evidence she wants to present against you, to explain why she did what she did, would come into play."

"So what happens next?" Peter asked.

"That's what we were just discussing. They've released her on bail and scheduled a pre-trial hearing for two weeks from now."

"They released her? You've got to be kidding me," Peter said. "Does everything she admitted to already mean nothing?"

"There's no reason not to release her on bail. The judge doesn't feel like she's a threat to anyone. She didn't do what she did because she wanted to keep your baby for her own, she's not planning on going after any other babies or pregnant women, and she's not likely to run. She wants this fight; she's not going anywhere. There was no reason to hold her in jail. She's certainly no danger to anyone but you two, and she means you monetary and business harm at this point, not personal or physical harm."

"So she gets everything she wants, then? She gets to give away our child, stay out of prison and drag us through the mud as her defense of the unthinkable thing she admits to doing. Do I have all this right?" Brooklyn asked.

"If she's convicted..." Forest said.

"If? So she may or may not go to prison for

stealing our child, but either way we could lose everything? How is that fair?" Brooklyn asked.

"Speaking of your child," Dee said, trying to steer the conversation back to preparing for court instead of a debate on fairness. "The first step is to prove that the baby is yours. I'm assuming neither one of you have a problem with being cheek swabbed and having your DNA run against the baby's?"

"Of course not. The sooner, the better," Peter said. "How soon can we get the results?"

"Well, the good thing is that this kind of testing is fast and easy," Dee said. "It's not like in a murder case where we have to try to get DNA out of multiple blood pools or teeth or fabric swatches, and then run them in the system and hope for a match against some unknown sample. This is more like your basic paternity test, so you're talking a few days to a few weeks. Depending on the lab. A private lab would be best. No real backlogs there, unlike with trying to do it at a police lab. We'll easily have the results back before the pretrial hearing."

"If we can prove by then that it was your baby she gave away, maybe we can get her reasons for why she did it thrown out as inadmissible," Forest added. "She had a contract with you through the surrogacy company, so maybe we can focus on that. Basic contract law. The baby wasn't hers to give. She's guilty, who cares why she did it? Legally, I mean. The public will care, but the law? Maybe not. We'll see. We'll work on that by the hearing. Maybe we can keep your business practices out of it completely, as the contract was between you all personally. The center had nothing to do with anything on that front. The where and why she did what she did may be a legal non-issue we can get blocked from even being admitted as evidence."

"That would be ideal," Brooklyn said. "So, best case scenario and that happens, how soon until we can get the adoption overturned or voided? How soon until we can have our baby?"

"Well, that'll be a separate matter entirely, won't it?" Forest said, for the first time looking rather uncomfortable. "Once the criminal aspect of all this is put to bed, whatever ends up happening to Sarah, the adoption issue itself then flips to the jurisdiction of the family court. Just like any previous time that one of the adoptions that took place through the center were challenged."

"But," Brooklyn said, looking between both attorneys and Peter, "None of our adoptions have ever been overturned. They've been upheld every single time."

"I know," Forest said, starting to squirm and looking a little pale. He opened his mouth to say more, but shut it again after darting a glance to the criminal attorney beside him.

Whatever he wanted to say he obviously thought better of it and Brooklyn knew they had to get Forest alone. For multiple reasons.

She had some questions for him regarding how to handle the family court judge and getting an adoption overturned for the first time, but something else was starting to nag at her. Something he said triggered the beginnings of a realization, but before she could pin it down the other attorney spoke up again.

"So, let's address the other elephant in the room now, shall we?" Dee said. "It hasn't been released publicly yet, but it's just a matter of time. This unnamed birthmother. I see from the records you brought to this meeting that the same Carole Scott that is listed on Sarah Scott's original birth certificate is also the name of one of your employees. Anyone care to fill me in?"

"About that," Peter jumped in. "Sarah said on live TV that she did this alone. And that the birthmother, Carole, didn't even know who she was when she was living there because she just went by her first name of Sarah and no one knew her last name was Scott. Including Carole. I'm calling bullshit on that. I don't think it's at all possible for Carole to be uninvolved."

"Because Sarah knows too much?" Forest asked. "I was going to bring that up, as well."

"Sarah said that her birth mother contacted her at eighteen and she didn't even know she was adopted before that first contact happened," Dee said, agreeing. "If your employee Carole is her birth mother, however they lost contact when Sarah was a baby, she had two years or so to get to know Sarah before all of this happened. Online or in person, they would've at least exchanged pictures. Spoken on the phone.

"If Carole knew enough about her to be able to find her and contact her at eighteen, then she knew that Sarah's name was Kristine Armstrong. So when she supposedly went missing, surely Carole knew that it was her daughter who was missing. If she was truly innocent, and she'd just recently found and contacted her daughter after eighteen years apart, and then after just two years of being in contact with her she up and disappears? And she never mentioned a thing to anyone? Including the police?"

"Yes, exactly," Peter said. "Plus, Sarah would've had to get this outlandish story of being stolen from

Carole. I mean, who else would make up such a story? And, all this information, and this supposed proof she supposedly has, it would have to come from someone inside the center. There's no way Sarah could just come upon any of this by herself. Carole has to be in on this."

Brooklyn was nodding her agreement, but something Forest had said earlier was still bugging her. Nudging at her.

"It sounded like, in that interview, that she did get a lot of information from her birthmother. She said as much. It seemed like she was saying though that her birthmother hadn't known anything about her plans to take your baby and then go public. We don't know if that is true or not yet, but it seemed like that was the part she was saying that she'd acted alone in. Saying she did it for Carole, just not with Carole," Dee said.

"Even if they'd supposedly only been in online contact initially," Peter continued. "Likely exchanging pictures and stuff over two years, like you said, had they really never met in person in all that time? And if they had met, wouldn't Carole recognize her at the center, even pregnant, with her hair cut and dyed? Especially using the name Sarah?"

As the three of them bantered ideas back and

forth, the missing piece slid into place for Brooklyn. It was something Forest had said earlier that finally did it. It should've dawned on her sooner, but in the stress of the past few days she'd almost missed it. But she wasn't missing it anymore.

Chapter Twenty-Seven

Peter turned on Brooklyn the minute they were alone.

They'd arrived at the meeting with the attorneys in separate cars, and as they stood between those cars before heading off again after the meeting, Peter tried to convince her to settle.

"The lawyers think we should try, Brook. You heard them in there. Dee thinks..."

"I don't care what Dee thinks, you heard Forest, too. Maybe he can get Sarah's plans blocked before trial."

Brooklyn had missed parts of what Dee said, as her own thoughts and realizations had started to fall into place. She did remember hearing the part that

Peter was referring to, though. The part where Dee tried to warn them about what might be coming if this whole trial mess was allowed to continue.

"Other people are already starting to come forward, according to Sarah's attorney," Dee said, before the meeting had ended. "Past birth mothers, I mean. And it's only been about 48 hours since Sarah was on TV. We've got two weeks to go before the pre-trial hearing, even longer before there's an actual trial. That's plenty of time for others to come forward as well. Maybe we should think about settling. Contact Sarah, and Carole too, since we're thinking she's likely involved."

Brooklyn had already started shaking her head, but the attorney kept on.

"We can still spin this, adoptions are difficult and emotional in the best of times and most of these women coming forward are talking about cases two decades in the past. Times were different then, not to mention statute of limitations have expired. We could put out a statement and try to settle this between you somehow. Out of court. You're all very well acquainted with NDA's, from my understanding. Maybe all they're really after is money..."

"Over my dead body," Brooklyn said, still

shaking her head. "Sarah planned this. She came after me on purpose. The worst part is that she stole my baby. She did so in an unmerciful and unheard of manner and who knows when I'll be able to get my baby back. It was deliberate and cruel. On top of that, she's slandering me and my company in a very public way. I'll never settle."

The meeting had wrapped up quickly after that, there hadn't been much more to say. Dee came prepared with a paternity swab kit from a private lab, saying that she'd assumed everyone would want answers as soon as possible and she had a preferred company she liked to work with that was fast and reliable.

She'd had both of them rub the kit-enclosed swabs on the insides of their cheeks before the meeting concluded. She mentioned that Sarah's attorney would do the same with Sarah and that they'd send someone by to swab the baby as well.

The baby was currently being allowed to stay with the adoptive family she'd been given to, pending the DNA results and further decisions of the court, because if the baby's DNA ended up showing that Sarah was the biological mother, even if that result was likely improbable, then that part of the case would stop there. There was no reason to upturn their lives any further until there was proof. And until there was proof, the adoption stood.

The part that killed Brooklyn was the possibility that it might still stand even after it was proven that the baby wasn't Sarah's. But that was a bridge she knew she'd need to cross later, with Forest and whichever judge got assigned their family case after this criminal case finished, if she wasn't able to handle that aspect on her own.

"Why not try to settle? What would be the harm? I don't get it," Peter said between their cars, still pleading his case.

What would be the harm? In giving in to them?

His words only reinforced the realization she'd come to just moments before the meeting had concluded. That the person working closely with Sarah and feeding her inside information wasn't Carole at all.

"You don't get it?" Brooklyn asked. "No, I'm the one who doesn't get it. Why would you do this to me, Peter? Why do this to us? Why do this to us personally, and why go after our company? And why like this? So secretive and so convoluted and cruel?"

"In trying to settle? What are you talking about?"

"It was Forest who made me realize. When he

said in there just now that we had a personal contract with Sarah through the surrogacy company and the center had nothing to do with that aspect. He was talking about getting Sarah's plan to come after us shut down before it legally began, as an inadmissible contract law matter, but it made me realize that it was you all along. You had to be the one behind all of this, not Carole."

"I still don't follow."

"All that stuff you said in there, all those questions you asked, trying to make sure everyone was thinking that Carole had to be involved. You said you didn't think that Sarah could've done any of this alone. *Where would Sarah get the idea that she was stolen from Carole? you asked. Where would she be getting all this information? All this supposed proof would have to come from someone inside the center,* you said. Then you said, *There's no way Sarah could just come upon any of this by herself. Carole has to be in on this.* And you're right. Sarah can't be doing this alone. She has to have someone on the inside helping her. Only it isn't Carole at all, is it? It's you!"

"Now you're talking nonsense. Why would I..."

"I don't know why," Brooklyn hissed the words between her teeth, trying to keep her voice down but too furious to wait to confront him. "That's what I'm asking you. Why, Peter? Why would you do this?"

"I didn't! I'm not..."

"Then how do you explain Sarah ending up as our surrogate? Cause that's the key. It was a private contract, like Forest said. Not only was the center uninvolved, it was our secret. Yours and mine. No one but you and I knew we were even looking for one. We kept everything about that a secret. No one else knew we were even thinking about surrogacy. No one knew which company we decided to use, Carole didn't know anything about any aspect of that. No one at the center did. We even kept everything about the surrogacy a secret from our household staff. Carole couldn't have fed Sarah anything on when or how to apply to the surrogacy company, or what to put on the questionnaires to get matched with us."

Brooklyn was so angry, felt so betrayed by this newest realization that she was shaking with it.

"The only insider Sarah could be working with is you, Peter."

He just looked at her stunned.

"Do you realize how sick that is?" Brooklyn kept on. "Especially now that it's come to light who Sarah really is? Who our supposedly random stranger of a surrogate actually was? Whose daughter Sarah is? Carole never contacted her, did she? You did. You found her. You fed her all these stories about being stolen and you gave her all the information she needed to take me down. Did you pretend to be Carole online?"

He was shaking his head, but she wasn't done with him. All her thoughts and realizations just tumbled, one after another, through her mind.

"Those diary entries, were they true?"

"I already told you a million times, no. None of that is true. None of what you're saying now is true, either. Brooklyn, you're insane."

"Did you sleep with her? Even knowing...?"

"No! I didn't sleep with her, I didn't contact her and I didn't feed her anything. And I didn't know who she was until after you did. Would you listen to me? You're wrong about everything. I've no idea why she wrote those things in that diary."

Brooklyn thought fast, more and more pieces falling into place.

"Then maybe she did it to blame you, to make you look guilty. She's not only coming after the center, she's not only coming after me personally, by stealing my baby. She's coming after you, too. To implicate you. She pointed her finger right at you from that diary."

Brooklyn was thinking out loud, trying to understand. Hoping against hope that her own husband hadn't betrayed her so terribly, but all the evidence pointed to him even as he stood there denying it.

"She went on TV and said that she did this alone, but that can't be true. Even you said that, Peter. But she specifically said Carole had no idea, that no one in the center knew who she was. Maybe that part was true. Maybe they really hadn't met in person, cause Carole never contacted her, you did. It's the only thing that makes sense."

Her head swam with all the various possibilities, but each time the puzzle pieces came together they showed the same picture.

"No wonder Carole didn't recognize her in the center. No. It really can't be Carole; it has to be you. You set all of this in motion but you gave her too much information while you were pretending to be Carole online, didn't you? And she double crossed you. She made sure you, Peter, looked guilty in that diary, whether you slept together or not. She knows, doesn't she?"

"Knows what? Brooklyn, none of this makes any sense. I'm innocent."

"The last thing you are in any of this is innocent," Brooklyn said. "We've got days, Peter. You heard them. Days to weeks before that DNA comes back. You and I both know what the DNA is going to show. Does she?"

Chapter Twenty-Eight

Brooklyn allowed the DNA swabbing because she didn't feel she had any other choice, standing there with everyone just assuming she too wanted the results to come quickly. She did, of course. But once they came, then where would she be? It would all be over, for sure.

Although, depending on how thorough they were, maybe not. If they just compared her DNA to the baby's, that would be ideal. And fast too, with just a one-on-one comparison. Even running both hers and Peter's DNA against the baby's would be fine. She was confident in the baby's bloodline, that wasn't the issue.

The issue was in processing Sarah's DNA with this whole story about her having been stolen being bandied about. Brooklyn had seen some of the online armchair quarterbacking going on, in comments on Facebook and on news sites under the articles, after Sarah had gone on TV. People were throwing their own warped and illicit ideas around as possible twists that might come out of this whole thing.

After everything Sarah had written in her diary about her and Peter becoming involved, people were saying things like, *wouldn't it be something if the baby ends up being Sarah's and Peter's?*

But others, in Facebook comments, were quick to point out that she'd written in her diary that she and Peter didn't become intimate until after she was round with Brooklyn's baby. They pointed to the entry where she said that the first time they'd even touched was when he wanted to feel his baby moving inside her, so Brooklyn wasn't giving that theory much regard. Whether or not her husband had actually slept with Sarah, Brooklyn didn't think it would've been early on. She fervently hoped it hadn't happened at all, but Brooklyn knew that baby was hers.

No, it was the stolen baby aspect of Sarah's DNA that was keeping her uncomfortable, though she hadn't heard of any rumors about them swabbing Carole. Maybe she'd get lucky and Forest could shut down that entire line of questioning and they wouldn't even run the swab they had on Sarah at all. A girl could hope. For expediency all they really needed to run was the baby against Brooklyn anyway, to prove Brooklyn was the only mother with the right to put the baby up for adoption.

Brooklyn shook her head as she drove away from Peter. She was ruing the day she'd chosen Sarah to be their surrogate. She should've waited, let other possible matches come through the agency over time, instead of jumping on the first one. But Sarah just seemed so perfect. Too perfect, Brooklyn thought in hindsight.

It's got to be Peter, it's the only thing that makes sense across the board.

Peter denied everything, but he would, wouldn't he? He'd denied the redhead until there was video proof in Brooklyn's hand. Why wouldn't he deny being behind all this, too?

"Are you coming home?" Peter had asked her before they'd gone their separate ways after meeting with the attorneys. They'd stayed together for appearances until this was all over, but they were sleeping in separate bedrooms and largely avoiding each other unless they were out in public. They'd come in two cars because he'd gone to the meeting from the center and she'd gone from the house, but it was getting late and neither had any work to do before heading home.

She said yes, she was planning on going home, but she'd be a bit behind him. She had a few stops she wanted to make on her way. Brooklyn only had one stop in mind but she didn't want to give Peter any kind of a head's up. Him thinking she was running errands would buy her some time.

As she drove, she thought her situation through. She was glad that she hadn't fired Carole when she initially thought that Carole was neck deep in all of this. Not only was she convinced now that Peter was behind everything, but this way, with Carole still living and working at the center, she knew where everyone was at almost every given minute.

And with Sarah having been released on bail, Brooklyn was pretty sure Sarah would be staying with Carole at the center. There were plenty of rooms available, after all. Business was way down so she could easily see Carole spending her time getting to know Sarah better while they waited to see what the court verdict would be.

Brooklyn thought Sarah should be locked up, but whether she would be or not remained to be seen. Of course, Brooklyn thought, Sarah could also just go back to the apartment she'd been living in by the university, but if she really was Carole's long-lost-daughter, why wouldn't they want to reconnect?

Brooklyn thought it would be funny to be a fly on the wall during that conversation. Either Sarah was lying and saying it was Carole who had first contacted her, to protect Peter, or it was Peter pretending online to be Carole. So, if Peter really was the one who first contacted Sarah, then Carole hadn't known anything about anything and was likely as shocked at Sarah turning up as the rest of the world was. But either way, their post-bond release conversation was bound to be a dozy.

With Carole and Sarah both likely to be at the center and Peter heading home, she was free to do what she needed to do with no surprises. Brooklyn rubbed her belly as plans started to come together in her mind. Forget letting the law handle this. Forget going to court. Forget Peter. Forget the center and forget Sarah, too. None of them mattered to her anymore. The only thing that mattered was her baby.

Sarah had called it. Brooklyn was going to take her baby and run.

Surely no one would expect her to do it now, not after Sarah had warned everyone on live TV. She obviously couldn't do like Sarah thought she was going to, by knocking on the door and saying, 'Hey, paperwork issue, I need to take her for a couple days' or anything like that.

No, she'd have to steal the baby in a different way. She'd have to watch. She'd have to spend these next few days to few weeks, the only window she had until the DNA comes back, smartly.

She figured she could spend the next little bit watching the house, watching their routine. Try to figure out the best way and time to take her baby and run, with the intent being to steal the baby from her stroller outside if she happens to be left out there for a minute, or watch their schedule for other possible chances. Knowing that newborn parents are tired, she could see how well they locked their doors and such, with the intent of stealing the baby out of the crib. Something like that.

She parked her car in a strip shopping center a few blocks away from the house where the people who'd adopted her daughter lived. She swapped the heels she'd worn to meet with the attorneys with a pair of running shoes she kept in the car, popped some headphones in her ears without turning any music on, to look the part of a woman getting a walk in after work, and headed off.

She circled their block a few times, but never saw

any movement either inside the house or out. She'd told Peter that she'd be right behind him, so she didn't dare circle long. Besides, someone grabbing the baby and running, throwing the kid into the back of a car with no car seat and taking off like a bat out of hell would likely just get her caught, so she made a few plans while she walked and watched.

She'd use this errand time to pick up a car seat and some baby supplies. No, too many cameras inside stores nowadays, she thought. She'd take supplies from the center instead.

She'd come back and watch the house some more once Peter was in bed for the night. It would be even easier to do tonight, since they slept in separate beds, than it was the night she snuck out to go to Sarah's apartment when she first went missing.

That night seemed like forever ago to her. Everything had changed since that night. She was even calling her surrogate by a new name. She shook her head at the enormity of everything as she headed back to her car to prepare and wait.

A few days later, after seeing absolutely no life happening at the house she'd been watching, she started to wonder. She'd already tried the doors and peeked in the windows the night before, desperate to finally get a look inside. To catch a peek of her baby.

She'd even entertained the idea of breaking a window. She had everything she'd need to run with the baby ready to go in her car, she was just lacking the baby. But she was too afraid of being caught in the act. She knew she'd never get her baby back, legally or illegally, if she was arrested for breaking and entering with the intent to kidnap her own child.

So she called Forest, her attorney, instead and made an appointment to see him for a lunch meeting the next day, away from his office and any listening ears.

"Have you heard anything on the DNA results?" she asked him once the waitress brought their drinks, took their food orders and left them alone to talk at a corner table away from anyone else.

"No, nothing yet. Should be any day now though."

"I know what you said in that meeting with the criminal attorney, when I mentioned that none of my center's adoptions have ever been overturned. But between you and I, I've got to ask. Once the DNA does come back and we know it's my daughter that Sarah gave away, can't we just do what we always do? Pay the judge to do what we want?"

"I don't see why not. It's not a guarantee, you know that. But if it ain't broke..." he said, shrugging. He reached for his drink and took a healthy swig.

"I know you said that they weren't going to take my baby from its adoptive parents during Sarah's criminal process. So what do they do in the meantime? To make sure the adoptive parents don't run off with my baby or something? These parents are often pretty desperate, as you well know. Are they just letting them stay at their own house? Have they been moved? Are they under some kind of protective custody in some safe house or hotel somewhere? This case is big news; big news attracts crazies. What if someone wants to take my baby and run?"

With a deep, booming laugh Forest said, "I can't imagine anyone else who would want to steal his baby but you."

Brooklyn looked around, wishing he'd keep it down. But she didn't see anyone paying them even the tiniest bit of attention.

"But even you wouldn't dare," Forest continued. "Because you know it's going to be a whole lot better if you get the baby back legally, in court, instead of having to steal it and run and hide for the rest of your life. That baby isn't going to remember any of this, so it's not like there's any rush. You and I both know you're going to get this baby back at some point.

"Besides, what do you need this one for? You look like you're going to pop any minute. You're bigger than you were just a few days ago when I last saw you. Let someone else deal with the midnight feedings on that one while you've got your hands full birthing this one."

Brooklyn didn't respond to that; it was beneath her to. He didn't have any children and didn't want any. Only someone who didn't like kids would think that she wouldn't want one just because she was having another.

She doubled down on what she really wanted to address instead.

"So, they aren't even watching them? They didn't move them into any kind of safe house or protective custody?"

"Why would they? There's really no reason to keep them under protective custody. But as it turns out, they're out of town anyway. We found out when we tried to swab the baby for DNA. We had to mail a kit to them at the adoptive mother's parent's house instead. They'd gone there, out of state, before Sarah's TV appearance, to introduce the baby to her grandparents once the adoption was finalized, and to get help with the baby's first weeks at the same time. They were surprised to hear from us, let me tell you. Apparently they hadn't heard anything about the case at all. They must've been living under a rock since this case is national news, but whatever. They know now.

"They're under court order to be back in time for the pre-trial hearing though. And they've already mailed their swab in, according to Dee. They gave us the tracking number off the kit when they sent it in, so we can monitor the results."

Brooklyn felt conflicting emotions at that revelation, but she didn't have time to sort through them sitting with Forest.

"When are you due, anyway?" he asked. "You aren't going to go into labor in the middle of the trial, are you? Although, that would be sensational. Not that this case needs any new twists to make it sensational."

"Should be any time now. I've heard that stress can trigger contractions, but as usual I seem to be doing things backwards. Apparently stress is keeping this baby from wanting to make an appearance."

The rest of their lunch was uneventful and took far too long to end, according to Brooklyn. She needed to get away from his constant chatter to think. She was glad that her gut reaction to seeing no activity at the house for days was wrong. They hadn't taken the baby and run to prevent possibly losing it, like she'd begun to think. But that meant that she couldn't either.

She was going to have to sit tight and wait until the pre-trial hearing, but she wasn't happy about it.

Chapter Twenty-Nine

Sarah was a nervous wreck. Sitting in the courtroom, her lawyer beside her and the judge in front of her, she was grateful that she couldn't see behind her without purposely turning around. The glimpse she'd gotten of the packed room when she'd arrived was more than enough.

She saw Janine in the crowd, sitting in the first row. Brooklyn and Peter were in attendance as well as Carole, even though none of them would likely be giving any kind of statements yet. The pre-trial hearing, her attorney told her, was for motions and discovery to be discussed, not for calling witnesses or giving testimony.

Basically it sounded like when she'd taken English classes and they'd had to turn in an outline for a grade long before the paper assigned was actually due. It was a peek at what was possibly to come, and the only way to hear things brought up if they were determined not to be allowed to be presented at trial later, when there would be a jury in attendance.

It was also open to the public, so it was no wonder the press seemed to take up half of the courtroom.

Her attorney, Dennis West, had asked her if she wanted him to file a motion to close the hearing to the public or the press, but that was the last thing she wanted. Too many aspects of the center were shrouded in secrecy, and the entire point to everything she'd done so far was to drag them into the light. She welcomed the press. She had no secrets, she'd already aired her dirty laundry in as public of a forum as she could find when she spoke with Kate Miller on TV. Yes, she'd have to give up details, on everything from her diary entries to her moment-by-moment accounts of where she was while the world thought she was missing, but that was fine by her. She had nothing to hide anymore.

She was still a nervous wreck though, but she tried not to look the part.

Since she was here on a criminal matter and it wasn't technically Brooklyn or her center she was fighting in court but the state vs Sarah Scott, aka Kristine Armstrong, the opposing counsel's table only held attorneys and those attorneys were volleying motions and arguments with both the judge and her own attorney as she sat quietly and listened.

The whole thing reminded her of a tennis match where the judge was the net and the opposing lawyers were wearing suits instead of tennis whites. They were throwing legal terms back and forth over her head faster than she could keep up, so she was grateful that her entire job this day was to sit quietly and keep her mouth shut unless the judge or Mr. West spoke to her directly.

"And the adoptive parents? The... uh..." the judge said, shuffling some paperwork, looking for the names that were eluding him. "The Williams family. They're under court order not to leave town again until all this is settled, but you said they've gone missing?"

That got Sarah's attention.

"Yes, Your Honor," the state's attorney, Dee Thomas, spoke up. "They were out of town already when this case came to be, visiting family with their new baby. We were in contact with them in regards to swabbing the baby's cheek for the DNA testing, and they were to be back in town by today, although not required to be present here. But they haven't complied."

"There was a sample taken before they disappeared, correct? We have everyone's DNA results?"

"Yes, Your Honor."

"But the child in question is...?"

"The best we can confirm is that they fled to the Maldives to avoid whatever the DNA tests were going to show."

"The Maldives."

"Yes. Apparently Mr. Williams is in the tourist real estate business and travels there frequently, but they also happen to be a non-extradition country. According to Mrs. Williams' mother, who said that she, and I quote, *never trusted that man,* that is where her daughter last contacted her from. She was letting her mother know that they were ok, but that they did not head back here like they were ordered to, because they had no intention of giving up the baby they'd, and again I quote, *adopted fair and square.*"

Sarah snuck a peek behind her to see Brooklyn's reaction and she was not disappointed.

Brooklyn's eyes met hers and Sarah felt the rage Brooklyn was aiming her way full force. Sarah didn't even try to hide the smile she felt begin to spread over her face. She turned back to face the front again because she didn't trust herself not to laugh at loud at this newest turn of events.

Sarah was ecstatic. She didn't think they could've given Brooklyn's baby to a better couple.

Try and overturn that, bitch.

Sarah restrained her smile now that she was facing the judge instead of Brooklyn, but inside she was dancing with joy as the discussions continued on all around her.

"Well, that is unfortunate," the judge said. "Of course their whereabouts only really pertains if it turns out that the baby was, in fact, the biological child of Mr. and Mrs. Taylor, and if the adoption gets overturned in family court, based on the findings of this court. Hopefully they will come to their senses before that time and return. Unless of course it turns out that the baby was the biological child of the defendant, Sarah Scott. Where do we stand in that regard?"

"The child in question is the biological child of Mr. and Mrs. Taylor, with 99.9 percent probability," Dee said.

Sarah had to duck her head and stare at her lap to keep the new smile on her face from being seen by the judge. There it was. Proof of what she'd done.

She still couldn't believe that she'd been able to pull it off. She bit her lip to keep her laughter inside. She knew when she started down this road that she'd have to pay for this sin, but if keeping a straight face could cut a few years off of whatever sentence she ended up with, it would be worth controlling her emotions until she was alone.

Revenge was sweet. She'd been stolen from her rightful mother by Brooklyn, and she'd stolen Brooklyn's daughter in turn. And then the adoptive parents had stolen her again, from Brooklyn's reach and from the court process. The universe was on her side today.

She knew that the memory of this feeling would help keep her warm for years to come as she sat in a jail cell paying for this crime. Oddly enough it was something her adoptive mother Janine used to tell her growing up that she thought of now. *You can do whatever you want, as long as you're prepared to face the consequences.*

It was one of Janine's favorite expressions, and Sarah heard it on many occasions. When Janine would lecture her as a teenager about everything from missing curfew to driving to staying off drugs. *Everything has a price, Kristine,* she'd say. *Miss curfew if you want, but be prepared to be grounded when you're caught. Speed if you must, but be prepared to pay the speeding ticket if you get caught. If you're going to do the crime, don't complain when you have to do the time. Take your lumps without whining. If you don't want the consequences, don't go outside of the lines.*

Janine thought she was teaching her to be a good citizen, a law-abiding member of society. And she was, over-all. But she doubted that Janine saw the irony in teaching her to be a good criminal at the same time. She'd do her time, get released, and enjoy the rest of her life with no regrets over the revenge she went seeking. Plus, she'll have a heck of a story to tell in the old folks' home, won't she?

"There was something else of interest in the DNA results though, Your Honor."

Sarah had almost forgotten that the case was still going on around her, she'd been so lost in her own satisfaction.

"The baby is related to the defendant, as well."

Sarah's head popped up at that. She looked from the lawyer to the judge and back, in confusion, and then chanced another glance behind her at Brooklyn, Peter, Carole and Janine before looking for answers in her own attorney's face. He just gave a slight head-shake to say that this hadn't been shared with him yet either, and no one behind her had met her eyes. They'd all been looking at the speaking attorney, so that was where she turned her attention, as well.

"According to the DNA results, Sarah Scott carried her own half-sister to term. We ran the results twice, to be sure. That's what took so long, and why opposing counsel hadn't been made aware prior to this hearing. We just got the final report this morning. Sarah Scott shares paternal DNA with the baby she gave up for adoption."

"What? What does that mean?" Sarah was surprised when her attorney motioned for her to be quiet, she hadn't realized that she'd spoken it out loud. She thought that the question was only echoing in her head, not the courtroom.

"It means, Ms. Scott," the judge said, flipping through his copy of the same report that the attorney was reading from. "That the baby's biological parents are Peter and Brooklyn Taylor, as we presumed. But your biological parents seem to be Carole Scott and Peter Taylor."

Chapter Thirty

*B*rooklyn wanted to wring Sarah's neck when Sarah looked back over her shoulder and grinned at the lawyer's announcement of her baby being taken to the Maldives.

Sarah looked so pleased with herself, Brooklyn wanted to crawl over the hip-height wall separating her from the woman who singlehandedly ruined her marriage, her hope for a happy family, her empire and her sanity all at once, and pummel her with her fists until her smug smile became a swollen, bloody mess. But she refrained.

Instead, to help her control her anger, frustration and desperation, Brooklyn was already mentally planning her own trip to the Maldives in her head, now that she knew where her baby was. Fantasizing about first beating Sarah to a pulp and then flying down and rescuing her daughter from the Williams' was the only thing keeping her butt on the courtroom seat when all she wanted to do was strangle the woman who'd destroyed her entire life, and seemed to be quite satisfied with herself about it, to boot.

Brooklyn did almost enjoy watching Sarah learn who her father was, though. Guess the little schemer hadn't known that bit. Apparently neither Carole nor Peter had ever filled her in on the why behind Carole's whole stolen baby story.

Like Brooklyn was going to just carry on while her cook raised Peter's baby? As if.

She certainly wasn't going to let Peter's illegitimate child with the help be raised underfoot like they were running some kind of feel-good free-love commune. If Carole had cared about her baby at all she never should've left her at the center to go visit her parents in the first place, even if it was Brooklyn who'd suggested it. Stupid move, that.

Peter had resisted selling his and Carole's baby at first, but he knew what was good for him, so it didn't take him too long to come around. He'd sworn Carole was the one and only time he'd cheated, he'd blamed alcohol and the stress they were under back then, but the recent redhead just drove the point home to Brooklyn that the man couldn't be trusted to keep it in his pants. He couldn't then and he couldn't now.

But she didn't need him now like she had back then. She didn't need him and she didn't need the center anymore, either. It had made her filthy rich over the years and she'd slowly siphoned a lot of it into overseas accounts to cover herself just in case a day like today ever came about.

Not that she'd ever thought she'd have to face any actual consequences for the sometimes grey-area'd way that she ran her business, especially in the old days when adoptions and maternity homes were less regulated. And she certainly never expected it to be Peter's bastard child who'd take her down, but be that as it may, she knew she was finished.

The press would be all over this. She could just imagine the headlines to come. And if Sarah somehow had even a fraction of the proof against them that she said she had, along with the other women from decades before who seemed to be crawling out of the woodwork with the seemingly sole intention of badmouthing her now, she knew her center was doomed to be closed down anyway. Life as she knew it was over.

But now she knew where to find her daughter.

Brooklyn would be just as missing as the Williams' by the time Sarah's actual trial was over. The state would continue to prosecute Sarah, and Sarah could present every bit of evidence she had against her and the center if she wanted to, Brooklyn just didn't plan on sticking around to watch any of it.

She rubbed her belly meditatively as the court proceedings carried on. Forest was right, the daughter that the William's had run off with wouldn't remember any of this, she had plenty of time to get down there. She had the rest of her life to find that child. She just had to get through the rest of this day first, that's all. She'd figure something out, she always did.

Everything moved quickly after the dual shocks came out. With everyone in attendance learning that the baby was gone, followed so quickly by the public revelation that Peter had fathered both Brooklyn's baby and Carole's Sarah, it seemed to be too much for everyone in the courtroom.

The judge banged the gavel a couple of times to quiet the people who began to murmur amongst themselves. When the courtroom, largely press, didn't come immediately to order the judge moved to recess court until after lunch. That was fine with

Brooklyn. She needed to get out of there before she screamed.

The court stood for the judge as he left the bench to head back to his chambers. As everyone else slowly began to disperse, some clumped into little groups, talking instead of leaving. Sarah's attorney spoke a few words to her before turning and speaking with the other attorneys. During that time Sarah took it upon herself to turn around and finally face everyone who had been behind her all morning.

She locked eyes with Brooklyn once again and it felt to Brooklyn like the two of them were suddenly the only people left in the room. Maybe in the whole world. That same maniacal grin started to spread across Sarah's face again, infuriating Brooklyn. A rage was building inside her, one unlike anything she'd ever experienced before, but it was Sarah's next words that moved Brooklyn into action.

"Karma is a bitch," Sarah said, staring straight into Brooklyn's soul. "And so are you. I can't decide if I hope that the baby you're carrying never finds out what an evil woman you are or if I hope that it does eventually find out, and you lose it, too. After everything you've done, you don't deserve even a moment's peace for all the babies you've stolen from their mothers. Not even a second's peace. You don't deserve to be happy."

She said it all quietly. Almost under her breath. But Brooklyn heard every word. And snapped.

She wasn't going to let Sarah get away with this. She wasn't going to just sit quietly by and lose everything. Not again. Maybe it was already too late, but she couldn't let Sarah just walk away unscathed. It was just too much. Even jail time was too good for her. Sarah had no idea what she'd done. Brooklyn had already lost everything once before, when she'd been discarded and abandoned by her supposed father, and now she was losing everything she'd built since then. She couldn't go through it, losing everything. Not again.

Her business was gone, or soon would be. It was only a matter of time, now. Her husband was gone, in all the ways that were important to her, and this... this child. This young, stupid, privileged, bastard child had taken away the only thing she had left. She'd exposed every one of Brooklyn's secrets. Or almost every one. The only secret she had left, the one secret she still carried, literally, inside her swollen belly, was all she still had, as of this morning. And although Sarah had no idea, she'd destroyed any way for her last secret to work itself out, too. She'd taken *everything* Brooklyn had, and she was going to pay.

Moving faster than any pregnant woman should be able to, Brooklyn was out of her seat and through the swinging doors that separated the spectators from the participants almost before she even knew what she was doing.

She had her hands around Sarah's neck. She felt detached from herself, almost like she was watching herself from above, or perhaps imagining the whole thing. She squeezed hard, pressing her thumbs into the soft flesh of Sarah's skin, pushing her against the defense table, bending her backward over it as Sarah clawed at her hands and tried to remove them from around her neck.

Brooklyn muttered things, low and guttural, that Sarah couldn't catch in all her surprise and panic. Brooklyn was so focused on strangling Sarah that she didn't see the people that ran toward them in Sarah's defense. Soon they were separated. Arms were holding her back from attacking Sarah. Other arms, attached to other people, were checking Sarah over, making sure she was ok.

And somehow, in all the mess and confusion, Carole ended up between them. She'd grabbed something off of the same defense table that Sarah had just been bent backwards over, and she held it high in one hand as she turned toward Brooklyn.

Brooklyn could still hear Sarah choking and coughing in the background but her eyes were now focused only on Carole. Or rather, her eyes were focused on the sharp-looking, ornate letter opener in Carole's hand as it glinted in the light of the harsh overhead bulbs of the courtroom. It seemed to be aimed directly at her stomach.

The letter opener descended toward her in what seemed like slow motion. Everything had slowed down, even the sound of her own blood throbbing in her ears in rage seemed to slow. An eternity passed between every heartbeat, and yet she had no time to get away. Her hands and arms were being held behind her still, so she couldn't fend off the attack or protect herself in any way. She was totally exposed. Vulnerable.

Her round, hugely swollen belly was all that stood between them. It almost seemed to be reaching out toward the pointed blade that was headed straight for it. She was past-due. Over her due-date now by almost a week. She couldn't help but think that if she wasn't, if everything had gone on as scheduled, if everything had *gone according to plan,* she wouldn't be here at all.

But nothing had gone like it was supposed to. Not even from the very beginning. And so here she was, watching it all come to an end as time slowed down and then stopped. At least for her.

She didn't even feel it. She saw it though. She couldn't help but see it as time seemed to stop for her completely.

The tip of the letter opener first touched the fabric of the maternity dress she was wearing, indenting it, pushing against the tautness for one helpless split-second before sliding deep. Up to the hilt.

Seeing it like that was surreal. The beautifully entwined filigree of its handle just sticking out so obscenely finally broke her trance.

She screamed.

Chapter Thirty-One

Sarah couldn't believe what she was seeing. Brooklyn was screaming bloody murder with a letter opener sticking out of her pregnant belly, and Carole had put it there.

All the arms and hands that had been helping Sarah a moment before, tugging her away from Brooklyn's attack and seeing to her welfare, let go, leaving her feeling momentarily unmoored and off balance as they all moved to assist Brooklyn instead. People were trying to pull Carole off of Brooklyn, but Carole wouldn't let go of the letter opener.

Someone tried to yank Carole back and away, but Carole held on tight. With all the yanking, the letter opener ripped a gash through Brooklyn's stomach where a puncture had been a moment before.

"No! No, no, stop," Sarah yelled, her voice too hoarse from being strangled to be heard by anyone above all the commotion. As others seemed to concentrate either on Brooklyn or on Carole, trying to separate them, Sarah was intent on everything that was happening in the space between them. She moved to the letter opener and pried Carole's fingers from the filigreed handle, still not fully comprehending everything but disgusted and flabbergasted by what Carole had done.

Sarah had just wished ill of Brooklyn and the child she carried, but she'd never wished for this. This was inhumane. This was insane. To stab a pregnant woman in the belly, to drive a letter opener deeply into an unborn child, hitting who knows what- an arm or a stomach or a soft spot on the baby's head- it was beyond unthinkable. It was *evil*.

"See? See?" Carole was yelling.

See? See what? That you're certifiable? That you're a bigger monster than the woman you stabbed? Cause that is what I see.

Sarah didn't dare yank the letter opener from Brooklyn's belly. What if it was plugging something vital? What if removing it caused more damage than leaving it?

"We need a medic! An ambulance!" Sarah shouted as best she could.

This was not how things were supposed to go. Brooklyn's life was to be destroyed, yes. But legally. By a court of law and public opinion, not by murder or attempted murder, of her or her unborn baby. This was barbaric. This was psychopathic. This was... not bleeding?

Why was there no blood?

Why were Brooklyn's screams sounding more and more like anger tinged with madness instead of pain?

"Even her pregnancy was a lie. A trick. A con," Carole was still yelling even as a court officer subdued and cuffed her with her hands behind her back.

Sarah pressed on Brooklyn's stomach and Brooklyn fought against her but she still made no sounds of pain, just rage. Sarah stuck her fingers into the slit Carole had caused, pulling the fabric of Brooklyn's dress apart. The sound of tearing cloth ripped through the courtroom as all eyes turned to Brooklyn's stomach now that Carole was cuffed and out of commission.

"It's fake," Sarah announced to the room, her voice scratchy with both injury and disbelief. "It's a good fake, it's silicone or something. Maybe even medical grade, but it isn't a baby. Brooklyn isn't hurt, and she isn't pregnant. No need for an ambulance after all. There's no baby in there."

"You can uncuff me now," Carole said, smug. "I didn't hurt anyone, I only exposed another lie, that's all. I protected my daughter and exposed her attacker. I committed no crime."

"That remains to be seen," the court officer said, but he didn't look too sure of himself.

"That felt good," Carole said back. "I've been waiting a long time to do that. I've been waiting a long time for a lot of things."

Sarah stepped back and away from Brooklyn, lowering herself down into the chair she'd been sitting in all morning. She watched all the commotion as Carole was officially arrested and read her rights while Peter gathered Brooklyn and ushered her out of the courtroom.

Sarah was surprised that Brooklyn wasn't being arrested too, alongside Carole, since it was Brooklyn's attack on Sarah that had started everything. It must've been the shock of Brooklyn's fake pregnancy being revealed so dramatically that made everyone forget that she'd been in full-on attack mode when she'd been stabbed.

Sarah's attorney must've thought the same thing because he ducked down beside Sarah and asked her if she wanted to press charges against Brooklyn.

"I... I don't know," Sarah told him honestly. "Should I? I'm just so... what just happened?"

"I think you should. You can always decide to drop them later, if you change your mind. Her attacking you will be in all the papers no matter what you decide, but having official charges against her can only help your case. If people hadn't been here to pull her off of you, there's no telling how that would've ended."

"Yes, you're right. Of course."

He stood, got a court officer's attention, and said he wanted Brooklyn taken into custody as well, for assault on his client.

As the officer raced out to catch her in the hall before they got too far, the lawyer leaned back down beside her and asked her if she was ok. Before she could answer, Carole called out to her as she was being escorted out a different door by another officer.

"My purse and keys are on my seat, Sarah. Take them with you, please."

Sarah nodded at her numbly as she was led away.

They'd ridden to court together with Carole driving. She'd been staying with Carole at the center since she'd been released on bail but she'd never expected to have to go back there alone.

After Carole was taken away, Sarah's lawyer started talking about her welfare again.

"You should at least get checked out. Make sure there's no lasting damage to your throat. Document it. Make a report."

"That sounds exhausting. I just want to get out of here and go home."

"Ok, no doctor then. But I'm going to get one of the medics over here for a once over. No arguments."

"Fine. Then will you follow behind Carole and be her representation?"

Sarah wasn't sure how she felt yet about what Carole had done, but she knew the woman would need a lawyer, regardless. She'd have to sort out her feelings over all the new developments later, but in the meantime, Carole needed someone.

"No. There will likely be a conflict of interest with everything else going on. I'll send someone to take care of her, but she's going to need her own lawyer, the way this case is shaping up."

"The way this case is shaping up is full-on crazy.

Are you wishing you hadn't volunteered for this madness yet?"

"Nope, no regrets. At least not yet. It's definitely been the most interesting case I've had in a while, though."

"And this is just the pre-trial hearing."

Chapter Thirty-Two

Brooklyn was still fuming as Peter picked her up after her release from jail. Humiliated and angry, she tore into him the whole way home.

"What good is having an attorney for a husband if he can't keep me out of jail? I swear, I have to do everything myself. Just once it would be nice to have someone be there for me."

"What are you talking about? Everything I do is for you. To try and make you happy. I helped you start the center because it was what you wanted to do. I let you sell Carole's baby because it was the only way to keep you happy..."

"*Carole's* baby? Like you had nothing to do with it, right? I'm the one who had to clean up your mess there as well. You can't even cheat without screwing everything up for us, can you?"

"I let you talk me into getting a surrogate," he continued, gaining steam. "I even kept up your charade of still being pregnant after you miscarried again this last time. And here I am, bailing you out of jail after you lost your mind and strangled the woman who already let it be known that she was out to take us down. You attacked her in public, in a courtroom full of witnesses, bailiffs and reporters for God's sake."

"I guess I should just be grateful then that you weren't *out of town* when I needed you to bail me out."

"What's that supposed to mean?"

"You know exactly what. You're always conveniently gone when I need you here. You were gone when they retrieved my eggs, you were gone when they implanted Sarah, you were gone when I found out I was pregnant after she was, you were gone when I lost it. I'm shocked you were even around to make it but I guess I shouldn't be. Making babies seems to be the one thing you do stick around to do. I'm surprised that redhead hasn't shown up again, carrying another one of your babies. That would be the icing on the cake now, wouldn't it?

Everyone getting to have your baby but me, your actual wife."

"Brooklyn, I..."

"No. You don't get to talk. You don't get to try and make excuses, not anymore. Do you have any idea what it's like to be me? To be the only one trying to make a life for us? A marriage for us? To try and make a family out of nothing but my own blood, sweat and tears? Do you?"

"Maybe it's time to stop trying."

"It's just so humiliating, Peter. The only thing I want more than anything, I can't have. Every time I get close, every time I think *this time will be different,* it's the same thing all over again. I lose it. Again and again, it slips out of my grasp. Maybe if I didn't have to do it all alone..."

"You haven't been alone."

"Where were you when I found out I was pregnant again? When I tried to call you and tell you?"

When he didn't answer she said, "Exactly. You were out of town. And then, when I lost it? When I was further along than I'd ever been before, being so careful? Were you here helping me? Knowing that something could go wrong at any moment, with either me or our surrogate? Where were you?"

"Brook, come on."

"Don't *Brook, come on* me. Were you here? Were you here when I needed you? Were you here when I started cramping, *again*? Were you nearby to help me, to be there with me when I lost our baby? Or did I have to go through that all alone? Again? *Where were you?*"

"Out of town."

"Exactly. Anywhere but with me. Do you know what it was like for me? Having to show up at our surrogate's appointment after that and see her still pregnant and radiant and watch our baby's heartbeat on that monitor knowing that the heartbeat I'd carried had stopped beating, yet again? Do you know what that day was like for me? Do you know what every day has been like for me since?"

He answered her by hitting the garage door remote above his head on the visor as they neared the house. He pulled in the garage, parked and went inside. She followed him silently, all the way to his study, where he tried to swing the door shut behind him.

She blocked its arc, pushing it back open as she followed him inside. She wasn't going to let him block her out any more. She wasn't going to just turn around and go off to do her own thing any more.

He turned around halfway to his desk to face her

but she passed him. She went to the drawer he kept his liquor in and opened it. She figured she needed it more than he did this time.

After months of abstaining, even in here in private, she poured herself a double and downed it before pulling his chair out and plopping down in it as he stared at her in silence.

"What?" she asked him as she refilled her glass and settled in to have a discussion that was long overdue.

"Nothing."

"So now you're judging me for drinking?"

"No, but you've been able to drink now for months. I just don't get why we even had to pretend here. In our house, with no staff around, we still had to pretend. How was I supposed to be there for you when I had to pretend nothing was wrong with you even in private?"

"I had to keep up the pretense, even here. You know that. If I let my guard down at all, even here, there's a chance I'd forget in public."

"That's exactly the problem, don't you see that? You never let your guard down. Ever. Even with me. You say you want me to be there for you but you really don't. You shut me down every time I've ever tried to be real with you. So yeah, I've stopped even trying. I do your bidding at the center. I do your bidding here. I knock you up and leave you to it cause that's all you want from me anyway. You don't want my real thoughts or feelings. You don't want my advice. When I tried to talk you out of buying those stupid fake pregnancy bellies, what did you tell me? To shut up and mind my own business. You won't let anyone help you, Brooklyn. You never have. You've always insisted on doing it your way. No one else even gets to have an opinion. So yeah, I go out of town every chance I get. Does hearing it make you happy?"

"Nothing about you makes me happy."

"Yeah. Tell me something I don't know."

"Ok. I know what else you keep in this drawer with your liquor. Did you know that?"

His face went pale.

"What do you mean," he asked.

"I mean," she said, putting her drink on the desk and reaching for the drawer in question. She pulled it back open again and reached far back into it, behind the liquor bottle, to the very back of the drawer. "That I know what's behind this false back."

She gave it a practiced tug and then pulled out a small, snub-nosed revolver. She placed it on the desk between them before reaching back into the drawer and coming out again with an even smaller USB drive. She set it beside the revolver and tilted her head at him while she waited to see his reaction.

"Care to tell me again how rarely you've cheated on me in all these years?"

"How did you...?"

"Charles gave you up. For cash, of course. For a lot of cash, actually. He told me that he found it when you hired his security company to upgrade and install all of our cameras. He just didn't know where you put it after he'd found it and given it back to you, after blackmailing you for it. He got money out of both of us for the same USB drive, he was quite the double dipper. But once I knew it existed it wasn't too hard to find. Apparently our house isn't the first place you've ever installed cameras, is it Peter? You had to have moved some of that footage from VHS to disks to USB over the years. I've got to admire your dedication."

His complexion had gone from pale to flushed and she could hear his every exhale from across the desk as he stared her down from the center of the room.

"Imagine my surprise," Brooklyn continued. "At seeing myself as a minor, from back when we first met. When you told me I was special. When you told me that being kicked out of the system at eighteen didn't have to be scary, because you'd help me every step of the way. Imagine my surprise when I realized that I wasn't the first minor you offered to help. Nor was I the last."

His face turned to stone as she spoke. She'd shocked him with her knowledge, but he'd recovered quickly.

"I guess you're not the only one with secrets," he finally said with a shrug.

"Sarah's diary held the truth, didn't it?" Brooklyn said. "I could tell that she was shocked to learn that you were her father, but you knew, didn't you? You've been behind everything from the start. She was starting to realize, wasn't she? She even mentioned her suspicions about you and some of the women on this USB drive. The women in the maternity ward. She mentioned how you likely dipped into them as a pool for your warped entertainment. That's bad enough, but she had no idea she was sleeping with her own father, did she?"

"You're wrong! I never slept with her, I swear. And you found out who she was before I did, when you checked her records. I had no idea she was my daughter. I never slept with her. Actually, this proves my innocence there. You didn't see her anywhere on that USB, did you? If her diary was true, I'd have had multiple opportunities to put a camera in her apartment. She's not there. So, yeah. I haven't been faithful. I've made a lot of mistakes, but none of them involved her. I was never with her. And I wasn't behind her taking our baby like you think I am, Brooklyn. I had nothing to do with any part of that. Or her."

"You expect me to believe you? You never come clean until you've got the proof shoved in your face. You didn't come clean about cheating with Carole until she was carrying your child. You denied knowing who threw the rock into our window until I watched it on video. And you've denied being with anyone else all these years, but there's the proof of your lies again, right there on that USB drive. So what I know is that you lie. No, I didn't see her on it, but I didn't watch it all. But you know what I did see? Minors, Peter! Going back more than twenty years. Going back to before me. And women in our center. Women supposedly under our care."

"What do you want?"

"I only want two things. My daughter back and the truth of your involvement. You can help me with one of those things. Only you knew we were looking for a surrogate, to be able to send Sarah to me, and only you knew I was faking my pregnancy. You had to be how Carole knew that. You had to be behind Sarah stealing my baby. It all comes down to you, Peter."

Instead of answering her he lunged for the desk. So did she, a spilt second behind him. Only they each reached for separate things.

He grabbed for the USB stick as she grabbed for the gun. They moved almost simultaneously again. He picked up the evidence and dropped it into her almost full glass of whiskey as she raised the revolver and fired all six bullets into her husband.

Chapter Thirty-Three

Sarah made herself a post-dinner snack by scavenging food from the maternity home's large kitchen. Dinner was long over and had been a simple one, she and the one remaining pregnant occupant, Tamika, had warmed up leftovers from the previous night. They'd split the last of the spaghetti and garlic bread that Carole had made, while discussing how weird it was to not have Carole around. She'd never not been there to make dinner before.

Afterward Sarah was left to her own devices when Tamika headed to her room for the evening, but she couldn't sit still after the eventful day. Instead of reconvening after lunch like the judge initially decreed, he'd adjourned everyone until morning instead.

Sarah came back to the center the minute her lawyer was satisfied that she was ok and the medic released her. She hadn't heard from Carole and didn't know when she would. She felt weird being there all alone but for one other soul tucked away in a bedroom. It hadn't been busy at the center by any means since she'd come to stay with Carole, but she'd had Carole herself to hang out with and get to know, and she'd enjoyed her time with her birthmother immensely. She wasn't sure what to do with herself without her.

She also wasn't sure she wanted her to come back tonight, either. She'd stabbed Brooklyn in the stomach! Had she known the stomach was fake? It sounded like it, the way she was yelling, "See! See!"

And what about that, anyway? It seemed like faking a pregnancy all the way to term was a lot of work. It required multiple size bellies, just to start with. Why had she bothered with any of it when she had a surrogate? So many lies.

So many new truths had come to light just that morning, Sarah still wasn't sure what to think about any of them but she didn't have Carole to ask. And boy did she have questions. *Carole and Peter?*

She couldn't wrap her mind around her DNA results. Carole had never said a word in all their conversations about who her father was. She'd glossed over it so well that Sarah almost assumed it was just some old boyfriend that never stuck around. Carole lied. And Sarah didn't like being lied to. She thought she'd found an honest victim in her birth-mother from all the conversations they'd had in the two years since Carole had found her.

She'd been ripe for a mother figure since Janine hadn't really been much of a mother to her since Robert had died. Carole had swooped in and made her feel important. Missed and wanted. She'd hunted her down and found her and reached out to her the day she legally could.

Then to find out that Janine and Robert had lied to her throughout her whole life by not mentioning that they'd adopted her, Carole had been in a prime position to sweep into her life and stir up her sense of justice and fairness, and maybe that's all the stabbing was about too, since Carole hadn't technically hurt anyone. But still...

Sarah felt overwhelmed by everything. The last two years had gone by in a blur of new knowledge, then planning, then executing the plan. Sarah hadn't stopped to think in all the last year if she was really doing the right thing in growing Brooklyn's child to give it up out of revenge for the mother she'd just found. At least not since she'd been accepted as Brooklyn's surrogate. Once it had been official, she just let the plan sweep her away.

Maybe she shouldn't have been so eager to trust Carole. Carole lied. Carole never told her that Peter was her father. Carole never told her that Brooklyn was faking her pregnancy. What else was she not telling her? Was everything Carole ever said about Brooklyn and Peter a lie? Was all her supposed proof a lie? Had Brooklyn really stolen her from Carole as a toddler or had Carole given her up since she was fathered by another woman's husband and just made up the story about Brooklyn adopting her out from under Carole's nose while she was out of town?

She didn't know what to think or who to trust anymore. Had she made a huge mistake? Had she been played all along? Used? Was Brooklyn innocent in all this?

No, she couldn't be. That fake belly said a lot.

She was so deep in thought that she didn't hear Brooklyn let herself in. Suddenly Brooklyn was just in the kitchen with her. And she was holding a gun.

Chapter Thirty-Four

"What's going on? What are you doing?" Sarah asked in a panic.

"Where is Carole?" Brooklyn asked in return, ignoring Sarah's questions while pointing the gun at Sarah's face.

She looked very different without the large pregnant belly preceding her. She'd showered and changed since Sarah had last seen her at the courthouse as well. Probably needed to wash the scent of the back of the police car and the jail holding room off of her, which Sarah understood completely.

"What do you want with her? Why do you have a gun?"

"You had me arrested," Brooklyn said.

"You tried to kill me in court."

"Well now I'm here to finish the job. Get in the walk-in."

"Now just hang on a minute."

"It wasn't enough for you to ruin my life? You took everything from me. My husband. My life's work. My reputation. My secrets. *My baby*. And then you had me arrested. They fingerprinted me, like some common criminal. I have a record now. A mugshot. They had a female officer search me for weapons. Do you know how humiliating that is? Oh, yeah. I guess you do, don't you? They search *everywhere!*"

"Then I don't even want to know where you were hiding that gun."

"I found this in Peter's study just now. He hid a lot of secrets in there." Brooklyn sighed as she said it, shaking her head. But her gun hand stayed steady. "Now get in the walk-in fridge, like I said."

"Look, I didn't know," Sarah said, shaking her head too, mirroring Brooklyn. "Ok? I didn't know that Peter was my father. Carole never told me that. I get it now, why you wouldn't want me around. Why you'd adopt me out. What really happened back then? I don't know who to trust anymore. Did Carole give me up back then? Did she make up the whole story she told me? About you stealing me from her? To get me to help her?"

"You can stop pretending it was Carole, I know it was Peter that was behind everything all along."

"What are you talking about? Wait, how are you even out of jail?"

"The same way you got out, I'd guess. Apparently no one cared about what they watched me do to you any more than they cared about your on-air confession. Which makes me think that Carole should be getting out soon too, if she isn't already here."

"She isn't."

"Then I'll just have to wait for her, won't I? Do you want to wait for her with me, alive in the walk-in or do you just want me to shoot you now right here? Cause I'd rather wait and shoot you in front of her, but I'm not going to tell you again."

"What do you want from her?" Sarah asked, letting herself be herded to the large, restaurant-style walk-in refrigerator, trying to buy herself some time. She eyed every counter as she slowly moved in that direction, hoping to grab a knife or something to defend herself with. But she didn't see anything she could use as a weapon between her and the large, stainless steel fridge she was being directed toward.

"Answers, of course. Confirmation, really. Since Peter denied everything. Not that I believed him, but still. I want to hear the truth for myself. From you two. How did you and Carole know I wasn't pregnant?"

"I didn't know. How would I? I still don't understand why you were pretending to be."

"Then you're dumber than I thought. Which only reinforces my belief that you didn't plan any of this yourself."

"So tell me," Sarah said. "Maybe we're both victims here, because I'm starting to doubt a lot of things I was so sure of before. I've already laid everything on the table. You know what I did, I admitted to it fully. I'll answer anything you ask me honestly. If you do the same, maybe we'll both get to the truth together."

"You are no victim. You're a baby thief. You stole my daughter right out from under me."

"Really? You're claiming a moral high ground on stealing babies? I stole one. How many have you stolen?"

"How did Carole know I wasn't pregnant?"

"Why were you pretending to be?"

"I've got the gun."

"Then shoot me, and see how many answers that gets you."

Brooklyn's nostrils flared in rage. They were standing just outside of the walk-in and Brooklyn motioned for Sarah to open its large door.

Sarah complied and a rush of cold air rolled out to greet them as Brooklyn motioned Sarah backwards, until she was fully inside the walk-in. She looked for any weapon she could find on its cold shelves but all she saw was salad makings, milk and defrosted chicken breasts within reach.

"You were our *secret* surrogate," Brooklyn continued, standing just outside the walk-in.

Brooklyn had her free hand resting on the fridge's door, ready to swing it shut. It had a handle on the inside, so no one could accidentally get trapped inside it, but Sarah had a feeling it wasn't going to do her any good.

"No one but Peter and I knew you existed, outside of the agency. Once you gave birth I was going to take possession of my baby, take a maternity leave, and later on go back to work, flat stomached and carrying the baby you grew for me. And no one would've been the wiser. No one would've known that I couldn't have one. That I was broken. But then you disappeared, and well... you know how the rest went."

"Why go through all that trouble though? You as well as anyone know how common it is to not be able to have a child. No one would have judged you. Think of the PR if you'd have adopted from your own agency."

"*I don't want someone else's trash baby!*" Brooklyn yelled. "I want *my* baby. My blood. The stupid, desperate women who come here, who knows what crap blood runs through their veins? Even *they* don't want those babies, but that's fine. I'm happy to give them to people who do, because they don't deserve to have them in the first place. Blood family is..."

He was right not to want me, wasn't he? The thought hit Brooklyn out of nowhere. *I mean, look how I turned out. He knew. He knew there was something wrong with me even back then. He couldn't get away from me fast enough. He didn't love me. Neither did Peter. It's because I'm unlovable. Unforgivable.*

I'm the throw-away trash baby.

Her non-gun holding hand rose of its own accord, to her face, to finger her scar while she fought her thoughts. The fridge door started to swing shut, but Brooklyn stopped its slow swing by sticking her foot out and blocking its path.

But maybe I wouldn't have turned out like this if I hadn't been given away. If I hadn't lost my mom. My blood. I can't lose my daughter after all of this. What will she become without me? I have to save her. I can't lose her, and I won't.

"No," Brooklyn continued after a moment. "My motives are none of your business. Now, again I ask you, how did Carole know I wasn't pregnant?"

"I don't know. She didn't share that part with me, just like she didn't tell me that Peter was my father."

"Peter must've told her, like I thought," Brooklyn said. "How'd you know I was looking for a surrogate to begin with? Peter is the only one who knew that, too."

"Carole told me. Carole has been my only contact."

"It could've been Peter pretending to be Carole online."

"It wasn't. We didn't stay online long. We moved to phone calls and video calls pretty fast. It was Carole who contacted me, not Peter. She and I built a relationship slowly these past couple of years, from the day I turned eighteen. She planned it all, she was the one who told me you were looking for a surrogate. Peter didn't tell me anything. The only times I've ever had contact with Peter was with you, too. We've never seen each other or spoken to each other outside of your presence. We've had no other contact. No email, no phone calls, no texts, nothing."

"But, the diary..."

"Everything in that diary was a lie," Sarah said. "We got the idea from *Gone Girl*. Every word was to make him look guilty, to make the world's eyes turn toward him, and by default you and your center. It was Carole's idea to write all that and leave it where it would be found."

"How did you know so much about the center's past? Where did you get all the proof you say you have for court?"

"I told you. Carole. The only thing I lied about in that news interview was when I said I did all this myself, for Carole. I did do everything for Carole, to help her get revenge against you. But I didn't do it alone. I lied about that part. I didn't just do it *for* her, I did it *with* her. It was her plan."

"He must still be behind it. No one else knew I was seeking a surrogate, or knew that after I miscarried I started faking my stomach. He must've fed Carole all the info, and she in turn fed you. They had to be in it together, then. They went behind my back once before, to make you. They must've done it again, or maybe they never stopped. He denied everything, of course. The whole way home after I was released. The whole time we fought at home in his study, before I came here, he denied it. He can't deny anything anymore, but that doesn't matter. I know the truth."

"Oh, God. What do you mean by he can't deny anything anymore? What did you do to Peter?"

"Nothing he didn't deserve."

"Did you shoot him?"

"I didn't do anything he didn't deserve," Brooklyn repeated, neither confirming nor denying.

Sarah didn't want to think that Brooklyn had shot and killed Peter. She didn't want to think that she could be capable of it, but desperate people were often driven to do desperate things.

"What do you want from me?" Sarah asked.

"I want my child."

"I mean now. Here. You got all the answers I can give you. I can't give you your baby, even if I wanted to. It's too late for that, it's out of my hands. What do you want from me now?"

"To kill you, of course. You've taken my entire life away. You and Peter and Carole. It's only fair that I return the favor. I have nothing left. But that also means I've got nothing left to lose either. You said it yourself, karma's a bitch. Goodbye, Sarah. I'll see you in hell."

Brooklyn raised the gun again and this time only two deafening shots rang out instead of six. She was saving the rest for Carole. The shots drove Sarah backwards. She hit the stacks of shelving behind her and dropped like a rock.

"It shouldn't be too long before Carole gets here," she spoke again quietly, closing the fridge door on Sarah as the whole kitchen still echoed from the gunfire. "They won't hold her forever. I'll get my answers from her, and then I'll kill her, too. And before anyone finds any of your bodies, I'll be in the Maldives going after my baby. I hadn't planned on killing the Williams' but what's two more bodies after yours, Carole's and Peter's, right? In for a penny and all that."

Chapter Thirty-Five

arole heard multiple sirens in the distance as her Uber driver pulled into the maternity home parking lot. They sounded like they were getting closer and she contemplated their background noise differently than she ever had before, since she was coming home from her own dealings with the law.

She wasn't surprised to see her car in the parking lot, since she'd told Sarah to take her purse and keys hours before, but she was surprised to see Brooklyn's car sitting right beside it.

This can't be good.

The two cars looked chummy sitting side by side, the only two vehicles seen on the property's grounds.

They looked like lover's cars, meeting up in an empty, vacant lot. Seeking privacy. Up to no good.

Carole was just as surprised by what she didn't see. No news vans. Business had been beyond slow lately. With only one woman left in the home as of this morning, the rest of the center hadn't even carried a skeleton crew. For days now it had just been Carole, minding the one resident, with Sarah to keep her company. The midwife was on call, for when their last resident, Tamika, eventually went into labor. She could be here quickly once called, but until then there was no need for her services. With no other babies, the adoption side was equally empty.

But with the way the pre-trial hearing had gone, Carole had expected her Uber driver to have to fend off hordes of newly back-on-the-property reporters and camera crews, but other than the duo of cars, the lot was empty.

After her driver dropped her off Carole found herself still eyeing Brooklyn's car instead of heading inside. Lots of truths had been exposed today, and Carole was tired. She wasn't sure she had it in her to deal with whatever Brooklyn was here to discuss, but she knew she couldn't put it off for long by standing outside the center and hoping.

She wondered if Brooklyn was still wearing that stupid stomach she'd been parading around in for the past few months now that the gig was up. Maybe she'd come by to fire her? Or maybe she was hoping to get in and out of here for some reason before Carole got back? She hoped Sarah was tucked up into the spare bedroom she'd been using and wasn't taking the brunt of Brooklyn's rage, but she figured there was only one way to find out.

She finally turned her attention away from the pair of cars and toward the front door instead. As she let herself in underneath the angel wings that hugged the doorframe, she noticed that the sirens had grown even louder while she'd been pondering. She wondered where they were headed, it sounded like they'd grown in number as well as volume. She gave a quick prayer up for whoever was needing their services tonight, victim or villain, as she stepped inside the maternity home and shut the door behind her, bracing herself to find Brooklyn and get this over with so she could go to bed.

She crossed the entry room, headed for the kitchen as she called out, "Brooklyn? Where...?"

Brooklyn entered the room from the direction of the kitchen before Carole had the chance to finish yelling her question. "Oh, there you are. I must say I was surprised to see your car parked on this side. Where's Sarah?"

"On her way home, I'd imagine."

"Home? What home?"

"Her eternal one. Why'd you stay, Carole? All these years?"

"What? You're not making any sense."

"How'd you know I wasn't pregnant? Did Peter tell you?"

"No."

"You're lying. He's the only one who knew. Are you still sleeping with him? Is that why you stayed all these years? Is going behind my back and laughing at me part of the appeal?"

"The appeal of what?"

"Of ruining my life! Are you still sleeping with my husband?"

"Good Lord, no. I try not to make the same mistake twice."

"Police! Open the door!" The masculine voice yelling from just outside the center startled Carole, making her jump. It was accompanied by a sharp, loud knocking on the door that she'd just come in through.

"Did you call them?" Brooklyn asked.

"No, why would I?"

"You said you saw my car outside."

"And? You own the place. Why would seeing your car make me call the police?" Carole asked, turning toward the door so she could open it to the knocking officer.

"Don't," Brooklyn said, her voice suddenly sounding strange to Carole's ear.

"Don't open the door to the police? You're kidding, right? What has gotten into you today? Of course I'm going to open it."

"Do it and it'll be the last thing you ever do."

Carole paused in her approach to the door. She looked back toward Brooklyn in shock, to see a gun in Brooklyn's hand, pointing right at her. Carole's hands rose instinctively, imitating everything she'd ever seen on TV. Palms up and open, she tried to calm Brooklyn.

"Relax, would you? And point that thing somewhere else. Why do you even have that? Where'd you get a gun anyway?"

"I'll be asking the questions, not you. How did you know I wasn't pregnant if Peter didn't tell you? And don't lie to me or I'll shoot you, too."

"Too? Who did you shoot already? Where is Sarah?"

"Relax, I just shot Peter, that's all. I don't know

where Sarah is," she lied. "Maybe she's the one who called the cops, but I'm not letting you answer that door until you answer me first."

"*That's all?* You just shot Peter? Where? Is he here? Is he ok?"

"HOW DID YOU KNOW I WASN'T PREGNANT? It's driving me crazy, I have to know."

Carole looked at Brooklyn silently for a long time. The officer yelled out again, ordering them to open the door, but she didn't dare move. Brooklyn's eyes were wild but the gun she held was steady. Steady and pointing right at her. Hoping not to get shot but wanting Brooklyn to know exactly who really was behind the ruining of her life if she didn't survive the day, Carole spoke the truth.

"The same way I knew *everything*. The same way I knew you were looking for a surrogate. The same way I knew how to find Sarah after you stole her from me. You asked me why I stayed all these years? To get revenge. To destroy you like you destroyed me.

"I've waited 20 years to do this. I didn't know what I was going to do back then, when you stole Sarah from me and I lacked the money, the knowledge and the skills to get her back, but I knew I had to do something. So I stayed. When you took Sarah from me right as I lost both my parents, I knew the only way I could survive was if I destroyed you like I was destroyed. So I learned.

"Over the years, I learned. I started with picking locks so I could break into your filing cabinets back before technology. I learned who you gave Sarah to. I kept up with their whereabouts. As tech became more of a thing, I learned computers. I learned how to set up hidden cameras, how to bug phones. I learned about key tracking software, I knew your email passwords, I knew *everything*.

"When Sarah turned eighteen I contacted her so I could finally have a relationship with her, but I still didn't know how I was going to get my revenge. The right plan never presented itself. I did little things over the years to sabotage you as I could, but it wasn't much. Throwing wrenches into your plans for the center. Feeding the girls here as I could, with warnings. The ones who weren't sure about giving their child up, I did what I could to help them. But there wasn't much I could do that would help them, so I waited still. I bided my time. And I learned some more.

"I was already in contact with Sarah when I learned from bugging your and Peter's phones and watching your emails that you were thinking of getting a surrogate. It started as a spark of an idea that I drip-fed to Sarah. She already knew my story by then. We'd had the 'why did you give me up' conversation long before, when we first connected. She knew I never gave her up, she knew she'd been stolen from me. I hadn't told her back then, at the beginning, that you were the one who took her, but I did direct her to books and movies.

"I told her to read *The Girls Who Went Away*, and other books like it. I told her to read *The Adoption Machine* and *The Butterbox Babies*. I told her to look at Georgia Tann's story too, to explain what happened to me without spelling it out. I told her the times were different and I had no recourse. I couldn't undo what had been done to me.

"But then. Then I found out you were thinking of using that surrogate company. I'd known of your trouble, of course. From tracking everything else of yours for years. I'd already told Sarah by then more particulars of my story. That you were at the heart of everything, and that I'd only stayed on to stay close to you, in the hopes that someday...

"And then one day I threw the idea out there, almost as a joke. *Wouldn't it be something if we did to Brooklyn what she'd done to us?* And she liked it! She jumped on it. *And it worked!*

"So do what you want to me, Brooklyn. I don't care. I got my revenge. It was a long time coming, but I finally did it. So shoot me. Whatever. You can't do anything to me now that would hurt me more than you've already done."

With that Carole turned her back on Brooklyn with every intent of opening the door to the police who were probably preparing to break it down or break a window to lob in smoke bombs or flashbangs or whatever else they did to take control in hostage situations but Brooklyn stopped her again by the words that popped out of her mouth.

"I bet I *can* hurt you more. I've got Sarah. Again. Only this time I'm not giving her away. And this time you can't get her back."

Chapter Thirty-Six

Carole abandoned all thought of dealing with the police at the front door. She turned to Brooklyn and asked, "Where is Sarah? What have you done to her?"

"Why don't you come and see for yourself?"

Brooklyn motioned toward the kitchen with both the gun and her head, the two moving in unison to guide Carole into the kitchen ahead of her.

Carole did as she was told. As she turned around she caught a glimpse of movement down the hall to her left. She squinted in that direction and caught sight of their only resident at the end of the hall. Way back, where it turned a corner to go further into the center, she saw Tamika's face and belly peeking around the corner. She seemed to be on the phone, whispering words into the device quietly, trying not to be seen by Brooklyn.

Carole kept going, following Brooklyn's directions. She opened the door to the kitchen, muttering things to keep Brooklyn's attention on her so she didn't also see Tamika. Carole passed through the door with Brooklyn right behind her. She could almost feel the gun pressed into her back, like in the movies, even though Brooklyn was trailing her by a couple of feet.

She didn't see Sarah as she entered the kitchen but directly in front of her on the counter was the TV Carole usually watched while she cooked. The TV she'd caught Sarah's live newscast on what seemed like forever ago to her now. Currently the TV was broadcasting the same news station.

They were showing another live feed, with a reporter right out in front of the center. They must've arrived immediately after Carole had come inside, along with all the police cars she'd heard getting closer when she'd been dropped off.

The volume wasn't on but she could see what was happening. The words *Breaking News* were hung at an angle in one of the upper corners of the screen while the words on the banner underneath the reporter said that they were responding to an armed hostage situation called in by a resident of The Brooklyn Taylor Center.

Seeing Tamika in the hallway made more sense now. She was obviously the police link to inside. Tamika had to be the one who had called them. Carole wondered if Brooklyn even realized that they still had a pregnant woman in-house. And she wondered what Tamika had heard that made her call in the first place. Shots?

Brooklyn said something about shooting Peter, though she'd denied knowing where Sarah was. Was that a lie? Or was her saying that she had Sarah in here a lie? She didn't see either Peter or Sarah in the kitchen.

Keeping herself between Brooklyn and the TV, Carole walked straight toward it and powered it off before turning around and leaning against the counter it sat on, to face Brooklyn.

Brooklyn's gun still pointed at her and Carole's eyes kept darting between Brooklyn, the gun, and the rest of the large, airy room. Taking quick, desperate glances around, she tried to see where Sarah could be. She was half hoping to see her so that she could check on her wellbeing but she was also half hoping that Brooklyn was lying and Sarah wasn't even here.

"I shouldn't have come here. I can see that now," Brooklyn said.

Carole wasn't sure if she was speaking to her or to herself. Brooklyn's eyes were wild with pain and regret as she continued. "I wanted answers, but having them hasn't changed anything. Shooting Peter didn't give me what I want. Shooting Sarah didn't either. I thought it would feel good, though. Destroying the ones who destroyed me. But it didn't."

She spoke louder, definitely talking to Carole, "Shooting you probably won't help me either, but maybe I can use you instead."

"Where is Sarah? You said she was in here."

"It doesn't matter. You're too late to save her anyway," Brooklyn said. "But she's over there. In the walk-in fridge. I was planning on killing both of you and then leaving before anyone found your bodies, like with Peter. But I didn't expect the police to get here before I even finished with you. I didn't expect to feel no relief after it all, either. No, I played it all wrong. I should've headed to the Maldives straight away, without coming here. The only thing that will make me feel better is getting my baby back. Answers don't matter without her, only she matters now. And you can help me get to her. You're worth more to me as a hostage than a body."

"I'm not going to let you do anything with me or to me until I check on Sarah," she said, heading to the walk-in.

"You'll do as I tell you, actually. But go ahead and look. I want you to see what will happen to you if you give me any trouble."

Carole barely heard her, all her concentration was on opening the walk-in to get to the daughter she'd only recently been reunited with. When she swung the heavy door open she was met with chilly air and a heartbreaking sight.

Sarah was slumped on the cold, concrete floor. Her back was against the shelving but she'd tipped over to one side. She looked like a homeless person sleeping one off in some back alley. Except for all the blood.

It was pooled under and around her, a thin trickle flowing down the angled floor, toward the drain in the middle of the walk-in. She didn't look to be breathing.

Carole squeezed her eyes tight, closing them not

against Sarah but to remove herself from the situation just long enough to collect herself. To breathe, to get a handle on her emotions so she could think how best to handle this instead of getting herself shot, too. All she wanted to do was turn around and bum-rush Brooklyn, regardless of the danger. But she knew all that would accomplish would be her own death, her blood mixing with Sarah's and draining away as she joined her daughter in a heap on the floor.

In the tomb-like silence of the walk-in, her eyes still closed tight, she thought she heard the faintest intake of breath before the fridge's motor kicked on to replace all the warm air that was pouring in through the open door with cold once again.

Carole opened her eyes as she moved forward and knelt in front of Sarah, her fingertips reaching out, searching for a pulse.

She found one, though it was weak.

She heard Brooklyn somewhere far behind her, giving her orders, but her full attention was on Sarah so the words didn't quite register as Carole gently probed and prodded, trying to determine how many times Sarah had been shot, and where.

Before she could determine the extent of Sarah's wounds, she felt herself being yanked up and out of the fridge by the back of her head. This time the gun she felt pressing against her back at the same time wasn't imagined. Brooklyn had grabbed ahold of her hair, fisting it against her scalp with one hand as the other held the gun pressed into the side of her spine.

"I said it's time to go."

As Brooklyn guided her rather forcibly away from Sarah and toward the door that separated the maternity home from the rest of the center, her thoughts followed down the same path that Brooklyn's muttered words had forged. Brooklyn had realized that she'd gone about her escape all wrong, in coming here instead of heading to her daughter in the Maldives and Carole's thoughts couldn't help but follow a similar path.

She too realized that she'd gone about everything the wrong way, but not just today. Her regret spanned an entire twenty-year period. If she hadn't left Sarah here when she was an infant, to deal with her dying parents. If she had fought harder to overturn the illegal and immoral adoption. If she hadn't stayed here for twenty years, letting pain and anger become seeds of revenge. If she hadn't gotten Sarah involved in her hateful and convoluted idea to do to Brooklyn what had been done to her. If she hadn't... if she hadn't... if she hadn't...

Then Sarah wouldn't be in that walk-in. She

wouldn't be hurt and dying. She wouldn't be facing a legal battle and years in prison for a revenge plot that should never have been carried out, let alone even planned or imagined in the first place.

It was all her fault. She'd blamed Brooklyn for two decades, but where they were *now* was Carole's fault. She could've walked away from this evil place twenty years ago, the minute she'd learned who adopted Sarah. She could've kept an eye on her from afar, contacted her just the same way that she actually did, only she wouldn't have had twenty years of festering hate and revenge plans bubbling just under the surface when they reconnected.

Sarah embraced her with open arms when she contacted her. If they'd gotten to know each other and bonded over love instead of hate, gratitude instead of payback, where would they be now? Certainly not here. Sarah wouldn't have been shot and left for dead in a walk-in fridge and Carole wouldn't be a human shield, held hostage at gunpoint, helpless while Sarah died.

They wouldn't have been just as guilty as Brooklyn, having stolen a baby from its mother, and Brooklyn wouldn't have shot her husband and Sarah out of rage and desperation.

She was just as guilty as Brooklyn.

That realization tore her up inside almost as much as the realization that she was going to lose Sarah all over again. All because she'd spent the last twenty years seeking revenge instead of justice. Until this very moment, she hadn't realized there was a difference.

Chapter Thirty-Seven

"I don't want to leave Sarah," Carole said.

"Nobody asked you what you wanted."

"Where are you taking me?"

"For now? To my office. I need to see. The windows are mirrored and it sits on a corner. I need to assess my options."

"The cops are already here. Both of our cars are on this side of the building, with the cops, and Sarah has the keys to mine anyway. You're out of options. You shot two people, they aren't going to just let you leave."

"Shut up and keep walking. I can't think with you talking."

"I wasn't talking when you shot Peter or Sarah. My talking obviously has nothing to do with your lack of thinking. You aren't thinking at all. You're reacting."

"What would you have me do?"

"Give yourself up."

"Ha! Give up? Like you did? You waited twenty years to get what you wanted. You didn't just give up. If you had, we wouldn't be here."

"I knew I was stuck twenty years ago. I couldn't do anything then, like you're stuck now. You can't do anything either. There's no way you're getting out of here. Even if you did, by some miracle, there's no way you'll get to the Maldives, find your daughter, get her from them and be able to raise her in peace. Do what I did. Realize you're stuck and do what you can. Turn yourself in, do your time, and maybe you can reconnect with her later, like I did with Sarah."

"No. I refuse to give up on her. She's my daughter, I have to get her back."

Carole wanted to say so many things in response to that. So many retorts sat on her tongue regarding all the other daughters, and sons, that Brooklyn was responsible for taking from so many other parents. But she knew that wouldn't get her anywhere. So she tried to connect with Brooklyn a different way instead.

"It's going to be easier to get her back after you face this and do your time than it will be if you die trying to get to her. One way she gets to know you, maybe from prison, maybe after. The other way she'll never know you. She'll only know what she hears about you in the press coverage."

Brooklyn didn't say anything back, she just kept prodding Carole with a fist in her hair and a gun in her side toward her office. She made Carole open all the doors on their way, since she was the only one with free hands.

"You can't really think this is going to work, can you?" Carole asked. "Come on, Brooklyn. You know there's no way out of here now. Even with me as a hostage."

When Brooklyn still didn't respond, Carole kept on.

"You're a survivor. You're smart. Ruthless. You'd have better luck paying people off for lenience and early release than trying to carry out this half-baked plan you kicked off when you shot Peter and came here. Be smart, Brooklyn. You know there are only two ways out of this. Handcuffs or a body bag. And only one of them will allow you a chance at seeing your daughter again."

They were almost to her office before Brooklyn spoke again, quietly this time. Almost to herself.

"She'll hate me if I wait. She'll know too much by then and she'll never be able to forgive me. But if I can get to her, raise her, she'll just know me as her mother. She won't know anything about my life before her. And if I die trying to get to her, then I'll never have to see the unloving, judgmental rejection in her eyes. I couldn't stand seeing that. It would kill me. And it would be there. Cause I know I'm unforgivable."

Carole felt the truth in her statement. It was a bitter truth, and she felt it resonate in her core. She didn't think what she did, what she pulled Sarah into, was forgivable either. She understood exactly what Brooklyn meant.

"You can be forgiven," Carole said, unsure of the truth herself but needing it to be true of Brooklyn if she was to have any hope of it being true for her own parts in this tragedy. "Come clean. Serve your time. I reunited with my baby after I lost her. You can, too. But you need to become someone worthy of her by then. Pay for your sins first. Become someone she can be proud of."

"I can't. I can't make her proud if I'll never be able to be proud of myself first. Getting to her young is my only chance. I'll still be unforgivable, but maybe she won't ever have to know."

Brooklyn forced Carole into her corner office, butting the door closed behind them with a hip as she said, "I'll succeed or I'll die trying."

As they passed Brooklyn's desk, headed for the windows, Carole reached out. Desperately grabbing onto the only thing she could reach that looked at all like it could be used as a weapon, her fingers wrapped around the heavy glass and wood award she'd presented Brooklyn with just a few weeks before. She twisted toward Brooklyn, pirouetting against the grip Brooklyn had on her hair.

Her sudden movement surprised Brooklyn, causing her to fire the gun in reflex.

Carole felt pain rip through her right breast as she continued her twist, swinging the award up at an angle until it connected with Brooklyn's face.

Brooklyn instinctively let go of everything then, releasing Carole's hair and the just-fired gun at the same time, in order to try and protect herself. She covered her face with her hands as she lost her balance and fell off her feet.

Carole tossed the lifetime achievement award

aside and dropped to the floor to grab the gun. She stood up with it, bleeding and swaying in pain. She held the gun in both shaking hands and aimed it at Brooklyn's slit open and bleeding face.

Chapter Thirty-Eight

"Do it," Brooklyn said, looking up at her through a waterfall of gushing blood. "If I can't get out of here and get to my daughter, I don't even want to live. So, go ahead. Do it. Put me out of my misery. Please."

Carole stood above her, unsteady on her feet. The gun shook in her hands but as close as they were, there was no way Carole could miss.

They say that your life flashes before your eyes when you're about to die, but Brooklyn was glad that wasn't the case for her. She didn't want to see all her mistakes again on repeat. There were too many, it would take another entire lifetime to watch them all play out again.

"They'll have heard the shot," Brooklyn said from the floor as Carole's blood dripped down on her. "This office is about to be crawling with cops. Don't let them take me alive, I'll never survive in prison. Shoot me. They'll understand, it'll be considered self-defense after what I did to Peter and Sarah. Finish it, Carole. You wanted to end me, now is your chance."

Brooklyn watched conflicting emotions flit across Carole's face.

Carole shook her head, lowering the gun. "There's been too much destruction already. Killing you won't solve anything. It won't undo anything; it'll only add to the pile of wrong choices I've already made. That pile is already too big, killing you will make it insurmountable. I'm sorry Brooklyn, you're just going to have to deal with whatever demons come the same way we all do. Alive and facing ourselves in the mirror for the rest of our days."

Brooklyn heard the sounds of feet running toward them from down the hall. Multiple heavy steps meant that the police had gotten inside and were closing in, just outside the door.

Still keeping the gun pointed at Brooklyn, Carole made her way to the office door. Before she opened it she yelled out, "This is the hostage speaking. I'm going to open the door, please don't shoot me. I'm already shot."

A male voice yelled back through the door, "This is the police, I hear you. You can open the door, but do it slowly and then step toward us, keeping your hands where we can see them. Can you do this?"

"Yes," she answered. "I'm putting Brooklyn's gun down now, just inside the door. Brooklyn is on the floor by the windows, I knocked her down. She's hurt too, I hit her in the head. I'm about to open the door slowly."

When she finished speaking she laid the gun down at her feet, stood back up and slowly swung the door wide. Holding her hands high she stepped out into the hall where she saw two officers braced, pointing their guns her way just in case she'd been lying.

One took charge of her until they could determine the truth for themselves and the other turned his attention to the office where Brooklyn lay.

"I need to see my daughter. I need to go to Sarah, can you take me to her before you do anything with me?" Carole asked the officer who was patting her down. "She's in the walk-in, Brooklyn shot her. She needs an ambulance."

"So do you, you've been shot, too."

Before she could reply she heard the other officer bark out behind her, "Put the gun down! Don't move!"

Carole tried to turn back but the officer beside her grabbed her tight.

"Brooklyn, no!" She yelled the words back toward Brooklyn's office, but no one heard them because multiple shots rang out to cover them. From such close range the shots hurt Carole's ears, making her jump and cringe.

The officer with her twisted them, pushing her behind him as he went to back up his partner, but no such activity was needed. Brooklyn was no longer a threat to anyone.

"She crawled, she grabbed the gun from the floor and aimed it straight at me," the officer inside Brooklyn's office told the other officer. "I had no choice."

"Suicide by cop," Carole muttered, despondent. "I didn't think she'd... I never thought she'd really..."

The officer who'd patted her down and put himself between her and the office looked hard at her, his eyes narrowed.

"When I got the gun away from her she told me to finish her. I couldn't. But I didn't think she was serious. I thought it was just her pain and anger talking. She was nowhere near the gun and she was hurt. She was down. I only put the gun down for you, right when I came out. So you wouldn't shoot us." Carole's words faded off again. "Is she... Is she dead?"

Chapter Thirty-Nine

When Sarah woke up she didn't know where she was. She heard voices around and above her but when she tried to open her eyes and put faces to the voices, everything swam and blurred. A beeping sound that she hadn't noticed yet sped up and got shriller, awakening a headache she hadn't realized she had either.

"Sarah? Sarah, hello. Can you open your eyes for me?" The voice came from far away but as Sarah focused on it, it seemed to get closer. Then it moved away again, saying, "Hang on, let me mute this real quick. There now, that's better, isn't it? Sarah? Are you with us? You gave us quite a scare."

"Who...? Where am I? What happened?"

"You're in the hospital. Let me see those pretty

eyes of yours and I'll tell you all about it. Can you open them for me?"

"Sarah honey, thank goodness," another voice chimed in. This voice Sarah recognized.

"Carole? What happened?" Sarah pulled her eyelids apart by pure will, needing to see what was going on for herself.

"Yes, it's me. Your doctor and I were just talking about you," Carole said as Sarah finally got her eyes to focus on various items in the room. A TV sat high in the corner, up by the ceiling. Flowers covered the surface of the table underneath it.

She turned her head and saw the doctor Carole had been talking about beside the bed she was laying in. Beyond it, Sarah saw Carole. She was in a bed similar to herself, the beds parallel to each other in the small room.

The head of Carole's bed was cranked way up, so Carole was more sitting in it than laying. She was propped on one elbow, her body twisted so that she could face Sarah better while still lying beside her.

"What happened to you?" Sarah asked her, making Carole laugh.

"The same thing that happened to you," Carole said. "I got shot. I got it in the boob though, but you got it in the side. You're down a kidney, with some damage to your stomach and liver as well, but all in all they say you're going to be fine. If you're going to get shot in the gut, well, you did it in the best way possible."

"What?"

"Janine is here, too. She just left to get something to eat after your doctor here gave us a full report. She'll be right back, I'm sure. The doc and I were talking about other things when you started waking up."

"I'm glad I was still here," the doctor said, pulling Sarah's attention to her. "Let me look you over while you wrap your mind around everything Carole just told you, and I'll answer any questions for you, OK? How do you feel?"

"I... I don't know. I feel like I'm coming out of a dream," Sarah tried to brace her hands against the bed, at her hips, and scoot herself into more of a sitting position, but her body didn't want to cooperate.

She tested various things while the doctor looked her over. She moved her feet and stretched her legs as best she could, grateful that everything below her waist at least operated the way it was supposed to. She used her hands to feel around on her trunk and her palms were met with the roughness of gauze and tape underneath her thin hospital gown.

She rolled her shoulders and played with her head and neck, tilting them one way and then the other. Her headache renewed itself and her abdomen held whispers of soreness largely dulled by what she assumed was good drugs.

The doctor completed her assessment of everything, from checking her pupil dilation to changing the dressing covering her bullet wounds. She said, "You're very lucky it was just .22 caliber bullets. Anything bigger and you may not have made it."

"Peter didn't," Sarah heard Carole say.

"Peter didn't make it? So Brooklyn really did shoot him too, huh?" Sarah asked, bits and pieces starting to come back to her.

"She did, with the same gun she shot us with. Only she shot him six times."

"Holy... Six times?"

"Yep, she emptied her entire revolver into him. Then she reloaded and came looking for us," Carole said. "She got you twice. I took one, and there were three still in the gun when she pointed it at the officer, only he fired first."

"She tried to shoot a cop, too? Wait, he shot first? He shot her? Is she...?"

"She didn't make it, either."

"So Peter and Brooklyn are both dead? When? How long have I been out?"

"Three days," the doctor said, adding her first contribution to the discussion in a while. "Three days and two surgeries. But everything looks good. We've just been waiting for you to wake up. Oh, Janine is back."

"You're awake!" Janine said, putting her coffee off to the side, on the table that held all the flowers. "We've been so worried about you."

"We?" Sarah asked, looking back and forth between Janine and Carole with surprise. "You two are... good?"

"We're good," Carole said.

"We've been getting to know each other," Janine added. "Sarah honey, I know we've had our differences but..."

"We don't have to talk about that now," Sarah said. "But you don't need to worry about that, either. I've been doing a lot of thinking, or I had been, before Brooklyn showed up. I know I've made a lot of mistakes, I didn't handle anything the best way I could have. I know that."

"You're right," Janine said. "We don't have to talk about it now. Your first priority needs to be healing. I just wanted you to know that I'm here, that's all. And I love you. The rest can wait. We'll figure it out, I'm not worried."

"I've been doing a lot of thinking too," Carole said, looking back and forth between them. "I've got a lot to apologize for as well. I let my quest for revenge take over and you got hurt. Two people are dead and I..."

Carole shook her head as her words faulted and failed her.

"We've all made mistakes," Sarah said, beginning to tire but grateful that all three of them were together. She then repeated Janine's words, aiming them at Carole. "We'll figure it out."

The three got quiet and the doctor excused herself, saying she'd be back to check in soon.

"So, have you told her?" Janine asked Carole after a few minutes.

"No, not yet."

"Told me what?" Sarah asked.

"The court case. It got dismissed," Janine said.

"It did? How? Why? I still did what I did, getting shot doesn't change that."

"No, but both Peter and Brooklyn dying does," Janine said.

"The public is going nuts," Carole added. "Half of them are still calling for your head. The other half thinks you're a hero, exposing Brooklyn's business practices like you did. Especially after the police found evidence of more and different stuff against Peter in a USB drive they fished out of a glass of whiskey in the room where they found his body. What's on it hasn't been confirmed yet, but there are rumors."

"Either way, the district attorney's office decided to drop the whole case against you, since neither Peter nor Brooklyn are alive to take care of their baby you had. And her adoptive parents are in the wind anyway," Janine said with a shrug.

"I guess it beats going to foster parents," Sarah said. "Unless...?"

"Unless what?" Janine asked.

"Maybe I should... I don't know. She is technically my half-sister. Should I try to do something?" Sarah asked.

"I don't think you can do anything. For better or worse, regrets or no, our plan worked out well. Maybe too well," Carole said. "There's no way you'll be able to undo the adoption. Besides, would you truly even want to? Do you want a child? Would you want to raise the half-sister you gave up in a revenge plot? Maybe it's better this way. She gets to grow up away from all of this."

"I didn't know she was my half-sister when we started down this road," Sarah said, looking pointedly at Carole.

"I know. I have some things to answer for, like I said. Some things I wasn't straightforward with you about."

"You think?" Janine added, causing all eyes to turn in her direction.

"Don't even," Sarah said. "You've got no room to talk. You never even told me I was adopted to begin with. You may not be as in as deep as the two of us, but you're not squeaky clean, either. I found out my whole life was a lie at eighteen. Even after I turned eighteen, you never said a word. At least not until you told the world at large. Maybe if you had, I wouldn't have..."

"Disappeared on me? Faked your own kidnapping? Given away a baby you had no rights to?" Janine said.

"Been susceptible to what I thought was an honest, hurting, aching woman who also happened to be my real mother?"

"What was I?" Janine asked. "Imaginary? I was real. I am real. I changed your real diapers and I nursed you through real sicknesses and I loved you with real love."

"I know that. I do. I'm sorry, I..."

"I had no idea how you came to be up for adoption, all we knew was that the center gave us a baby when we couldn't have one. We thought we were doing a good thing, Kristine. Sarah. Whatever you prefer to be called. A great thing. And now you don't even want the name we gave you. Was life with us, with me, really so bad? So awful that you didn't even think twice about letting me think something tragic had happened to you?"

Sarah was quiet then. She brought her hands to her head and started massaging her temples.

"I'm sorry," Janine said. "This isn't the time for this conversation. We both already said we weren't going to talk about this right now. You should rest."

"No, I'm sorry," Sarah said. "For all of it. For everything. You're right, I never should have... I don't know how I ever..."

"Later," Janine said. "Thankfully you're alive, that's all that matters. We have time. But don't think that I'm going to let you push me out of your life, because I won't let that happen."

"I don't want to push you out. I don't. I don't know what I want right now, but I've had to face a lot of things about myself in the last little bit and I do know that I won't be any kind of a better person without you in my life than I will be with you in it. Either of you. I have regrets, I've made mistakes. I'll own them. But I want to continue to do so with both of you in my life."

Janine was tearing up with relief and couldn't answer so she just placed a hand on Sarah's and Sarah held it tight. It was Carole who spoke next.

"The three of us figuring this out together would be wonderful. Besides, who else would even begin to understand?"

Sarah snorted an unexpected laugh and Janine began to giggle wetly through her tears.

"I think you may be right, we're stuck together now. Three peas in one very twisted pod."

Chapter Forty

EPILOGUE

"May I have your attention, please," Carole began. "Welcome to The Brooklyn Taylor Center's annual fundraising dinner. As most of you know, it's been quite a journey."

A smattering of laughter broke out around the room at her understatement. It had been five years since Carole had stood in the same spot, awarding Brooklyn Taylor with the lifetime achievement award she'd then gone on to use as a weapon against the woman the center was still named after. Many of the people gathered had come back every year since, continuing to support a cause that they still believed in, even as it transformed, changing shape over the years since the center's founders had died.

"I want to start my speech tonight by first

thanking you all for coming, and secondly by answering the question I get asked more often than any other question, which is why in the world did we not change the name?"

Carole paused and smiled as laughter broke out all around her once again.

"Well, we thought about it," Carole continued. "But we weren't sure calling it the Kristine Armstrong Foundation would go over any better."

Even more laughter followed this time, as Carole embraced the awkwardness of the entire situation and ran with it.

"We also toyed with calling it the Sarah Scott Foundation. But again, we found ourselves in the same boat. Then we thought about going very generic, but in the end, we decided to just keep the original name for two reasons.

"One was because, no matter how we got here, we knew that we wouldn't be here at all without the center's namesake. That's just a fact. Without Brooklyn and Peter, this place never would have existed. It wasn't all good, we know that. But it wasn't all bad either. This center was largely above board back then, just not completely.

"That brings us to the second reason we decided to just keep the name. We knew that the only way this place had a chance of surviving was if it was oriented and run completely differently. No more secrets. No more private adoptions. We needed everything to be open, honest and transparent. And how much more transparent can you get than to keep Brooklyn Taylor's name on the building?

"All it would take, ten years from now or a hundred years from now, would be to research the name Brooklyn Taylor and the center's entire history, good, bad and ugly, will be there to be seen. And we decided we were more than fine with that, because, for once, this center has nothing to hide."

The applause from that was deafening and encouraged Carole to keep going.

"As most of you know, once all the legal dust settled, this center was ultimately inherited by Sarah Scott, which would've upset Brooklyn to no end, ironically.

"Now, in most states, adopted children inherit only from the parents who adopted them, not from the biological parents they were adopted from. But in Brooklyn's case, she was rather obsessed with biology, and Peter and Brooklyn's wills were worded in such a way that their blood relations inherited everything. Meaning that both Sarah and their biological daughter who was adopted and taken out of the country also inherited.

"Now, that child is still a minor and, as far as we know, hasn't reentered the country yet, but once she is of age she too will be recognized as a rightful heir. But in the meantime, that leaves the infamous Sarah Scott in charge, whether she wants to be or not."

The laughter that brought on was even louder.

"And speaking of Sarah Scott, this night is also a celebration for both her and her other mother, Janine. I am very pleased to announce that both of them have recently graduated from our nearby university, together, with brand spanking new degrees. Janine now holds a bachelor degree in science with an aim toward social work, and Sarah holds a bachelor degree in business with an aim toward eventually taking over the center in actuality instead of largely in name only."

The applause that time went on so long and was so loud that Carole waved both women up to join her on stage so they could bask in the glow beside her. After a few moments, Sarah stepped up to the mic, giving Carole a hug before she started to speak.

"Standing here between two amazing women, I can't even begin to describe how I feel tonight looking out at all of you. You guys stuck with us. I'm so grateful.

"Carole here keeps saying that I'm in charge, but she's being too humble. She's continued to run the maternity side of things throughout this whole transition, and she's done a fabulous job doing so."

"It's all I've ever known that's all," Carole said, deflecting. "I love taking care of my girls. I always have. I'm just glad that I can continue to do so."

"And we have all of you to thank as well," Sarah said to the crowd. "To those of you that stuck with us from the beginning, through the scandal, thank you! To those of you who've just recently joined us on this adventure now that it's being run transparently, thank you, too! We would not be here without you.

"We are growing in leaps and bounds after an interesting reboot, and I'm very happy to announce that the Brooklyn Taylor Center has been able to come back bigger and better than ever and it is our hope, no, *our promise,* that we are going to continue to turn this center into what it could have been, and should have been, from the beginning.

"Thank you for your support!"

Acknowledgments

I would like to thank my own mother for the bits of truth at the kernel of the original idea that eventually lead to this fictional story. Very, very, very loosely based upon some real events, I'd just like to say: Mom, you're amazing. You were a warrior back then and you're still a warrior today. And I see many of those same warrior traits in my child as well. How the warrior genes passed me by, I've no idea. But I'd much rather write your stories than live them, so there is that, lol.

I'd also like to thank my indispensable writer's group, DD, and all the friends I've made therein. Especially those who gave me feedback on this story in particular as it progressed, and especially especially to Sydney James for being there throughout the entire process. F yeah, bouncing rainbow sheep to the lot of you.

9 798985 130706